One Small Candle

One Small Candle

Janet Mary Tomson

ROBERT HALE · LONDON

© Janet Mary Tomson 2005
First published in Great Britain 2005

ISBN 0 7090 7906 0

Robert Hale Limited
Clerkenwell House
Clerkenwell Green
London EC1R 0HT

2 4 6 8 10 9 7 5 3 1

Typeset in 11/13½pt Palatino
by Derek Doyle & Associates, Shaw Heath.
Printed in Great Britain by St Edmundsbury Press
Bury St Edmunds, Suffolk.
Bound by Woolnough Bookbinding Ltd.

For Frances
With Love

Author's Note

In 1587, Francis Lamb, aboard the privateer *Leopard*, intercepted the Spanish galleon *Fortunate* as she left the Caribbean port of Cartegena. It was fortunate indeed – for Francis. The galleon was loaded to the gunwales with gold. On his arrival at Tilbury, he rode hotfoot for London and in a gesture he was instantly to regret, he offered half the bullion to Queen Elizabeth. Her Majesty took it all, but in return she knighted Sir Francis and awarded him 500 acres of rich farmland in Somerset on which he built himself a fine manor house. He called it Cartegena. A year later he married Elizabeth, a neighbouring heiress. Thus began a dynasty that lasted for 389 years.

One

'I have decided to open Cartegena to the public.'

The words hung in the air like the sword of Damocles. Shirley Weeks stared at Lady Lamb with barely concealed disbelief, stifling back the words, 'You can't.' She could. The house was hers to do with as she wished.

'Only on Sunday afternoons to begin with.'

From her tone, Shirley wondered if the older woman was trying to appease her. It was foolish, of course, this feeling towards the house. Shirley had never supped at the dining table nor slept (officially) in any of the many creaky cavernous bedrooms, although she'd swept and polished them often enough. But she felt as if in some way Cartegena was hers and as such she had a right to be consulted about the house's future. Perhaps she was in danger of becoming one of those old retainers, a pitiable figure with no life of her own, living vicariously through the tiles and stonework of this unattainable mansion.

Obviously sensing that Shirley was not going to make a fuss, her employer said, 'I have been in touch with one of those marketing companies. I have given them access to the family papers and they are going to arrange everything – a guidebook, postcards, everything.'

The heat of resentment notched up a degree or two. Shirley knew this house, loved it. Why should Lady Lamb even contemplate needing strangers to delve into its secrets? For a moment an old disappointment threatened to submerge her. The feeling had been there since she was approaching eighteen, leaving school with three good A levels under her belt and the prospect of gainful employment confronting her.

'What do you want to go to university for? People like us. . .' Her father's voice, growly, one of a long line of sons of the soil.

'Because . . .' How could she ever explain to him about the grammar school, what it was like to sit in a classroom and watch the windows of her mind open, the doors swing wide to reveal things she had never even thought about? The next step, the natural progression to university, gleamed on the horizon like some golden Shangri-la only to be lost in the fog of her family expectations.

'With your education you could get a job in a bank.'

The resentment never quite went away.

Shirley dragged her attention back to the present. Lady Lamb naturally assumed that because she hadn't been to university, because she still spoke with a Somerset accent, she wouldn't know how to research the house's history, how to write an authoritative and interesting guidebook. Lady Lamb had not been to university either. She had had a tutor, gone to some sort of finishing school in Switzerland. The clear, cultured rounding of her vowels might make her sound as if she was the fount of all knowledge but in reality she was rather a feather-brained woman, certainly not one with Shirley's passion for English and history.

As if still trying to placate her employee, Lady Lamb said, 'I thought that perhaps you, Shirley, might like to help with the guided tours.'

'Me?'

She had been to numerous stately homes and followed the crocodiles around between the red guide ropes, always comparing the house in question unfavourably with the place that she worked in and loved. Dates, famous visitors, provenance of pieces of porcelain and pictures on display were deferentially spelt out by the guide but it took more than that to impress a woman who had grown up against the background of Cartegena's perfection.

'You could always read the guidebook when I get one,' said Lady Lamb. 'You could take notes. I wouldn't expect you to remember it all . . .' Her voice trailed off and Shirley noticed the confusion in the older woman's eyes. She suffocated her own affront. The decision to let in strangers must be a difficult one for Florence Lamb, raised as she was to take her privileged life for granted. She might say that she had reached the decision but in reality it had probably been thrust upon her.

Her husband, Lord Lamb, had died nearly two years ago. The family finances were in a muddle, everyone knew that, and the black cloud of death duties fogged out the future. Besides, there was no son and heir.

Shirley's heart tightened. Not the time to think about Guy Lamb; not now, with his mother standing so close.

'Well—' Shirley could feel herself weakening. If anyone was going to explain about the house then it should be her. She could not tolerate the thought that her employer might bring in strangers. The decision, though, to turn Cartegena into a stately home was unsettling, the first step in accepting the inevitable, that sooner or later Lady Lamb would die and then the house would be at the mercy of a predatory world. Nothing lasted for ever.

'When will we be opening?' she asked.

'On Easter Sunday.' Lady Florence leaned more heavily on her stick. Her hip gave her trouble these days and she walked badly, although she never drew attention to her increasing infirmity.

'I – I have quite a lot of notes of my own.' Shirley recognized the edge in her voice. Years ago she had been to the local record office, looked up the house's history, kept her own chronicle of events. It had never occurred to her that in the house itself there was a treasure trove of information that she might have access to. Her own ambition got the better of her.

'Could I use the library? Research a few more things?'

'If you wish to.' Florence Lamb looked genuinely surprised. It would not have occurred to her that anyone like Shirley would be interested in the dusty tomes and documents that had lain undisturbed for so long.

'Thank you.' Shirley felt the tingling anticipation somewhere under her ribs. Perhaps she had neither the training nor the experience to know how to produce a guidebook for publication but she already knew all those interesting anecdotes that would enhance a visitor's tour. As she put on her coat she began to warm to the idea, imagining the day when someone – Lady Florence herself, perhaps, or the manager of the unknown marketing company – would say to her, 'Our visitors keep asking about the talk you gave them. Where did you get your information?'

'I researched it.'

'Well, might it be possible for you to update the next edition of the guidebook? Your version is so much better than ours.'

'Will that be all right then?'

With an embarrassed start, Shirley realized that Lady Lamb was watching her. She blushed, afraid that her thoughts might be transparent.

'You'll help with the guided tours?'

She gave a single nod of her head. Without needing to think, she had agreed.

The prospect of the changes swarmed around her as she walked home. Sometimes she cycled to work. In bad weather she took the car but whenever it was possible she preferred the walk along the quiet country lane, arriving at the wonderfully ornate wrought-iron gates set into a creeper-strewn wall. Their beauty still entranced her, standing as they did, seemingly in the middle of nowhere. Once inside she trudged along the leafy driveway edged with trees, some older than the house itself. Occasionally she saw a tree creeper, even more rarely you heard a nightingale, at dusk eavesdropped on the migrant nightjars before the trees halted abruptly and the vista opened on to Cartegena itself.

The house was nothing short of magic, a perfectly proportioned, symmetrical building in muted stone, with large Georgian windows, the original Tudor timbered wing at the back giving on to the courtyard, stables, fountains and statues. The walkways had been laid out by the great Capability himself. This was the backdrop against which Shirley identified who she was, the stage for her childhood adventures, the happy-ever-after of her teenage dreams. The warning tension of regret forced her to think of other things.

As Lady Florence Lamb was the last of the line, so in her modest way was Shirley. An only child, she had never questioned that she in her turn would have a family but somehow that had always been in the future, a future that now found her at thirty-five years old, with no husband, no boyfriend, and no sense of direction.

Reaching the cottage, she let herself in. Unease surged at the edge of her consciousness.

'Is that you, Shirley?'

The inevitable question. Who else would it be?

'Yes, Mum. It's me.'

The local paper was stuffed in the letterbox. As she pulled it through she noticed the date, 17 February. It would have been her grandmother's birthday. She had forgotten. There was something else, too. Something else had happened on that date seventeen – no, eighteen – years ago.

She filled the kettle and placed it on the Aga, now beginning to show signs of its great antiquity. Her hands tingled and trembled slightly. Eighteen years ago today – it was there again, that warning sensation, like the distant awareness of an avalanche that might at any moment engulf you, sweep you over the edge and into a bottomless limbo. Think about something else, anything else.

Grandma Morris, who had died seven years ago, had always dressed in black. She had been the first one to take Shirley to Cartegena where once in the mists of time, before Shirley's mother was born, she had been in service. In later years, when Shirley was a toddler, Grandma returned daily to help with cleaning and, latterly, to supervise the meals for Lord and Lady Lamb, although they were both ten years younger than she was. When Grandma died, it was Shirley's mother, Maud, who took on the role of cook and bottle-washer. Now her mother was losing the battle with arthritis and it was Shirley who made the daily pilgrimage. Unlike the olden days, though, the days of her mother and grandmother, she was the only employee in the house. Gone were the maids and footmen, gone were the cleaners and handymen. Now there was Shirley and old Moses Jenkins, whose gardening efforts gradually succumbed to the encroaching wilderness outside that had once been the pride of Cartegena.

'How are things at the house?'

It was like a play, a matinée repeated every afternoon. Mother had her lines and Shirley had hers.

'All right.' She fetched the tea caddy, spooned in the leaves. Something new today, though.

'Lady L is going to open the house to the public.'

'She's never!'

'I expect it will help with the debts.'

Funny, really, how indestructible the Lambs had seemed when she was a young girl. Even in her teens, when her social-ist beliefs were at their height, she didn't really include Cartegena in her brave new world. Get rid of the church, the royal family, the House of Lords. Turn Buckingham Palace into flats for the old folks of London. Not Cartegena, though.

'I'm going to fetch some washing.'

She delivered her mother's tea and escaped upstairs. Her clothes from yesterday were strewn on the floor – jeans, polo, off-white bra and sagging panties. Suppose she bumped into an Adonis and in a moment of sheer madness invited him in? How was she to let him rip off her underclothes when they looked like something from the cleaning basket? She realized that she didn't even know what women were wearing these days. Bloomers, drawers, knickers, panties, bikini pants – what was it now? She thought about Lady Lamb, the pure silk and lace, old as the hills but still indicating 'breeding' and self-respect.

She remembered what she had been wearing on *that* day, 17 February 1967. A mini-skirt. Soon they would become much shorter but at that time they were in their infancy. They had hardly reached outside of London. In fact, she was the first girl in the village to stride out with six inches of leg showing above the knee.

'You'll catch your death.' Her father.

'You'll be giving people the wrong idea.' Her mother.

The wrong idea – what was that, that she was easy, anyone's? Their very doubts bolstered up her determination to be differ-ent. Brown mini, tan-coloured polo, black tights, flat shoes. It must have been fate that gave Grandma the worst cold she had had in decades and made her mother make an emergency appointment with the dentist because her dentures were cracked.

'You'll have to go, Shirl. The shepherd's pie is all ready. You've only got to put it in the oven. They can have tinned peas. They won't mind. And peaches. And evaporated milk.'

The prospect of dishing up anything to the Lambs left her paralyzed with fear. Although there were only the two of them, they always ate in the dining room at exactly one o'clock. The linen napkins came out, silver cruet set, crystal tumblers for water; only the cutlery was stainless steel because there was no-one left to clean the silver.

'I don't—'

Her mother cut her short. 'Put the peas in a serving dish. Don't forget to put out serving spoons. They'll do the rest themselves.'

She'd done it, somehow. Heated the food, carried it with trepidation to the dining room, placed it on the mats to protect the mahogany of the table.

'Thank you, Shirley. It was good of you to come. I hope your mother and your grandmother will soon be recovered.'

Shirley mumbled some sort of a reply.

'I like the skirt,' said Lord Lamb, flirtatious.

She didn't know whether to be embarrassed or shocked. Well, she had wanted to be noticed, hadn't she? Not by Lord Lamb, though, certainly not by Lord Lamb. By whom, then? There wasn't anyone else around whose opinion might matter.

When they had finished she cleared the table, washed up, put the things away, hoping against hope that she wouldn't have to come back another day. She couldn't afford to take time off school.

As she marched down the drive, anxious to put the ordeal behind her, she heard the distant clang of the iron gates, the vroom vroom of a car's engine. As she rounded the bend, a low, green motor was coming towards her. It slowed down as they drew level.

'Hi. I remember you. Sheila, isn't it?'

'Shirley.' She bent down to see through the window. Behind the wheel was Guy Lamb, nineteen, up at Cambridge. 'What are you doing here?' She didn't know what made her ask.

He grinned. 'I'm in a spot of bother. I've been sent home for the weekend to "think things over". Why don't you get in? I'll give you a lift.'

'But you're going the other way. You've only just arrived.'

'Not a problem. Besides' – His grin widened – 'I'm not looking forward to facing the old folks.'

In a daze Shirley walked round the sleek green bonnet, opened the door and slid into the leather seat. It was on the tip of her tongue to ask him what he had done but she thought better of it.

Guy leaned back to see her better. She was aware of his eyes, blue, green, oddly speckled, taking in her breasts, her legs. She resisted the urge to try and pull the skirt down further.

'I like the skirt.' Unlike his father, she found his comment exciting. When she didn't respond, he asked, 'Where are you going?'

'Home.'

'You live on the green, don't you?'

'Hawthorn Cottage.' The modesty of the dwelling weighed her down. It was part of a pretty row of stone cottages – thatched roofs, roses round the door – that coaches made a detour to point out to their mostly American passengers. Normally she felt smug about living there, the object of other people's envy, but today, with Guy Lamb, the reality of class differences clouded her self-image.

The thought that they had no bathroom and still used an outside loo embarrassed her.

'Are you working for my family?' he asked.

'No.' She blushed. How dare he assume that! The fact that her mother did so, and her mother before her, did not lessen the humiliation.

'I'm in the sixth form at King James Grammar.'

'Are you now? A bright girl.' He seemed to reappraise her. 'What are you going to do when you leave?'

What was she going to do? Study history? Simply be an

undergraduate? The universities must be full of boys like him. She had no words to articulate her hopes for the future. Just over a year to go before her A levels, then she would see.

'What are you studying?' The car was through the gates, down the lane. She wished, hoped, that someone she knew would see her.

He shrugged. 'Classics. It's not my thing but you've got to do something. It's the sport that really matters.'

'What do you play?'

'Rugby, squash. I row, do a bit of running.'

She had a vision of him in white shorts and vest, white socks, long muscular legs, lithe and lanky, pounding round a race-track. A surge of heat engulfed her.

Changing gear at the junction, he said, 'One thing I'm not going to do is to come back here, run this old pile.'

She was aghast. 'Don't you like it?'

He glanced at her. 'Do you? Would you want to live in a museum?'

'Yes!' She couldn't believe him. Didn't he know that people like her would sell their souls to have such a heritage?

He chuckled. 'You're welcome to it. It's like some huge cuckoo gobbling up everything we have. It keeps us poor.'

'I still think it's beautiful.'

'Do you? Why don't you come over tonight then?'

'I can't. It's my grandmother's birthday.' She blushed as she said it. It sounded such a feeble reason, like saying you were washing your hair.

He shrugged as if it was of no importance. A golden opportunity was running away from her.

She said, 'I'm not doing anything tomorrow, though,' and instantly felt mortified at such a pathetic display of keenness.

He glanced at her again and grinned. 'All right. You're on. I'll pick you up.'

'Shirley! Get me some aspirin, will you? My back's aching something rotten. I think I'll have to see the doctor again.'

Her mother's voice jerked her back to the present.

'Just a minute!' She tried to quell the resentment, the uneasy sense that in her illness her mother had found the ideal tool for keeping her at her beck and call. As she fetched the box and tumbled two tablets into her mother's gnarled, arthritic hands, she felt that crushing shame, that anger with life for dealing her so short. Perhaps if she were a better person, life would be kinder to her.

She said, 'Lady Lamb asked me if I'd like to do guided tours around the house.'

'What did you say?'

'I said yes.'

'Wouldn't you feel funny, talking to strangers?'

'Why on earth would I?'

Didn't her mother know that she had done presentations in that last year at school, seen herself lecturing in eighteenth century social history? Of course she didn't – the whole concept was light years away from her mother's expectations compared with her own. What had happened to make her so different?

Anyway, it didn't matter. It was too late now. Here she was, fast approaching middle age, stuck in the country, with only the house she loved to keep her from despair. Then she thought back to that evening. There were parts of Cartegena she had never then visited, rooms kept locked, corridors permanently in darkness. Those childhood fantasies were back. Was there someone locked away in one wing of the house, some mad person like Bertha Mason? Was treasure piled up behind one of those bolted doors? She grinned at the remembered foolishness but then another foolishness began to take hold of her. Guy, the *Honourable* Guy Lamb. Lightly waving brown hair that he had a habit of flicking off his face, a voice of delicious culture, dimples, crooked grin. She had seen him nearly all her life although the two years' difference in their ages, the fact they were different sexes and that other unmentioned social factor meant that they had hardly passed the time of day. That afternoon, though, he had noticed her all right. That was when the dream began, that dream that never could and now never would be fulfilled, born on her grandmother's birthday. Eighteen years later and she still knew of no way to make it go away.

Two

It wasn't until that night, when the last minutes of the day were tipping over into tomorrow, that the memory of Guy's first invitation to visit Cartegena returned to haunt her. Maud was in bed and Shirley had been dozing only briefly when she awoke with the instant knowledge that she was not going to get back to sleep. Her mind scrabbled around for something soothing to focus on but nothing would stick. She tried itemizing the things she must do the next day – send her cousin a birthday card, collect Mother's medicine from the chemist, change the library books – but gradually, implacably, like some slow-moving bed of lava, the memory of the meeting with Guy forced itself into the nooks and crannies of her brain. She switched on the light, glanced at her watch, switched it off again and succumbed to the thoughts.

As the afternoon in question had progressed, the reality of going to Cartegena in the evening began to take on insurmountable proportions. It was 18 February. The air was dripping damp and so cold that snow seemed almost inevitable. What excuse could she possibly have to go out on such an evening? Then there was the question of what she could wear – something that wouldn't arouse parental suspicion but felt right. Another hurdle loomed before her: when she reached Cartegena how was she to make her presence known? What if Lord Lamb answered the door – or his wife? She began to flounder with confusion. What should she say to her mother? It was unthinkable simply to tell her that Guy Lamb, the *Honourable* Guy Lamb, had invited her to visit. Apart from anything else, her mother would instantly want to know who else would be there and what they were going to do, and where. *How are you going to get there – and get home? If he had any respect for you, he wouldn't let you walk. He'd come and pick you up in that car of his – not that I want you riding round the countryside in a car. Goodness knows what the neighbours will think.*

Then would come the disapproving downturn of the lips. People like the Lambs didn't invite people like the Weeks socially. Young Lamb should know better. Shirley shouldn't be so silly as not to see that it wasn't appropriate.

'I'm going to pop round to Amy's. We're doing a project together.' Her voice sounded stilted as if it was being forced through the very narrow constriction that was her throat.

'Wrap up warm, then, it looks like snow.'

Her mother did not object. She approved of Amy. One hurdle completed.

She indeed had to walk to the manor. Reluctantly she dismissed the idea of wearing her new shoes with the stiletto heels. That would certainly cause comment. Her boots, though, were clumpy, old-fashioned. Perhaps somehow she could take them off before she actually went into the house. And walk around barefoot? She abandoned the thought as foolish.

As she stepped outside she braced herself for the journey. It would be all right crossing the green, taking the narrow lane that fronted a row of detached houses just on the edge of the village, but after that it was countryside, a good quarter of a mile before you came to the gates of Cartegena. Then came the chilling trek along the blackness of the drive, where trees that by day were calm and solid metamorphosed into the stuff of nightmares. She drew in her breath, assuring herself that the friendly trills and rustles of daytime creatures could not be transformed into hunting beasts with claws like daggers, slaver-ing mouths, their eyes the blood-red of hell. In spite of her sensible voice, though, only the overwhelming wish to see Guy again gave her the courage to face the intervening distance like some intrepid explorer entering head-hunting territory.

Somehow she forced herself to maintain a steady walk, not to startle like a nervous horse at the slightest creak or whisper. As Cartegena came into view, several lights beckoned her on, although by the time she was anywhere near the door, she stumbled to a halt, paralyzed by the prospect of making her presence known.

Before she could decide what to do, she heard the ancient latch of the front door grind open, saw the heavy ring of the handle jolt sideways, and the door swung inwards to emit a muted carriageway of light across her path.

'Hi. I've been looking out for you. I wasn't sure you'd come.'

Guy stepped back to allow her inside. He wore a cream shirt and jeans and his feet were bare. Something about the sight of the splay of his toes with their neatly clipped nails sent a trill of embarrassment through her. Her own boots swelled in her mind to monumental proportions. Mortified, she handed him her school coat – the only one she could possibly wear on such a night. He hung it on a stand in the hallway while she struggled out of her boots, mumbling something about them being muddy and pushing them close to the coat stand.

'Come along. We'll go up to my room.'

The churning continued. Should she be going up to his room? What would his parents think if they caught her red-handed, creeping up the stairs?

Mrs Weeks, I feel it is my duty to inform you that your daughter visited Cartegena yesterday evening. She spent time unchaperoned in the chamber of my son, an unmarried man. I thought you would wish to know.

'Come on.'

Cringing with every creak of the stair treads, she followed him up, turning along the landing that formed a gallery looking down on the hallway below. The wall was lined with family portraits: men in wigs, women in dresses that lifted their bosoms until they must surely fall out of the bodices. She slowed down to look but Guy had already opened one of several identical doors and she scuttled inside.

She hadn't really thought what his room would be like but even so it surprised her. No four-poster bed left over from centuries ago. No tiger-skin rugs or antique vases. The floor was carpeted in grey, with vivid zig-zag black and red patterns over it. The walls had been plastered and were painted a smooth bluish white but much of the area was covered by a built-in wardrobe and a set of drawers and shelves on which were stored various silver cups, a radio and a record player. Clothes were spilling out of the bag he had clearly brought home for the weekend and a guitar leaned drunkenly in the corner.

The idea of having entertainment in your bedroom was completely novel. True, sometimes Shirley read in bed, but that was difficult because the central bulb cast only a miserly light so that she had to lean awkwardly to the right to be able to see. Guy, she noticed, had a light directly over his bed and also a table lamp. Like Blackpool illuminations, she thought, knowing that this was the sort of remark her mother would make.

'Sit down.'

She didn't know where. There were some files on the only chair but rather than face the alternative of the bed she moved them to the floor and seated herself. While she was doing so, Guy put on some music. She was fascinated to see that his record player was the sort that would play several records one after the other. The frenetic pulse of 'Satisfaction' by the Rolling Stones filled up the emptiness around her.

'How did you get on?' she asked, and when he looked surprised, she added, 'What did your parents say about your coming home?'

He shrugged and turned the music down a decibel or two.

'Fortunately for me, the old man had just gone out. Mother was all of a flutter but I persuaded her not to tell him. I'm going back tomorrow. I've promised to eat humble pie, apologize, that sort of thing. It's important to her that I observe the rules.'

'What did you do?'

He shrugged, sinking on to the bed and drawing his legs up. She noticed the bones of his ankles, the hint of fair curly hair disappearing beneath his trouser legs.

'You'd expect a university to be a seat of enlightenment, wouldn't you?' he started. 'That's not the way I see it. One of the lecturers, in particular, he's a fascist. I listen to him bleating on about the glory that was Greece but he dismisses the slavery, the inequalities and superstitions. It's turned into a sort of running battle between us, more of a debate than a lecture. He doesn't like it, especially as some of the others are beginning to see things my way.' He shrugged, leaned over and opened the bedside drawer.

'Want a smoke?'

She shook her head. It took her ages to realize that he wasn't talking cigarettes here, not Embassy or Consort. He was moistening thin Rizla papers, sticking them together, filling them with desiccated green leaves.

She knew that it was illegal. Didn't drugs do things to your brain? She didn't belong here; wished that she hadn't come.

'He says I'm disruptive,' Guy announced, drawing long on the fragile tube and inhaling deeply. His eyes half closed to avoid the smoke and his expression reminded her of the way the cat sometimes looked at her, although in the case of the cat she had always thought of it as slavish devotion.

He held the cigarette out to her. 'Go on.'

Again she shook her head.

'You afraid?' he asked. 'It's all right, really. You should never believe everything that the powers that be tell you. It will make you feel good, relaxed. If everyone in the world smoked, there would be fewer wars.'

She hesitated, torn between her naturally law-abiding persona and the desire to please him. Hesitantly she reached out and took the spliff, putting it to her lips and taking the merest intake of breath. The presence of the smoke in her mouth was alien. She coughed, a response over which she had no control. Was it her imagination or did her head already feel strange? Quickly she handed it back.

'You're a timid little thing, aren't you?' Guy said.

She wanted to deny it but couldn't find the words.

He said, 'There's a big world out there, Shirley Weeks. Don't turn your back on it. Get out there as fast as you can and experience it.'

'I will when I've taken my exams,' she countered.

He smiled, a turned-down, ironic twist of the lips that denoted someone disillusioned by the world. 'University isn't all it's cracked up to be. Why don't you travel? Tell you what—' He sat up and leaned forward, his eyes now wide with enthusiasm. 'Why don't we, you and I, take off somewhere – Africa? India? We could really experience life.'

She shook her head, laughing. It took her several moments to realize that he was serious.

'I couldn't,' she said.

'Why not?'

Hundreds of reasons. She had no money, no passport, no courage either. Besides, her parents would never allow it.

'If you want to,' he said, 'you can do anything. Here.' He moved over on the bed, encouraging her to join him.

She felt all sort of stirred up inside. To say no would look stupid. Besides, there was so much about him that she wanted to experience. His look was intent, gentle. He seemed vulnerable somehow. She wanted to be closer to him, to smell him, to feel his warmth, to touch his skin. Knowing that this must be dangerous, she still moved to the bed and plonked herself down awkwardly, stiffening into a resistant skeleton of her real self.

'Come on, lean back, relax.' She allowed her back to press against the pillows, felt his arm resting against hers. 'Don't be afraid,' he said. 'I'm not going to rape you, nothing like that. I don't believe in violence, not of any sort.'

The tension eased away. Guy put the tiny remains of the spliff in the ashtray and leaned back. He closed his eyes. 'This feels good,' he said. 'I like you, Shirley. I think you're a nice person. I think you're pretty too, not in a conventional sort of way but – attractive.'

Immediately she felt mortified. He didn't think she was beautiful then. There must be beautiful undergraduates, girls with long hair and classical features, lithe, sexy bodies. And surely he was the sort of boy they all wanted – handsome, charming, kind, intelligent and rich. This last thought rose like a spike-topped barrier, separating him from her. Somewhere inside of her a hollow opened up and she knew in that moment that she would never be able to fill it.

They talked for ages and far too late he said he would take her home. Again conflicting desires tore at her. She didn't want this evening to end, not ever, but at home the spectre of her parents loomed. Her mother would be looking out for her.

Perhaps by now she had walked along to Amy's house, discovered that she wasn't there, phoned the police, sent out a search party.

The evening was ruined. All the negative implications swamped her.

'I'll drive you,' Guy said.

'All right.'

She didn't want him to stop anywhere near the house in case her parents saw them. How could she face the embarrassment of her mother coming out and telling Guy off? She would die of shame.

As they approached the village, she said, 'Drop me here.' In the dark she felt him glance at her in surprise.

'Afraid what Mummy and Daddy will say?' he asked.

'No!' She felt so ashamed, such a gauche, naïve creature. How could she ever compete with the sophisticated elegance of the college girls?

He pulled in on the far side of the green and switched off the engine. 'Better get along home then. I wouldn't want you to get into trouble with your parents.' He hesitated then added, 'I wouldn't like them to disapprove of me either because – well, I'd like to see more of you, when I come back at the end of term?'

Her heart, at one moment so constricted and in pain, soared. He was saying that he wanted to see her again, wanted her to be his girlfriend?

'I could write,' she said.

'So you could.' He gave her the name of his college, his room number. All the time the seconds ticked away and the desire to hurry home and yet to stay with the magic of him pulled her in all directions.

'Well.' He turned in his seat and his hands came to rest on her upper arms. 'Good night, then, Shirley Weeks.' Even in the gloom she could see the intensity of his gaze and slowly, in a moment-by-moment movement, he leaned closer and his mouth rested against hers. This intimacy, the taste of his slightly salty lips, the cold of his cheek against hers, engulfed her. Something happened then. She stepped through a portal and there was no going back, no going back – ever.

*

Much to Shirley's surprise, Lady Lamb remembered their conversation about the library.

A few days later, on a wet Sunday afternoon, she said, 'Shirley, whenever you want to, do come up and have a look at the library. There are lots of old files and things apart from the books.'

'Thank you, I will.'

She could have stayed on then but her mother would be waiting for her. She could phone home but it took Maud an age to struggle from the chair. Better just to wait.

The next afternoon, though, she did stay behind, armed with writing pad, two biros and great expectation. Now that it came to it, however, she wasn't sure what she was looking for or where to begin.

The library had a low ceiling, a polished wooden floor and fully panelled walls. The smell of old leather and wood oil permeated everything. About thirty years ago electric lighting had been installed and power points fitted into the skirting boards. As she pressed down the brass knob of the switch, muted light embraced the room. A large rosewood table and four chairs, their backs carved in an elegant fretwork, filled the central space. It was a place that Shirley regularly entered but only to dust and polish. Now she looked around it as if she was a stranger.

The bookshelves were in rows of five, jumbled with leather-bound volumes. Plato's *Republic* rubbed shoulders with two green tomes on woodland maintenance. The letters of Oliver Cromwell were squashed between the *Bloodstock Breeders' Handbook* for 1952 and Carlyle's *French Revolution*. A few jarring paperbacks squeezed in here and there. On the bottom shelf some boxes of papers were carelessly pushed in.

Shirley started with the boxes. The first one she pulled out held black and white photographs. She drew in her breath, knowing that her mind was about to lurch off on one of those tracks like the map of a tube line. Would she follow the self-deprecating line or the daydream line? Which would arrive first

– the practical train of thought or the nostalgia branch?

The first photographs were postcard sized, pictures of a young Lord Lamb and his slender wife, out on the lawn, standing or sitting beneath the cedars. Lady Florence wore a calf-length dress and a cloche-shaped hat, her short dark hair just visible as it followed the line of her jaw. Her husband wore flannels, a straw boater tipped back on his head. He had a dark drooping moustache. Two Labradors appeared in most shots, variously wandering around their owners' legs. Shirley tilted the table lamp the better to study them.

Carefully she laid them aside and picked up the next bunch. On top was a picture of a small child in a swimming costume, somewhere on a beach, his spade dragging in the sand. His head was tilted provocatively to one side, the hair almost white, hanging in long corkscrew curls, but there was no mistaking that it was a boy. No mistaking, either, that it was Guy. Shirley suspended breathing in her concentration, the pugnacious thrust of the lower lip, the chubby hand half covering one eye. He was perhaps two years old.

Shirley had not then been born. In fact her first memory of Guy was when she was about five and he was eight. It was summer. Guy was home from school, his second term at a prep school, something that Shirley thought of with horror. As far as she knew, no one else in the village went away to school, only the son of the people at the manor. It set them apart from ordinary people but to Shirley it was a cruelty, a punishment, something she could never imagine enduring. She pictured herself as she was then, skinny, bony knees above tumbling socks, dark eyes, thick brown hair invariably topped with a bow. She recaptured that feeling of suspicion with the rest of the world. Now she thought about it, she had only felt safe behind the closed door of Hawthorn Cottage, her mother a constant presence.

She loved her mother then with the unquestioning, self-interested confidence of a child. Her mother was always there. She would walk Shirley to school in the morning, wait outside the gates for her to come home at lunchtime, walk her back at 1.45 and collect her again at 3.15. She didn't work. Her role in life

27

was to cook and clean and provide for Shirley and her father. Her father, on the other hand, scarcely impinged on her life. When he was not at work he was in the garden shed or his allotment. As far as she remembered, he never went out to the pub in the evening. In winter evenings, therefore, he must have been at home with them in the kitchen, listening to the wireless, but she didn't remember him being there. There were times, though, when she would want to sit on his knee and comb his hair.

'Leave Daddy alone, he's tired.' Her mother's admonitions. He must have come home from work, worn out, too tired to face the attentions of a small, bored child. With hindsight, she realized that as life had progressed, anything that required her father's opinion was always filtered via her mother: *Daddy says, Daddy thinks*. Apart from the one memorable discussion over her going to university, she could barely remember a conversation.

She sifted through a few more photographs, mostly of Guy, older now. Here was the boy she remembered, in short flannel trousers, braid-trimmed blazer, similarly decorated cap. These had been taken when he was away at school. Strange how he looked the same to her now, not smaller, not a child, but the person as she then encountered him. The thoughts came in a torrent.

Each summer he would be at home, a stranger in the place where he was born. It must have been 1947 or 1948. His birthday was on 27 July, bang in the middle of the holidays. His new friends at the prep school lived miles away. Some of them flew out to exotic places – Hong Kong, Rhodesia – where their fathers had important jobs. Others went to the Continent or the States. This was what Guy told her.

'Jenkins can't come to my party, he's up in Scotland. Neither can Parks. He flies out to Barbados on Tuesday.'

The names caused her breath to ripple at the wonder of it. Their lives were as exotic, as unreachable, as the moon. Guy had been to France several times. Shirley had been to London, once. Her sort didn't go on holiday. Once a year or so they might take a coach trip somewhere, just for the day. Bath, Salisbury,

Stonehenge, these were the horizons of her childhood world.

It was because Guy had few friends in the neighbourhood that Lady Florence had invited Shirley, as the daughter of her cleaning lady, to his party. The doctor's son, Harold, had also been invited, as had the gardener's son, Frank Agnew. Frank was the same age as Guy whereas Patricia, the final guest and daughter of the housekeeper, was eleven. Poor Guy: what must he have thought about these uninspiring guests?

'You ought to take a present.' Her mum.

'They've got more money than we have.' Her dad.

She'd taken a wooden pencil case her Auntie Doris had given her. It had a sliding lid that was difficult to open and a painted rabbit on the top. It seemed babyish for an eight-year-old but Shirley took it anyway, wrapped in rather crumpled tissue paper with thin white string binding it. She had made a birthday card too, out of a sheet of folded lined paper, a drawing of Cartegena carefully coloured in with her crayons. Inside she wrote: *To Goy, happy berthday, from Shirley Weeks.* It was years later that she realized that his name was not spelt 'Marster Goy', as her family pronounced it.

The party was a revelation. Shirley wore her Sunday dress and new white socks, and a green ribbon in her hair. Granny had also knitted her a new cardigan in pale green and wearing it for the first time she felt the height of elegance. When they arrived they were shown into what she now knew was the ante-room; the drawing room, being full of delicate objects, was unsuitable for children. Being summer, they were soon chaperoned into the garden by Patricia's mother and set the task of hunting for 'treasure', hidden in an area of lawn surrounded by a thick hedge and known as 'the hideaway'. The treasure turned out to be sweets wrapped in shiny paper. Shirley, who was used to sweet rationing, could not believe the extravagance. She found four. Other games followed that involved running around – hide and seek, tag – and others that required you to pick a partner. Invariably Patricia was the first to be chosen, being the eldest and pretty. Shirley was almost always the last, but on one glorious occasion, Guy actually picked her first. The knowledge left a vapour trail of sheer delight.

The tea was something to remember for ever: neat little sandwiches cut into crustless triangles, filled with cream cheese and cucumber, silvery pink ham and something Shirley had never encountered before – Marmite. Thinking it was chocolate, she took a hungry bite from her first sandwich to be met with a violent, alien taste. Somehow she resisted the urge to spit it out, and searched around helplessly for somewhere to hide the rest. At that moment she spotted Hector, the Lambs' elderly spaniel, and surreptitiously slipped the offending remains to him. He obligingly wolfed it down.

There were jelly, blancmange, tinned peaches, biscuits, cakes and an iced sponge with Guy's name in blue icing and eight blue candles. It was the best children's party she was ever to attend.

In the way of things, the real surprise came later, though, unexpected, shocking in its suddenness. After tea they had been ushered back out into the garden to fill in the last half an hour before their parents arrived. Shirley was never sure what started it. She had wandered casually back into the hedged garden, hoping to find more sweets. From there she heard raised voices.

'You take that back!'

'It's true. Everyone knows so. You only got this lot by robbing the peasants.'

'We didn't. Queen Elizabeth gave it to my ancestor. He was a great man.'

'A pirate more like.'

Shirley hurried back to see what was happening. The idea of a pirate as an ancestor inflamed her imagination. Before she could pursue her thoughts, however, Guy repeated, 'You take that back.'

'Won't.'

'I'll fight you then.'

Frank Agnew, big for his age, snorted derisively. 'You and whose army?'

In a flash, Guy had his jacket off. He bunched up his fists and stood like a prize-fighter. 'Come on.'

Without warning Frank launched himself at his host, sweeping him bodily to the ground, and began pummelling him.

Shirley watched, thunderstruck. Fights, punching, violence of all kinds, unless you counted shouting, was outside her experience. For a terrible moment she thought that Guy would be killed, that Frank would be hanged for murder.

'Don't!'

The others stood around watching, various emotions playing across their faces. Harold looked superior. Patricia leaned forward, her eyes wide with excitement.

When nobody moved, Shirley rushed forward and grabbed Frank's shirt, trying to pull him away. 'Don't! You'll kill him.'

Her interference enabled Guy to scrabble to his feet and immediately he took up his pugilist's stance again.

'You're no gentleman,' he said.

'And you're a nancy boy.'

'Whatever is going on?' Lady Florence appeared on the scene. The whole group, fighters and onlookers, parted to let her advance. To her son she said, 'Whatever are you doing? This is no way to behave.'

'I'm sorry, Mother but this – this oik cast a slur on the family.'

'He's your guest. You should have been man enough to ignore it.'

Turning to Frank, she said, 'And you should know better than to insult someone who has invited you as a guest. I'll have words with your father tomorrow. Now you will both shake hands and ask each other's pardon.'

'But—'

Her look stopped them both in their tracks. Reluctantly, they both reached out a hand and mumbled a sorry.

Lady Florence declared herself satisfied. 'Right. Now you will go into the house and collect a little gift each before you go home.'

Her heart still beating unnaturally fast, Shirley followed the others towards the hallway. Ahead of her, Guy slowed down and waited for her to catch up.

'I say, thanks most awfully. It was jolly sporting of you to intervene on my behalf.'

She knew that she had gone beetroot red. She couldn't look at him but at the same time she swelled with the pleasure of his approval.

Once inside she received her gift – a small china rabbit nibbling a dandelion leaf.

'I know you like animals, Shirley,' said Lady Florence.

'Thank you, m'm.' She mumbled her thanks and pondered on the mystery that Lady Florence knew anything about her at all. She did like animals. Perhaps it was this love as much as anything else that shaped her future.

Whereas until that day Guy had been an almost alien figure whose life was as mysterious as a Hottentot, from then on he became the number one topic of Shirley's daydreams. At eight years old he was grown up, daring, the epitome of every prince in every story that had been read to her. It was he who aroused the Sleeping Beauty, placed the slipper on Cinderella's foot, metamorphosed from a frog. In each story, Shirley was the princess.

A week passed after the party when she did not go to the house, then on one magical morning, Granny offered to take her to work with her, Shirley's mum being struck down with some undefined illness. Thinking back, she guessed it was probably period troubles, or the early stages of a pregnancy that failed in the end to produce a longed-for brother or sister. Whichever, while Granny was washing up and preparing the dinner – which Lady Florence referred to as luncheon – she sent Shirley into the garden to play.

'Don't wander too far.'

'I won't.'

She made her way across the lawn to the hideaway with the hidden sweets, hoping that one might have survived behind a twig in the privet. While she was peering into the hedge, she heard someone coming. Turning round, she found Guy Lamb staring at her.

'What are you doing here?'

'My gran's in the house.' Even then, she didn't want to admit that her family worked for his.

'What are you looking for?'

'Nothing.'

They stood there for what seemed like forever, then Guy said, 'Thanks for the box, by the way. I hope you don't mind but I've found a different use for it.'

Shirley waited and with a nod of his head he encouraged her to go with him. He led her back across the grass, along the length of the ha-ha, through a wooded area and into a cobbled yard with various sheds and other outbuildings.

'Look.' He bent down and fished the pencil case from under a shed, carefully sliding back the lid that now worked perfectly.

Shirley leaned forward and peered inside. It was full of grass. She glanced questioningly at Guy.

'Wood lice. I'm carrying out an experiment to see if they breed in captivity.'

He must have seen the confusion on her face, for he added, 'I put them under the shed because they like cool, dark, damp places – sorry if it damages the box.'

Shirley peeped closer. Several grey insects scurried into corners, their feelers frantically searching for an escape route. She was surprised to notice that there was one that was a dark coppery colour and another that was blotchy, reminding her of a piebald horse.

'Lovely, aren't they?' Guy said.

Were they? Shirley had always regarded them with horror, squealing if she accidentally unearthed one.

'They don't really eat wood. I've put some earth and leaves underneath.' He suddenly looked regretful. 'I'm going back to school tomorrow so I shall have to let them go.' He regarded her speculatively. 'I don't suppose you—? No.' He shook his head, dismissing his own thought. 'In fact, I'll let them go now, in case I forget. I wouldn't want them to suffer.'

His words, the unthinking compassion for something so humble, sealed Shirley's fate.

With a deep intake of breath she pushed the photographs back into the box. This was no good. It was getting her nowhere. On the bottom shelf was a large, flat folder. She pulled it out instead and opened it. It contained various plans and letters relating to the layout of the garden. The plans folded out to reveal neat pen sketches. She recognized the front of the house, paths, a terrace, a shrubbery, ponds, the lake, fountains. With a frisson of pleasure, she realized that these must be the original plans drawn up in the eighteenth century. Laying them aside, she rummaged among the papers and found a list of employees, their jobs and their wages. It was dated 28 October 1784. Her heart thrilled as she read, 'Josiah Weeks, labourer, one shilling and sixpence.' This must surely be one of her ancestors. There was another Weeks, Isaac, referred to as an apprentice. She made notes, forgetting that it was the history of the house and not of her family that she was supposed to be pursuing. Had they too lived at Hawthorn Cottage? Was there an unbroken line of Weekses stretching as far back as the Lambs?

To her surprise, the library door opened and Lady Florence appeared, carrying a cup of tea. It shook dangerously in her hand.

'I thought you would welcome this.' She deposited it clumsily on the table. 'Have you found anything useful?'

'I—' Shirley showed Lady Florence the plans and together they picked out the features that were still familiar to them. All the time the essence that was Guy seemed to surround them. There was so much here in this room that seemed trapped in a kind of secrecy. She wasn't sure whether she should or could release it. She drank the tea in silence while the older woman peered down at the plans.

'Interesting,' she said. 'You will remember to turn out the lights, won't you?'

'I will. I was just going.'

She took the cup back to the kitchen and washed it up. The sandwiches she had made for Lady F's tea had been taken out of the fridge and stood on the table covered with a linen napkin. She tried to imagine spending every day here, every night, but couldn't. Everything seemed charged with uncertainty and there was nowhere for her thoughts to settle.

It was nearly dark when she left and she regretted not having brought the car. In the failing light, even in adulthood, the driveway seemed a different place, silent, waiting, almost hostile. She was glad to reach the gate.

As she swung it open, however, she was aware that a car was parked opposite and that someone was peering across at her.

Her discomfort quickened. Purposefully she turned and prepared to walk away but the driver wound down the car window and called out.

'I say, I'm sorry to bother you, but do you live here?'

She slowed reluctantly. 'No.'

'I – I remember this house from when I was a child. I used to come here sometimes.'

Now she was genuinely interested. She took a few steps back towards the car, leaning down slightly to see the driver.

He was possibly in his early forties, dark haired, with gaunt cheeks and deep-set eyes.

'I recognize you,' he said. 'Shirley Weeks.'

She nodded her head, still puzzled.

He leaned across and opened the passenger door. 'Do you still live on the green? Get in, I'll give you a lift.'

None the wiser, Shirley climbed in. As she shut the door and he put the car into gear, he said, 'You don't remember me, do you? I'm Frank Agnew.'

Three

Shirley absorbed several impressions all at once. The car was old and low slung with a throaty engine. Frank himself appeared to be dressed all in black which, combined with his dark curly hair, reminded her of a cat burglar. A map book and camera were jammed on to the top of the dashboard and for a fleeting and foolish moment she thought he could have been a spy. He exuded a pleasant aroma of soap, sharp and clean. She registered that he didn't smell of booze or tobacco.

'What are you doing here?' Her voice sounded accusatory. She had a vision of him hurling himself at Guy all those years ago in the garden. There had been a sort of fury about him then that went way beyond normal schoolboy scraps.

'Just visiting.'

She hadn't seen him for years. Briefly they had been at the village school at the same time, him at the top, her in one of the baby classes. She had known who he was even before the party incident. Agnew – you identified boys by their surnames then. At the age of eleven he had changed schools, taken the daily bus into Bath. Their lives had gone in different directions, no point of contact.

'How are your parents?' she asked, for something to say.

'Dad died eight years ago. Mother – I'm home for her funeral.'

'I'm so sorry.' She hadn't heard. In the village you nearly always heard of births, deaths and marriages. She felt rather than saw him shrug, a dismissive gesture.

'She hadn't been well for a long time.'

There was a silence in which they both mentally circled each other, looking for points of contact. Shirley was the first to speak.

'Where are you living now?'

'I've just come back from France. I've got a place out there.' His voice was different. Gone was the Somerset burr.

'You must speak good French.' It had been one of her subjects at A level. That sense of emptiness was there again, her wasted life. She dreaded his next question.

'And what about you? Where are you living now?'

'The same place.'

Same place, same life, nothing to report for the last quarter of a century.

'Your mother?'

'She suffers from arthritis. That's why – I can't really move away.' She felt that she had to explain herself. Even if she could move, she didn't know if she'd have the courage now. She'd probably left it too late.

Frank said, 'I haven't been home for five years. It seems ludicrous, coming now she's dead. There's no one else, though, no one to clear the cottage.'

'Did it belong to—?'

'No. It's leased, some ridiculous peppercorn rent. Part of the Lamb estate.'

It was there again. She sensed the disdain in his voice. At least her father had had the foresight to buy Hawthorn Cottage when, during one of those periods of financial crisis in the Cartegena fortunes, Lord Lamb had put some property up for sale.

Frank pulled the car up outside Shirley's door. She went to get out but he switched off the engine.

'What's happening then, at Cartegena?'

'Nothing really. Lord Lamb died three years ago. Lady Lamb is quite infirm.'

'She lives there alone?'

Shirley nodded. Hesitantly she said, 'You know that Guy . . . disappeared?'

He stared intently at the windscreen that was quickly misting up.

'So I heard. No news?'

37

'No.'

Cracks were threatening to shatter her calm persona. To steer the conversation on to safer ground, she said, 'The old place is in danger of going to rack and ruin. Lady Lamb's going to open it to the public at Easter.'

'Is she now?' He gave a derisive grunt. That silence again.

'Well . . .' Shirley hovered uncertainly, not sure if she was being dismissed. To ease the discomfort, she asked, 'When's the funeral?'

'Tomorrow.' He drew in his breath. 'The church is going to be pretty empty – the vicar, some woman from Social Services, and me.'

'Would you like me to come?'

She hardly knew Mrs Agnew, hadn't seen her around for ages. Theirs was a small village. She ought to be more aware of what was happening.

Frank said, 'I've told the vicar I don't want any claptrap. None of this bosom of the Lord stuff, no eulogies about my mother's life. He's new here; never even met her.'

Shirley imagined the scene: the vicar all twitchy and nervous, Frank a resentful presence and some woman he didn't know.

'I'll come if you'd like me to,' she repeated.

He shrugged a half acceptance. 'The service is at two o'clock.'

The funeral was indeed painfully short. An organist played background music but there were no hymns. The minister was visibly nervous, being unable to fall back on the safety of the service which by its very nature commended the deceased to her Maker. Frank stood alone in the front row, Shirley and the Social Services lady behind him. They nodded to each other, masking their discomfort, and faced the front, making the best of things.

When the minister had rambled through a few lines, the coffin was carried out into the churchyard and Mrs Agnew's earthly remains were laid with those of her husband. Again the vicar fumbled for appropriate words, being forbidden to offer sure and certain comfort in some future resurrection.

When it was over Frank invited them all for a drink. The vicar declined with indecent haste. The SS lady said that she had another job to go to. Frank raised his eyebrows and an amused grimace touched his lips.

'How about you then, Ms Shirley Weeks?'

'I'd love a drink.'

They went to the Dark Horse. Being a midweek lunchtime, the lounge bar was empty. Frank ordered a vodka and tonic for Shirley and a pint for himself. While he was at the bar, Shirley studied him, trying to marry the two images of an eight-year-old boy and the forty-something man. There seemed no point of recognition. As a child his hair had been light brown although curly. He had seemed plump, heavy, big built. Now his hair had darkened to near black and he was tall and catlike in his movements. He looked much younger than his years. She noted that he did not wear a suit, instead wearing navy blue trousers, a blue flecked jacket, white shirt and a black tie. He didn't look like an office type. She pondered on what he did.

He returned with the drinks and a menu. 'Might as well eat now.'

Mother would be at home, wanting her dinner. Shirley had told her that the funeral shouldn't last long. She had prepared things for Lady Lamb earlier that morning, when she had rushed up to tell her that she would be otherwise engaged.

She was about to say that she really should be getting home but this rare break in her routine made her suddenly rebellious. Mother might be incapacitated but she wasn't bedridden. She was capable of heating some soup, making a sandwich, boiling a kettle. She took the menu.

Once they had ordered, Frank stretched out in a chair and took a long, smooth draught of his beer. She watched him savour the flavour, assess it.

He said, 'I hardly ever drink beer these days. The French have a few good ones but it is the wine that matters there. I'm out of the habit.'

Shirley hardly drank at all. She hadn't anything against it but the chance rarely arose. She had tried having wine in the house, a bottle of sherry, but somehow alcohol had to go with relaxation, pleasure and good company. The atmosphere at home rarely gave itself up to any of these.

'When are you going back?' she asked.

He shrugged. 'A couple of days. I've got some house clearance company coming to take the stuff away.'

'It must seem strange, parting with your childhood.'

He looked at her curiously. 'My childhood seems a long time ago. Besides, it wasn't a happy time.' He took another mouthful of beer. 'I've kept a few small things.'

For a moment he seemed lost in his own thoughts and she tried to remember anything she had heard about him but nothing would come.

He said, 'How about you then? What have you been doing with your life all this time?'

It was her turn to shrug. Bugger all, she thought. Aloud, she said, 'I worked at the town hall for a few years but when my mother got sick I packed it in. I go up to Cartegena every day to cook the old lady a meal.'

'A sort of Samaritan, then.'

She didn't like the inference.

'Not married?' he asked.

Shirley shook her head, humiliated as if this represented yet another failure on her part. She struggled to hide her resentment at his question.

'You?' she asked.

'Not any more.'

'Children?'

He shook his head. 'You?'

'No!'

She felt foolish, this old maid assumption that only married women had children. Quickly she said, 'What are you doing in France?'

The food arrived at that moment and they waited until the waitress left before he said, 'I do a bit of everything. The neighbouring property's a vineyard. If I'm there I help with the *vendage*. Occasionally I do some labouring. I make the odd translation, grow my own vegetables. Mostly I take photographs.'

'What of?'

He gave an 'anything', gesture. 'There are several magazines I work for, one or two TV things. I get by.'

It sounded perfect: a self-sufficient, varied, independent routine in a foreign place with no one to answer to.

For a few moments they ate in silence, then Frank said, 'Why don't you come back to the house with me, see if there's anything of my mother's you might like? It's only old stuff, not to modern taste, but some of it is antique, if you like that sort of thing.'

As she went to refuse, he added, 'It's only going to the junk man or to the dump.'

Why not? The alternative was to go home and do the ironing.

He offered her another drink but she declined. Already there was a warning, floating feeling around the edge of her brain. Another drink and she might find herself saying something foolish. In silence they left the Dark Horse.

The cottage was in a state of limbo, things on chairs and in piles, cardboard boxes everywhere, some empty, some filled. Her eyes wandered over the contents lying around, trying not to feel like a dealer. On the mantelshelf were some vases. Without looking she knew that they were Minton. There were similar ones at Cartegena. Two pug dogs in Parian ware sat on either side of the vases, a statue of a highly coloured parrot on a china branch in the middle. It surprised her that the gardener's family should have such treasures.

She caught Frank watching her and felt uncomfortable, fearing that some avaricious streak might show through.

'I was thinking,' he said, 'that although I haven't seen you for what – thirty years – you still look the same. Weird, isn't it? You were a child then and you're a woman now, but you seem to be exactly the same person.'

Strange that she had thought the opposite about him; that he was not recognizable as the Frank Agnew of the infant school.

Seeing her glance again at the Minton vases, he said, 'Why don't you take those? That is, if you like them.'

'I couldn't. They are far too valuable.'

He shrugged. 'Take them to a charity shop then.'

'All right. I'll take them to the Red Cross.'

She didn't feel so bad now. He indicated a cardboard box and some newspaper to wrap them in.

He said, 'What about you then? What would you like?' She was about to say that she didn't want anything but he added, 'I'd like you to have something – to remember me by?' He gave a small, cynical grin.

Her cheeks grew warm. She suddenly wondered if by coming to the cottage she had agreed to some hidden agenda. She was out of practice. What would she do if he propositioned her? Scream? Behave like a fool? Go at it like a rabbit because she hadn't had sex for months, no, years?

She placed the vases in the box and stood up. Along the wall was an old-fashioned but rather elegant ladies' desk, narrow, with a drawer and two bookshelves beneath. It would fit ideally into her bedroom.

'I wouldn't mind that,' she said, 'but you must let me pay you for it.'

He gave her a hopeless case look. 'I keep telling you, it will either go to the dealer or the dump. I tell you what, I'll drop it round later – early evening? We could go for a drink?'

She barely nodded her agreement, disturbed at the prospect of continuing this acquaintance. Going across to the desk, she opened the drawer. It was stuffed with papers.

'What about these?'

'Dump them.'

'You shouldn't do that. There might be something important.'

'Put them in a carrier bag then.'

She found one and did so, wondering if he would simply throw them away later. Anyway, that was up to him.

She glanced at her watch. It was nearly three o'clock.

'I must be getting along,' she said.

'I'll give you a lift.'

'No, really, I could do with a walk.'

He acquiesced. 'All right then, Shirley Weeks, I'll see you this evening.'

'This evening.'

As she walked home she felt strangely churned up inside. Months of ignoring her emotions had them almost under

42

control. Now they were unleashed, her imagination conjuring up crazy scenarios. Did she want this? What did it amount to anyway, a polite invitation from someone who no longer knew anyone else in the neighbourhood? Perhaps he felt sorry for her; could see that she was a lonely, frustrated spinster. The thought that he might actually fancy her, a man who lived in France and travelled as a photographer, was laughable.

'You've been a long time.'

It was the greeting she expected from her mother. 'We went for a drink afterwards,' she said. 'I'm having some of Mrs Agnew's belongings to take to the Red Cross shop. Her son is going to drop them round later.'

She couldn't quite get her mouth to say that then they were going for a drink. Wait until he got here and pretend it was a spur of the moment invitation.

She picked up her mother's plate – she had boiled herself an egg. Shirley who had eaten vegetable lasagne, immediately felt guilty. She offered to make some tea and when she had done so, went up to her bedroom to decide exactly where she would put the desk. She felt ridiculously excited and girlish; this wouldn't do.

At about six o'clock there was a telephone call.

'Mrs Weeks?' It was an unknown female voice.

'Shirley Weeks.'

'I'm the receptionist at the surgery. Doctor McDonald was called out earlier to Lady Lamb? She had a bit of a fall. She's all right but the doctor thought someone should call in on her and she said that you were her daily. I wonder if you might—'

'Right. I'll pop up there now.'

'Thank you. Perhaps you could make her a hot drink, something to eat. A fall is always a bit of a shock at that age. We'd just like to satisfy ourselves that she hasn't suffered any after-effects.'

'Right.'

'Please call us if you have any concerns.'

'I will.'

Shirley replaced the receiver and told her mother.

'She shouldn't be living in that great house on her own,' Mrs Weeks said.

Shirley agreed that she shouldn't but couldn't think of an alternative. There certainly wasn't enough money for a live-in carer and the question of moving out and selling Cartegena was something that Lady Lamb would never countenance. Besides, the house was simply held in trust until such time – as what? Until Guy came back? And when he didn't? She had no idea what would happen when Lady Lamb finally died.

That sense that everything was transitory was back again. As she drove to Cartegena, she thought, One should live for today. All those other warnings drifted though her mind – this isn't a rehearsal, life is short, there might not be a tomorrow. Perhaps she should apply this to Frank Agnew?

When she got to the house, Lady Lamb was sitting in the parlour, her left ankle bandaged and resting on a stool. The fire was almost out and the room felt cold.

'Oh Shirley, what a nuisance. I did tell them not to bother you.'

'Nonsense.' Shirley busied herself, stoking the fire, fetching a shawl, making tea to which she added some brandy. She then prepared ham sandwiches, cut a piece of fruitcake and took them in on a tray.

'Please try to eat something. I'll go and put the heater on in your bedroom.'

'You are so kind.'

When Lady Lamb had drunk the tea and nibbled at the food, Shirley helped her up the stairs to her room.

'Do you need any help?' she asked.

'If you could just—'

Shirley helped her to undress. It was worrying because the old lady was independent. She must be feeling unwell to agree.

When she was in bed, Shirley asked, 'Would you like me to stay the night?'

'No, really. The telephone is to hand. You go along now. I – I won't get up until you get here in the morning.'

'Well . . .' She wasn't sure that she should leave but the old lady insisted. Besides, there was Mother at home. She had a momentary vision of a tug of war, two old ladies, one at each end of the rope, pulling her towards them.

Lady Lamb said, 'I promise that I will be all right.'

A sense of unease stayed with Shirley as she travelled home. Was this the beginning of a new phase in the old lady's decline? If so, what would it mean for Cartegena, for Shirley?

She parked the car in its usual place in the road, tucked under what in spring would be the flowering lilac, and let herself in. Standing in the hallway were several boxes and the desk.

'That young fellow called,' her mother said by way of greeting. 'He said he was sorry not to see you. He wanted to carry the desk upstairs for you but I said no.'

'Right.' She took off her coat, hung it up and tried to feel businesslike. It was already nearly eight. She couldn't phone Frank because she didn't know the number. Besides, there was probably no phone at Mrs Agnew's cottage. In one instant she considered and rejected the thought of going over to see him. Besides, he probably wouldn't be there. He'd probably gone to the pub, driven into town. Was he even now sitting in a bar somewhere chatting to a young woman? The tide of her feelings that had bubbled and frothed throughout the day suddenly drifted into the doldrums.

Four

F rank did not make contact the next day or the next. By the third day Shirley had to admit to herself that he must have left. A hollow sense of disappointment claimed her, something approaching despair that was way out of proportion to what had happened. She tried to convince herself that she was relieved, that she didn't want any complications in her life. It was all right as it was, steady, dependable, no troughs or peaks. Men, affairs, only meant trouble. The arguments raged in her head. It wasn't as if she even knew Frank. She had no idea what he thought about anything, what he thought about her, although perhaps that was pretty obvious, for she hadn't made sufficient impression for him to trouble to contact her. This voice from the past, though, however distant, seemed to represent some chance to go back, perhaps to make something happen, although she had no idea what.

As she went about her daily routine, the same thoughts kept coming up. She told herself that the only reason it mattered was that being now thirty-five years old, she needed some benchmark against which to measure her desirability, purely as an exercise. His failure to contact her proved that as far as he was concerned, at least, she was pretty low on the scale of sex appeal. She closed the subject with the jibe, 'I didn't fancy him anyway.'

The following Monday she took the vases to the Red Cross shop. The assistant viewed them with some suspicion.

'These are valuable,' she said. 'Do you have any proof of ownership?'

'I haven't stolen them,' said Shirley. 'The owner died. Her son lives in France and he asked me to give them to you.'

She knew that her face was taut, betraying a guilt that wasn't hers. Why couldn't even this act of kindness be straightforward?

'Well, we'll have to get them valued. Can I have your name and address?'

It was easier to give it than to try and explain again that she wasn't the owner. She left the shop feeling on edge. Everything, but everything, was unsettled; the only comfort was that Lady Lamb appeared to have made a complete recovery.

A few days later, just as Shirley was leaving Cartegena for the day, a car drew into the driveway. She waited on the step as the driver, a young man in a suit, got out, collected a brief-case and stood looking at the façade of the house. When he noticed her, he waved and walked over to her.

'Good morning. John Chambers, National Trust. I've just come to have a look round and advise on which parts of the house should be opened for public viewing.'

Shirley opened the door again, thinking that if she was going to be delayed she should phone Maud. While Florence would definitely have ideas, she probably wasn't up to trailing all around the building, so it would fall to Shirley to act as escort.

She showed Mr Chambers into the parlour where Florence was writing a letter, a weekly routine that kept in touch with Bunty Springfield and Dolly Haverton, two friends whose association went back to Florence's school days. Shirley thought that if you could collect all the correspondence together, it would make a priceless insight into twentieth century social history.

As they went in, the old lady put aside her fountain pen and gave them her attention.

'This is Mr Chambers from the National Trust,' Shirley started. 'He would like to discuss the tours with you.' Once the introductions were complete, she excused herself to go and make some coffee. When she returned, John Chambers had a clipboard and pen to hand.

Florence said, 'Shirley, will you show Mr Chambers round? You can take him anywhere he wishes to see, other than Guy's room, my bedroom and Lord Lamb's study.' She picked up her bag and produced a heavy collection of door keys, handing them over with the words, 'Just make sure you lock up when you've finished.'

When John Chambers had drunk his coffee, Shirley gave him a tour, starting with the ground floor, including the kitchens and utility rooms.

'This is amazing.'

He was a young man, slim to the point of being willowy, exuding that studious enthusiasm that laid bare his love for history.

'You have an interesting job,' Shirley said, as she tried to lure him out of the kitchen. He lingered to stare avidly at the deep sinks, the huge old fireplace where the spit and trivets still remained intact. 'These aren't still in use?'

Shirley smiled. 'Not now. Lady Lamb is the only occupant of the house. We don't roast sides of beef these days.' She pointed out the electric stove, the fridge/freezer, the toaster and kettle on the side.

'But this place has hardly changed. Everything has been kept. It's . . . amazing.'

He smiled self-consciously at her, embarrassed by his enthusiasm.

She showed him around the other rooms, down the stone-floored corridors, to let him peer into the storerooms and cupboards, marvelling at everything he saw. 'I didn't expect this,' he confessed. 'Most houses of this age have been modernized to a degree at least.'

Shirley felt an answering warmth. 'I think the Lambs come from a long line of hoarders.'

Upstairs he peeped into the bedrooms, all except the three forbidden by Lady Florence. When he glanced enquiringly at the doors, Shirley merely said, 'That one is private.' He did not question it.

In spite of a bright day outside, the house was always filled with shadows. They weren't oppressive, merely the legacy of 500 years of accumulated history. John Chambers stopped to stare out through one of the small leaded windows through which the world appeared in sepia.

'Amazing.'

As Shirley went to turn left, he hesitated at another door, set into the deep panelling. 'Where does that lead?'

'That's the long gallery. I'm afraid it is unsafe these days.'

'Could we just take a look?'

'Of course. We couldn't allow visitors in there though.'

She sorted through the keys until she found one that fitted the lock. It gave a satisfying groan as it yielded and the door needed some force to push it open.

'Wow, look at this!'

Shirley hadn't been into the gallery for ages. Now she was struck by its antiquity, its glaring legacy of history. The gallery was probably eighty feet long, the floor, walls and ceiling all carved in oak, now grizzled by age. Along the outer wall, windows admitted a grey-green light, while a soundtrack of groans and creaks from the ancient wood accompanied their progress. John immediately seated himself in one of the window recesses and gazed across the parterre.

'I'm flabbergasted.'

The inner wall was lined with paintings, portraits of past masters of Cartegena, and when he could tear himself away from the view, John Chambers gave them all his attention.

He stood in front of one of the oldest paintings, a man and his wife, he in satin doublet and jewelled jerkin, she in pearl-encrusted stomacher, her skirt held taut by a farthingale. 'These are . . .' He was running out of superlatives.

Shirley followed his gaze. The man in the portrait was fair haired, a hat in green silk, complete with feather held in his hand. On the desk at his side were parchments and an inkwell, a quill pen and a seal. In contrast the woman was black haired, oval faced, her hands having long, slender fingers that rested on the head of a small boy, a miniature version of his father. The faces were in a style that suggested fashion rather than a realistic portrayal of their appearance. In the background a Tudor version of Cartegena gave on to extensive hunting grounds and in the bottom foreground a large hound looked adoringly at the master.

'Was this the original owner?'

'I believe so.'

He shook his head in disbelief at the discoveries. 'You say it is unsafe?'

Looking along the length of the gallery, Shirley pointed out how it was beginning to lean crazily. 'It needs a fortune spent on it,' she said. 'There is no money to carry out the work.'

'That's criminal. This is . . .' He shrugged.

The tour continued and by the time Mr Chambers was ready to leave, he had copious notes. Shirley saw him to the door.

'Well, thanks so much for showing me round. I had no idea this was such a treasure house. It's made my day.'

She smiled. 'It's a wonderful house,' she started, and then the thought that it was on borrowed time filled her with a kind of anguish.

Over the next weeks, other men from the marketing company called and poked around, suggesting the routes around the house, advising on notices, entry charges and tickets and where to sell the initial souvenirs. Insurance was taken out, posters designed, an advert put out on local radio. The house appeared to be on line for an Easter opening.

Shirley took the opportunity to do some more delving into the library. In a black-edged envelope, she found a letter from Queen Victoria to Lord Francis William Lamb dated 29 May 1897, thanking him for his kind wishes for her birthday and her jubilee celebrations. His present, it seemed, was to be on display along with countless other gifts to mark her long reign. Shirley wondered what he had sent and where it was now. In another box she found some campaign medals from the South African war, awarded also to a Francis Lamb. The same one? This Francis, it seemed, had been wounded at somewhere called Ulundi, his gallantry noted in despatches. Another letter, from the Royal Society, and dated 1849, informed yet another Lamb, Algernon Francis this time, that the new species of rhododendron he had brought back from the Himalayas had been named after him: *Rhododendron orientális* subsp. *agnus*. Shirley thought of the avalanche of rhododendrons and azaleas that forested the park in spring. They should be in full flower at Easter. She wondered which one was this new species. Surely someone would know? Moses Jenkins was the most likely person, having worked in the garden since leaving school at fourteen. Perhaps the then head gardener might have told him. She translated the name – *Rhododendron eastern lamb*. It amused her.

She realized that Moses must have been working in the garden at the same time as Frank's father. She hadn't given old Mr Agnew much thought. In her mind's eye she had a vague recollection of him, middle height, slightly bowed, weathered skin, looking not unlike every other local man who worked on the land – same trousers, jacket, boots, cap. She wondered whether to ask Maud if she remembered him but thought better of it. Maud would want explanations, start sniffing around. Shirley had spent a lifetime hiding her thoughts from her mother. This was no time to change. She moved a vast Russian urn presented to Sir James Lamb by Tsar Alexander II that was shielding the light. She thought, 'Next time I see Moses, I'll ask him about the rhododendrons, perhaps mention Mr Agnew,' although with what intention she had no clear notion.

She returned to the task in hand. Jumbled among the papers were everyday notes, lists and letters from unknown correspondents. They were interesting but she couldn't decide how all the information could be put to good use.

As she was packing up for the day she remembered that there was a family tree hanging over the huge fireplace in what had been Lord Lamb's study. She had hardly ever been into that room. While he was alive, Lord Lamb had forbidden anyone to clean it and since his death Lady Lamb seemed to be upholding his wishes. Shirley remembered having looked at it only once when Lord Lamb was alive. She had for some reason taken the mail to his study. He wasn't there but the door was open so she had stepped inside, feeling like a poacher, and stared around. The tree soon captured her attention and for what seemed an eternity she studied it, marvelling at the idea of knowing so much about your roots. She didn't even know her mother's father's first name. She walked along the corridor and tried the door but it was locked. Further along on the other side was *that* room – Guy's. That was locked too and had been ever since . . .

51

Quickly she retraced her steps.

Lady Lamb was in what was called the morning or breakfast room, because here the early sun warmed the otherwise chilly dampness of the air. It was now afternoon, however, and that air of emptiness and neglect seemed to invade everything. Shirley wondered what the old lady might be doing, why she wasn't in the drawing room where a fire was lit every day right through until May.

Lady Lamb seemed confused to see her and for an awful moment Shirley wondered if she was beginning to lose her grip on things.

'I was just wondering,' she said, 'if I might have a look at the family tree in Lord Lamb's study, just to note down the main names.'

Lady Lamb nodded but did not move.

'I – I'll need the key.'

'Oh yes.' The old woman bestirred herself, rummaged in the voluminous bag she always carried with her that reminded Shirley of the knitting bag that her mother had once had in tow, before the arthritis defeated her. Unlike her mother's crocheted affair, Lady Lamb's bag was made of dark silk with a tortoise-shell handle. After a while she pulled out a large ring on which were several heavy-looking keys. Shirley thought of the time when the wives of lords of the manors carried the keys to the estate on a belt around their waists, ordering the households and keeping the accounts. In her youth, perhaps Lady Lamb had not been unlike them.

'It's one of these,' she said, holding out the ring.

'Thank you. I'll bring them back.'

She retraced her steps, stopping outside the study. The keys were heavy and old-fashioned. It was the third one she tried that opened the lock, already stiff from lack of use. As she withdrew it, a thought occurred to her. Surely another of these keys would open Guy's door? Her chest felt fluttery. No, this was crazy. Leave well alone. Pushing the study door open, she went inside.

The room was dark, the lowered blinds giving it a neglected feeling. Stale tobacco and dust disturbed by her sudden intrusion tormented her nose. Carefully she raised the blinds, fearful that they might stick. A reassuring burst of light bathed everything in sight.

Shirley looked across to the fireplace and the family tree. It was large and ornate, mounted in a gilded frame. The succeeding heirs to the house, starting with that Francis Lamb of so long ago, were printed in red. Near to the top, however, was one black entry, shrouded in drapes, announcing the intrusion of William Stapleton who had held the house for eleven years following the Civil War until King Charles II returned it to its previous owners, along with an elevation to the peerage.

Shirley counted down the lines. There were fourteen generations of Lambs listed: births, deaths, marriages, offspring. Her eye followed the line to the bottom.

The last two entries were incomplete. Edward Charles William, Lady Lamb's husband, had been born in 1903. He was forty when he married Florence Phyllida Charteris and two years later, their son, Francis Guy William, had been born. Shirley sank into Lord Lamb's chair. The baby must have been such a joy to them, such a relief to produce an heir at this late stage, to ensure the continuation of the Lamb line.

Seeing Guy's name on the tree like that was like losing your footing, stepping out on to something that wasn't there. No date had been inserted to mark the death of Edward, Lord Lamb, and as for Guy . . . How could there be?

The storm was brewing up inside her. This wasn't a good idea. All she must be interested in was the distant past, perhaps as far as Lord Lamb's father, probably the winner of the awards for gallantry? By noting down all the names and their dates, maybe she could discover something interesting about each one of them. Keep focused.

She scribbled the names of all the owners of Cartegena on her notepad, trying to ignore those distractions where several children had been born of the union. On two occasions a son had predeceased his father and then it seemed that a brother had stepped into the breach. Anyway, for the moment only the heirs to the house mattered, those who had continued the line right up until 1985, when Lord Lamb had died. She wondered about the contents of his will. Clearly for the length of her lifetime, at least, Lady Florence retained the right to live here, the mistress of the estate. Shirley looked back at the tree to the line before, where any brothers or sisters of Lord Lamb would be listed, for surely the inheritance would then pass to them or their heirs? As far as she could see, there was no one with an obvious claim.

For a while the preoccupation made her forget her turmoil but as soon as she stopped it was back again. Having done what she came to do she locked the door and returned the keys to Lady Lamb.

It was dark outside and she was glad that she had the car. On the drive home she tried to work out some plan of action, imagine a scenario where she was carrying out her first guided tour. *Ladies and Gentlemen, welcome to Cartegena, the family home of the Lamb family since (date?). The house takes its name from the Spanish port of Cartegena in (which South American country?)* There was so much that she didn't know.

When she got home she found Maud sitting near to the fire with a pen and notebook in her hand. She watched as her mother painfully outlined a column of words.

'What are you doing?'

'Making a list. I'm writing down the dates when everyone died. Since your dad went, I keep missing the anniversaries. I even forgot your gran's.'

Shirley took off her coat and hung it in the cupboard. Was this what it came to? Instead of recording each new birth in the family, were you reduced to notching up each death? What did it feel like to be alive when all your friends had gone? Did you feel a sense of one-upmanship, or was there a gathering sense of loss?

She wanted to give her mother a hug but they were out of the habit so she asked, 'Cup of tea?', falling back on the familiar. As she glanced out of the kitchen window she noticed that early narcissi were beginning to petal the bank under the hedge. They had survived another winter, overcome the hazards of scratching cats and nibbling mice to face another spring. The thought gave her a fragile strand of hope. Uneventful as it had been, she too had survived another year. Perhaps now was the time to grasp her future, bend it in some way that she wanted. She had no idea what that might be but the very thought brought a rare glimmer of optimism, displacing the gloom that had claimed her for days.

That first letter Shirley had written to Guy had taken a whole evening to compose. She decided on a friendly, chatty style, trying to think of witty things to write that would amuse him. In the end, though, the letter was short and formal. As soon as she had posted it she regretted having mentioned her cat, Herbert. He wouldn't be interested in such things. She should instead have told him about the hockey match, mentioned that she had seen his father outside the Dark Horse with Colonel Rainford from Thornton Grange, only she wasn't sure how she should refer to them. Her parents talked of Lord Lamb and the colonel in respectful tones. How could she use such titles without drawing attention to the differences in their stations?

The awaited reply did not come on Thursday as she hoped. In fact, it was Tuesday week before she came home from school to see a pale blue envelope propped up against her mother's wooden elephant that stood on the old radiogram in front of the window. Immediately her entire future teetered on the brink of a precipice. The contents of this letter would surely contain the most important words she would ever receive, and this included her O level results. How would she cope with the disappointment if Guy told her not to contact him again? Please God, she prayed, let him want me to write back.

'There's a letter for you.' Her mother was in the kitchen peeling potatoes. The kettle was already singing, part of the daily routine that greeted her from school. Their lives had been all routines then; days for doing the laundry, days for eating bubble and squeak, sausages, Sunday roast. Then it had seemed comforting, giving her a sense of assurance. Now the alternating routines of Mother and Lady Lamb were like chains, keeping her shackled to the neighbourhood.

Casually she dumped her school-bag in the living room and wandered across to the elephant. The letter almost seemed to taunt her – come and pick me up, if you dare. She did so. She did not know the writing but of course it was his. On the back of the envelope was a blue crest, some words in Latin. She wanted to push the letter into her bag to open when she was alone but to do so would arouse suspicion. Instead she hastily tore it open, hoping to absorb the pain before her mother came into the room with a cup of tea and two gypsy creams in the saucer.

The letter wasn't very long but her eyes scanned the page, looking for clues. Her gaze fastened on the last words – love Guy – and her spirits soared.

'Who's that from then?'

Quickly she pushed it into her bag.

'Just someone from school – someone who used to be at our school. She's moved away.' Since she had left the junior school and commuted into the town, her mother did not know all her friends or their families. She hoped the lie would go undetected.

'There's a blackbird making a nest out by the holly tree.'

She quietly exhaled her relief. Mother was not interested in her girlfriends. Surreptitiously she transferred the letter to the pocket of her school skirt and as soon as she could, used the excuse of feeding the rabbit to make her escape.

Flopsy the rabbit had survived into double figures, outliving his purpose as a young girl's pet. Arthritic and sleepy, he had long ago resigned himself to his captivity and roused himself from his torpor only when she opened his hutch to fill his feed bowl and replenish his water. Taking refuge in her father's shed where the rabbit food was stored, she drew the letter out and read it properly.

Dear Shirley,

So sorry to have taken such an age to write. I've been really busy lately, mostly sports fixtures although there have been a couple of outings – dance, theatre, that sort of thing – that has kept me from my studies. As you'll see, academia does not rate very high on my list of priorities.

I am sure that you are a better student than I could ever be. You seem to have ambition. Mine is to escape somewhere hot and peaceful and live out my life as a beachcomber. Shame, I hear you say.

I dutifully made my apologies to the lecturer in question, promised only to raise relevant points of debate and not rouse the others into rebellion! It won't last long – a man's got to do and all that.

I guess I am in limbo. I can't stop thinking about you. You have a fresh quality that no one else I know comes near to possessing. I don't know what love is, Shirley, but whatever I feel for you it is different from anything I have ever known before.

I will be away for much of the Easter vac – our college is on a rugby tour so yours truly will be trying not to break a leg – or worse.

Write again if you have time – and I hope you have.

A bientot,

Love Guy.

She leaned back against the door of the shed and lifted her face to heaven. There was a god. Her prayers, dreams, had been answered. From this moment forward nothing else mattered except that Guy loved her.

There were two more letters before the beginning of the Easter vacation but no further mentions of his feelings. Already Shirley was beginning to realize that there was no such thing as satisfaction in love. Be grateful that he has written, be glad that he likes you, be pleased that you will see him again one day during the holidays. . . . It was never enough.

Five

The guidebooks arrived a week before Easter. The sight of them produced in Shirley a strange anxiety as if their expertise might underline her own failings. The cover was stiff and shiny and a photograph of the house taken from the park showed it standing proud above the centre of the terrace, the foreground broken only by a statue of a boy and his dog and a few urns overflowing with flowers. The plants had been bought in specially, much to the disgust of Moses Jenkins, who took pride in growing his own. It was the wrong time of the year, though, and he had been caught out. The outer limb of a cedar tree extended fingers into the left side of the picture, adding balance. Shirley thought how serene it looked, how well maintained and timeless. The flaking plaster and the green water stains were not visible. Neither were the decaying window frames and the missing roof tiles.

She wanted to take the book into the library or even the kitchen to study it straight away, but there was too much to do. Agnes Selby from the village had been recruited to help with the cleaning. Douglas Kirk, who was Frank Agnew's distant cousin on his mother's side, was doing some hasty repairs. As Shirley went to put the washing away she found him in the corridor, fashioning a ramp that would give wheelchair access to the drawing room.

'All right?' He nodded to her.

Although he had been present in the village all her life, they had never had a conversation. Like Shirley's father, Douglas was one of those men destined to live and die in the same place, at peace with the small and familiar. Shirley smiled at him and squeezed past. Like Frank, he was dark, but there the family resemblance ended for Douglas had that sturdy quality that went with slow, laboured toil. Remembering Mrs Agnew's funeral, she guessed that the family ties were sufficiently remote for Douglas not to attend his aunt's interment. He had made her think of Frank, though, and that was unsettling. For the moment there were more immediate things to occupy her mind.

A conservator had been enlisted from the National Trust to instruct her in how to care for the more important objects around her – or more accurately to resurrect them from their present neglected state. A willowy, pallid girl called Rosina, who might have stepped from a Modigliani painting, examined the vases and glass and fabrics with disdain. She warned against detergents, astringents and hard brushes. The task of restoring the chosen rooms to their former glory was clearly unattainable so the most impressive items and the glaringly neglected pieces were picked out for attention. Once they had been soaked or buffed or beaten, though, it only seemed to draw attention to the neglect everywhere else. Shirley felt her spirits begin to flag.

'Do you know John Chambers?' she asked, thinking of the young historian's enthusiasm for the house.

'Oh, him.' Rosina's lips turned down derisively and her nose crinkled in disapproval. She clearly had nothing more to say on the subject so the conversation was closed. As Rosina left, Shirley feared that they would never be ready on time.

That afternoon she took the guidebook home to study. Once indoors her spirits lifted and she had to curb her impatience a little longer for Maud was avid for news of what they had done that morning and how.

'Vinegar, that's what you need for cleaning furniture,' she announced. 'A couple of tablespoons in a gallon of warm water and a good wipe over. Plenty of elbow grease with some beeswax and wood comes up like new.' Her expression conveyed her impatience with these newfangled methods. 'Pure soap,' she continued. 'Soap and water's best for glass and china. Many's the time I've had everything gleaming.' A hint of regret for things past pulled her mouth down at the corners.

Shirley didn't argue. Her mother had removed egg stains from silver breakfast forks, wine from table linen. She had polished brass and silver, ironed lace-edged pillow covers. Her methods had worked well enough.

As soon as she decently could, she smuggled the guidebook up to her bedroom. She felt guilty for not showing it to Maud straight away but she would do so later. For the moment she wanted to test her knowledge, to find some omission in the book that would boost her own sense of worth.

The contents were fine as far as they went: forty pages set out in chronological order, two columns to a page, interspersed with photographs of special items and portraits. Shirley flicked through the illustrations: a sword presented to Sir William Bouverie Lamb by Charles II; a Prussian helmet, trophy brought back by James William Francis following his escapades in eighteenth century Europe; an Italian table inlaid with various marbles, souvenir of a Grand Tour; the Lamb coat of arms.

In the centre of the book was a half-page reproduction of the Tudor portrait from the gallery, with the caption: *Sir Francis Lamb, the first owner of Cartegena with his wife Elizabeth Knollys and Francis, their first-born son. It is believed that the portrait was presented to Sir Francis by the Earl of Southampton and that on one of his visits he was accompanied by his protégé, William Shakespeare. It has even been suggested that Elizabeth might be the Dark Lady of the famous sonnets.* Shirley paused in her reading. Had Shakespeare really walked in the long gallery, wandered in the gardens, perhaps composed words now made famous? Did he have a flirtation with Lady Lamb or was it more intense? Could he and not Sir Francis have been young Francis's father? The possibility excited her so much that she put the book aside, trying to visualize the young Shakespeare, but the only portrait she had seen of him was with a high-domed head and a fringe of hair. Try as she might, she could not translate that into a romantic poet, wooing the wife of a wealthy lord. She picked up the book again, thinking what a pity it was that because of its precarious state, the visitors would not be able to see the gallery or the painting.

There were other things in the book that she didn't know – dates, statistics – but as she turned to the back cover with a photograph of the Talbot hounds guarding the front porch, the emptiness opened up inside of her again. It was what the text didn't say that gnawed at her. Lord Lamb dead, yes, his widow still living in the family home, yes, but what of the son who should even now be Lord Lamb? What of the future that no-one seemed to think worth mentioning? Suddenly, she felt very afraid.

That night she couldn't sleep. When her thoughts began to drift she was back in that first Easter, 1967, with Guy away on his rugby tour. He hadn't mentioned where they would be playing so she couldn't even try to picture where he was. Instead she fantasized about him telling the other players about his girl-friend, drawing comfort from the thought that he was bound to send her a postcard or two. She would have to be careful, though, to get to the mail before her mother did. But there were no postcards. The days dragged by and she tried to concentrate on her history revision, to struggle to read and appreciate the poetry of Alfred de Musset and Lamartine, but all the time her thoughts were elsewhere.

Then, just when the local schools reached the end of their holidays, her mother came home from Cartegena and said, 'Young Guy's back. He's been up in Scotland climbing a mountain or something.'

Until then, Shirley had not known it was possible to jolt physically at the very mention of someone's name. Carefully she set her history textbook aside.

'I'm just going out.'

'Where to?' Perhaps her mother didn't really sound suspicious and it was Shirley's guilt that detected the distrust in her voice. Even so, she found her face growing hot.

'Just to see Amy.'

'You've only just left her.' Maud sniffed at the foibles of young girls. 'Well, you can bring me in some milk. I think I'll make a macaroni cheese.'

The weather confounded her then, a sudden sharp shower

that made venturing out seem foolhardy.

'Surely you're not going out in this?'

'What about the milk?'

'That can wait until later.'

Shirley fretted. She wanted to see him. How much she wanted to see him. As soon as the shower eased, perhaps she could find an excuse to call at the house, say that her mum thought she had left her bag behind, except that Lady Lamb might ask Maud the next day if she had found it. Another thought occurred to her. Perhaps, just perhaps, Guy was even now driving down to call on her. The rain wouldn't matter in a car. What would she say, though, if he knocked at the door? How to explain? She couldn't invite him in without everything being awkward. She squirmed at the thought of her mum calling him Master Guy. Even worse, if her dad came home he might call him 'Sir', like he did the doctor. A sudden rebellion surged in her, anger with her parents. The Weekses were as good as the Lambs any day – better if anything, for hadn't her family always worked hard and produced useful things like food? As far as she could see, the Lambs had done nothing except fight and exploit the villagers.

It was in this mindset that she finally made her escape. Feeling that she had nothing to lose, she strode out in the direction of Cartegena. She'd think of something on the way. The nearer she got, though, the quicker her confidence ebbed. At the gate she halted, staring at the intricate ironwork, thinking how it was symbolic. Guy's world would always be closed against her.

'Fancy seeing you.'

She jumped at the voice, turning to find him behind her. All her sensible thoughts deserted her like rabbits fleeing to their burrows.

He said, 'I've followed you up from the village. Were you coming to see me?'

'No.' The inflection in her voice challenged his assumption. 'I just stopped to . . .' She couldn't think fast enough.

'I've just been for these.' He waved a packet of Guards at her, opening the packet and lighting one, drawing on the cigarette with obvious pleasure.

They stood there stupidly in silence until Guy said, 'Do you want to come in for a drink?'

She shrugged, but as he pushed the gates open she followed him inside.

'How was the tour?' she asked, for something to say.

'Tour? Oh, the rugby. Fine.'

More silence, except for their feet crunching on the gravel.

'Did you win?'

'It wasn't a competition. They were just friendlies.'

His reply made her feel foolish, as if she should have known. She was about to say that she had heard he had been moun-taineering but then he'd probably think that she had been talking about him so she remained silent. By now they were at the front porch. Her thoughts turned to his parents.

'Is anyone home?' she asked.

'Probably not.' He suddenly grinned. 'Lucky for us, eh?'

She didn't know how to respond.

'You sulking?' He gave her a quizzical look.

'Why should I be?'

'Why indeed?' He let them in and led the way to the kitchen. 'Tea or coffee?'

'Tea, please.' She saw with a sinking feeling that he made coffee for himself. She should have said coffee – that must be the thing to drink.

He carried the cups to the kitchen table and sat down, stretch-ing his shoulders as if they were stiff. She wondered if he had pulled a muscle with all his physical activity.

'So,' he asked, 'what have you been doing?'

She wished she could think of something interesting but she fell back on the truth.

'Studying.'

'Ah, studying.' His mouth twitched in amusement. 'You are a serious girl, my Shirley.'

My Shirley? The words took her aback. She was about to say that she wasn't his Shirley but surely that was what she wanted to be?

He gave a little sigh. 'Are you sulking because I haven't writ-ten?'

To her chagrin, tears began to prickle in the corners of her eyes. She couldn't speak for fear of betraying herself. He raised his eyebrows, forcing her to look at him.

'I've been busy,' he said. 'Moving around a lot.'

She wanted to know where and who with. There must have been girls where he had been – posh, good-looking, clever girls. What hope had she against such competition? She knew that she shouldn't have come. Her mum would call it making herself cheap.

'Hey, I've got something for you.' He got up and left the kitchen, returning a few moments later with a paper bag. The name printed on the side was Ferguson, an Edinburgh address. Carefully she opened it to find inside a slab of butterscotch. She didn't know whether to be pleased or disappointed. She decided to be pleased. At least he had thought about her once while he had been away.

'Thanks.' She put it in her bag, trying to calm herself. After a while, she asked, 'How long are you home for?'

'Just until Thursday.'

Only two days. The despair was there again, clawing at her.

She suddenly remembered the milk; remembered where she was supposed to be.

She gulped down her tea. 'I – I'd better go.' She stood up, feeling numb. This wasn't what she had dreamed of ever since that kiss, back then, 18 February.

'Shall I give you a lift?'

'No thanks.' Too dangerous, someone might see and tell.

'OK.' He followed her to the door. 'I'll see you around then? That is – do you want to come to the cinema tomorrow? They're showing *Yellow Submarine*.'

Her heart pulled back from the precipice. 'All right.'

'Shall I call for you?'

'I'll meet you outside.'

They arranged the time and, clasping at the straw of tomorrow, she stepped into the gloom.

'See you there then.'

'Until tomorrow.'

*

The film wasn't one she would have chosen. A love story would have been better but what really mattered was that she was with him. Part of her rejoiced in the fact that they were out together in a public place. Let her friends see them. Wouldn't they be envious! If her mother got to hear of it she'd say she'd met him by chance, happened to sit next to each other. She was supposed to be with Margaret Whitton. She'd say that Margaret hadn't been feeling well so she decided to go anyway, on her own. The lies came so easily.

When the lights went down he put his arm along the back of her seat, his hand resting on her shoulder. From the corner of her eye she could see its shape, the breadth across his knuckles, the long fingers. She kept very still, not wanting him to withdraw it. At the same time she feared that his hand might wander further down on to her breast. This was what her mum would call not respecting her.

In the darkness she thought of all the signs and signals, a labyrinth of possible misunderstandings. It must be different when you were serious about someone, though? Was he serious about her? What he had said all that time ago in his letter, surely that was proof of his feelings? She agonized about how to tell for certain.

An ice cream and the end of the film later, they stepped out into the gloom.

'I've got the car.' He slipped his arm around her shoulders again. She was contemplating the difficulty of letting him drive her the few hundred yards to her front door when he said, 'We could go for a little drive.'

In silence she followed him to the car. She didn't want their time together to end but neither did she know what she was agreeing to.

They drove away from the village, past the outlying cottages until they came to Moor Lane, a narrow track leading to Moor Farm. Just to the left was another track and Guy backed the car into it.

'There.' He turned off the engine and turned towards her.

'I—' She was aware of her stiffness, the tension in her neck and shoulders.

'You're not scared, are you?' he asked.

She wanted to say that she'd never done anything like this before, by which she meant she had never gone for a drive with a man in a car. As for anything else, what her friends called 'going all the way', well, she'd hardly gone any of the way at all; a few hugs and kisses endured from Eric Drew, an unwelcome grope from Peter Salisbury. Now she didn't know what she wanted. She was still a virgin. If what the others said was true, she was probably the only virgin in their class. Her body was sending out its own signals, spontaneous surges like invisible feelers reaching out in the darkness for some undefined fulfilment.

'It's OK. I'm glad.' Guy's face was close to hers. He nuzzled her cheek with his own, his hands resting on her upper arms.

'We won't do anything you don't want to do, I promise you.'

She felt the responsibility of being the one to have to decide the rules. If she said no, would he lose interest? If she said yes, would he dump her?

They went what she thought must be nearly all the way. She agreed to get into the back of the car because it was more comfortable. She put her arms around his neck when he kissed her so that her breasts were squashed against his chest, and the hardness in his jeans seemed to be feeling its way like some blind creature towards its burrow. Guy's hands travelled along her back, down her sides, across to her breasts where the answering jolt of response amazed her. It might be her body but it had a will of its own. She didn't object when his hand found its way under her skirt and into her knickers because she, her body, so wanted him to touch her that she would rather have died than stop him. Then he had his jeans undone, his penis warm and intent against the inside of her thigh.

'It's OK,' he whispered, 'I won't go inside you.'

Her legs clamped tight and held him as he moved against her until with a gasp— Of what? Ecstasy? Anguish? – he stopped and slumped back. Gently he kissed her temples.

'You're beautiful.'

Afterwards, he gave Shirley his hanky to wipe herself as he struggled to zip himself up. Surreptitiously, she pulled up her knickers; tried to capture the time and the moment. For a while she lay with her head against his shoulder, thinking that this was the moment she had been born for.

Too soon he said, 'Come on, I think we'd better go before the beast wakes up again.'

She hadn't realized that a man could be in this constant state of readiness. There was so much that she didn't know.

He parked across the green from her cottage. It began to dawn on her that the cinema had closed hours ago. She could see that both her parents' bedroom and the downstairs lights were on.

'I – I must go.'

'You're all right?' She nodded but the beauty of the occasion was spoiled by the thought of what faced her.

Guy said, 'I probably won't see you again before I go, but I'll write.'

'Promise?'

'I promise.' He kissed her eyes, his hands cradling her face.

'I love you,' she said.

'You're a very special girl.'

Hastily, unwillingly, she scrabbled from the car and took the short cut across the green. He must have been watching her until she reached the gate for as she unlatched it the engine exploded into life and the car crawled away.

Her mother was in the kitchen. She wore her dressing gown and slippers and her expression was that tight, gimlet stare that told of both relief and accusation.

'Where on earth have you been?'

'We forgot the time,' she said, hoping that would be enough, even though she knew that it wouldn't. It was impossible to know which line to take.

'And what have you been doing?'

Had her mother walked across to Margaret's house, wakened her parents and demanded to know where her daughter was? Her uncertainty must have shown in her face.

'The truth, young lady – who have you been with and where?'

'I – I just went for a walk with a friend, after the film.'

'And what friend would that be?'

'You don't know them.'

'Them? Do you mean *him*?' Her mother sniffed her distaste. 'You've been with a boy, haven't you? Who is it? What have you been doing?'

Shirley felt suddenly tired. She was cornered. She had no answers she could rely on. Changing tactics, she said, 'I'm old enough to go out with who I like.'

'Not as long as you are under our roof, you're not.' Mrs Weeks sighed. 'I can't understand you, Shirley, really I can't. You know as well as I do that going off with a boy like that, making yourself cheap, can only lead to one thing.'

The platitudes went on. Shirley took refuge in tears. They had the desired effect. At last her mother appeared to run out of steam.

'Right, you'd better get to bed or you'll be fit for nothing in the morning.' As an afterthought she added, 'Your father's been worried sick.'

As Shirley mounted the stairs she heard the steady, rhythmic snoring from her parents' room.

Like rain bouncing off cobbles, her memories disintegrated. She lay in the dark and the pages of the book that was her life fell open on the blank page of the present. Tomorrow would bring more cleaning at Cartegena, shopping for the Easter weekend before everything sold out. There were no treats in store, nothing to look forward to except the ordeal of the first guided tour.

I need a break, Shirley thought. I need to get away. She thought that perhaps her Aunt Jean might come to stay, look after Mum while she took a few days' break.

The prospect brightened her mood although she had no idea where she might go. Meantime, with Easter Sunday looming, she closed her eyes again and began to recite the speech she had planned: 'Good morning, ladies and gentlemen, welcome to Cartegena.'

Six

'Good morning, ladies and gentlemen, welcome to Cartegena.'

Six people stood expectantly in front of Shirley, the first tourists to experience the new venture. Faced with the reality of their presence, Shirley's throat threatened to seize up, her mind to empty of every thought. For a moment she scrambled frantically for the next sentence then, as the words began to tumble out, the fear abated. She led the visitors around the ground floor, explaining, entertaining, trying to gauge their reaction. Seeing the interest, her confidence grew.

The tours were scheduled to last for forty-five minutes, ending with a free tea or coffee and a biscuit, to be followed by a stroll in the grounds. For this, Moses Jenkins and Frank's cousin Douglas Kirk had been enrolled to potter in the garden and keep an eye on things. With trepidation Shirley asked if there were any questions and to her relief she found them easy to answer.

In the short break between the first and second tours, she manage to grab a coffee: so far so good. She felt suddenly exhilarated by her new guise as expert.

Lady Lamb herself had decided to take on the role of ticket seller. It was a sitting-down task, something she could manage. Besides, her upbringing dictated that as the hostess it was incumbent upon her to welcome the guests. Shirley hoped that she wouldn't get into too much of a muddle handing out the change.

Maud had been recruited too, to help with the teas and coffees. It was her job to spoon the coffee into the cups, top up the biscuits. Anything more was beyond her but her pleasure at being employed was pathetically obvious.

With a deep breath Shirley took a final gulp of coffee and

prepared for her second tour of duty. There were five people waiting in the gloom of the hall. She was surprised to see that one couple was Japanese and the second, who were talking intently, were clearly American.

'Good morning,' It was only then that she looked at the fifth member of the group and her voice faltered, for there, a quizzical grin on his face, was Frank Agnew. As she began to stumble over her words he nodded encouragement. Refusing to look at him, she said her lines, aware how stilted and uncertain they had become.

When the tour finished, the American man asked, 'Is the old lady taking the money the duchess?'

Shirley smiled. 'Actually she's a baroness – that's the wife of a baron, but her father was an earl.' His expression told of his fascination with the British aristocracy.

'What will happen to the house when she dies?'

Frank's question. The Japanese looked uncomprehending and the American man gave him a disapproving glance.

'That,' said Shirley, 'will depend on the conditions in Lord Lamb's will.'

'But he's dead. Don't you know?'

'No. I don't.' She turned her back on him and began pointing out a few final features. She felt angry that he should ask such a question and angry with herself that his presence should shake her confidence.

As the party left for tea and biscuits, Frank said, 'I'm sorry I didn't see you before I left.'

Shirley shrugged as if it was of no importance. 'Why are you here now?' she asked.

'I've come back to sign some papers.' He tilted his head to one side and studied her. 'You don't seem very pleased to see me.'

'Should I be? You'd better go and get your tea.' She felt pleased with her put-down.

Frank didn't move. 'Perhaps you'll come for a drink this evening?'

'I don't think so.'

He gave a small, philosophical shrug. 'That's a pity. I had something interesting to tell you.'

As she hesitated, he said, 'Tell you what, I'll call round about eight, just in case you change your mind.'

With a wave of his hand he disappeared in the direction of the refreshments.

There was no more time to think about Frank or what he had said because already more people were lining up for their tour. As she shepherded them from room to room, Shirley found herself glancing out of the windows, wondering if he was still in the gardens, but there was no sign of him. It took all her willpower to dismiss him from her thoughts.

Everyone agreed that the day had been a great success. In the six hours that they had been open, eighty-four people took a tour of the house. The shop had sold twenty-six postcards, five calendars and seventeen guidebooks. Both Lady Lamb and Maud looked tired but exhilarated and Shirley thought with some guilt how much better old people were when they were stimulated. She really should take her mother out more, find things for her to do. It was a familiar self-flagellation, beating herself up over her failings as a daughter, but when she did make the effort she found Maud's company unsatisfactory, her response to whatever Shirley planned not what she had hoped. The thought was always there – how much longer would her mother drag on? When would she, Shirley, be free to start living her life? The self-hate grew.

As her thoughts flitted fretfully, the knowledge of Frank's proximity settled around her like a gathering storm. The thought of going out with him filled her with panic. It loomed like an ordeal, some sort of dangerous test she must undergo. Yet she had a choice. She could say, 'No thanks, I'm too tired, too busy, I don't want to,' but even as she considered it she felt the desert of her life stretching ahead of her. Grasp the nettle, live for the moment, take the plunge – she knew that she had to go.

As she drove home, Maud wittered on about the trivia of the day. Shirley forced herself to listen, seeking refuge in the small and familiar. As she helped her mother indoors, she suddenly felt extremely tired. She thought about Lady Lamb and wondered if she shouldn't go back once Maud was settled. Then she realized what she was doing – running away from Frank's visit. Lady Lamb had only to sit in her chair and eat the cold meal that Shirley had prepared for her. Even her drink was heated and in a flask. The chair lift would carry her up to her bedroom. The toilet was next door. Around her neck she had the button that she could press in case of emergency and someone from the help agency would be round there like a shot.

'I – I think I might pop out this evening,' she said as she helped Maud off with her cardigan. 'Just for a drink.'

Frank called at eight. He wore a pale blue shirt and dark blue jeans. Shirley thought how youthful he looked, breadth of shoulder, flat belly, neat rounded behind, long legs. Even his face had escaped the ravages of time. It was disturbing. Shirley wore a skirt she had bought the summer before but only worn once. She was aware that her waist was thicker, her breasts heavier. She felt middle-aged, frumpy.

'You look good,' he said as if challenging her unspoken misgivings. She resisted the urge to say, 'So do you.'

He took her to the Bell and Candle. It was a tiny pub, an original village inn, only the village had moved elsewhere so that it was now somewhere people drove to for a bit of atmosphere, a quiet traditional pint. Shirley drank wine. Frank ordered a pint of beer.

'Do they worry about drinking and driving in France?' she asked.

'They do indeed.'

She tried to imagine what it must be like where he lived, but couldn't.

'Do you live in a town?' It was something to say.

'Good God, no, in the middle of nowhere. It what they call a *hameau*. A hamlet, three cottages, a farm down the lane, empty barns, birds, bees, sunflowers. You should come and see.'

The thought surged in her, seeming to fill her up. She felt choked by emotion, a thirsty prisoner offered a drink. She looked away.

Frank supped on his pint appreciatively. His glass was already half empty.

'Why did you ask about the house today?' The thought had been nagging at her.

'House?'

'Cartegena.'

He shrugged. 'I wanted to know.'

The annoyance surfaced again. 'Well, you might have picked a better time. I don't think it's something for public discussion.'

His look reminded her of a naughty schoolboy. 'Well, do you know?'

'No. It's none of my business.'

'And none of mine?' She got the impression that he was laughing at her. 'I get the feeling that you are very tied up in the place.'

'No, but I've been going there ever since I was a child.'

Tentatively, he said, 'It's a big world out there, Shirley.'

'Are you saying that I should get out more?'

'I'm saying life is short.'

For several seconds they were silent, then she asked, 'Where are you staying?'

'At the cottage.' He drew in his breath. 'It's a strange thing but there is something in the lease that states that the right to reside passes automatically to the next of kin of the last tenant. If I want to I can keep it on in perpetuity, it seems.'

Shirley pondered the strange bequest. 'Will you . . . keep it on?'

He shrugged. 'I might, for the time being. In general, though, I have little reason to come back to England. My home is in France.'

Why did his words make her feel so restless? Again she tried to picture his little hamlet with its farm and sunflowers.

'How far south are you?' she asked.

'About fifty miles south of Poitiers.' She vowed to look it up if she could remember the name by the time she got home. 'Now then.' He took another gulp of beer and settled down. 'What have you been up to since I left?'

'Getting ready for the tour mainly.' She was glad to have something, anything, to fall back on. Other than that there was nothing worth mentioning.

She began telling him about the conservation, but suddenly he said, 'You knew Guy Lamb pretty well, didn't you?'

His question jolted her into silence. She wondered what was behind it. Had he heard something? About Guy? About them?

'He was hardly ever here,' she countered.

73

'You must have heard things, though, being here when he disappeared.'

She wanted to shout at him to stop. Her eyes began to sting with the effort of keeping the lid on her emotions. Like a press statement, she said, 'He had taken a degree although he did badly. I don't think he cared because he wanted to travel. He left that spring, 1968, for South America.' She could hear his voice now: *Come with me; it'll be fun.* He was due back a year later.'

The last postcard was in her room, in the special chocolate box with the huge bow he had given her for her seventeenth birthday. *I can't wait to see you. So much has happened out here but I've had enough now, got it out of my system. It's time for you and me now. I'm leaving on the 19th. I'll be with you within the week.*

'What happened?'

She couldn't look at Frank. His intent curiosity held her like a butterfly pinned to a board.

Swallowing back her pain she said, 'They say he definitely got on the plane in Bogota – but he never collected his luggage at this end.'

It was as if the clock had stopped then, 26 May 1969. The police coming to Cartegena, her mother coming home full of the story, the press photographers, the hope – the awful hope. It was the year her life ended.

'And nothing since?' Frank asked.

She shrugged. 'Rumours of sightings. That's all.'

'The old folks must have been upset,' he said.

Shirley thought of Lord Lamb, stiff and unbending, carrying his loss like an albatross. Lady Lamb had aged a decade in a month. Aloud, she said, 'They never got over it.'

Nor have I, she thought. Nor have I. Already she had served a life sentence with little hope of a reprieve.

'Do you remember how he and I fought that time we went to his party?' Frank asked. His lips turned down in a self-deprecating grin. 'God, I hated him.'

'Why?' She couldn't believe that that event had stayed with him.

He shrugged. 'He seemed to represent everything I despised.'

'But you were only eight. Where did all those feelings come from?'

He raised his hands, invoking the gods. 'My parents, I guess. There was some deep-rooted antipathy to the Lambs even though my father worked for them. I always wondered why he didn't find another job, but perhaps they were hard to come by.' He shook his head, remembering. 'Anyway, it was a long time ago, as they say.'

Shirley nodded. A long time indeed. She longed to throw off the chains.

They chatted about other things but she was aware that in talking about Guy, his disappearance, she had brought it to the surface, faced it and survived the ordeal. As she started a third glass of wine she felt strangely liberated.

As it grew dark, Frank said, 'What would you say if I suggested going back to the cottage?'

Her mouth twitched. 'And why would you suggest that?'

'I've got a nice double bed there.'

'It isn't the one your mother died in, is it?'

'No. She died in hospital.'

She was buoyed up inside. The door of her cage was open. *Go for it, Shirley! Seize the day!*

'I would need to be home before daylight,' she said.

'The Dracula effect?'

'My mother.'

He grinned and slipped from the bench.

'Come along then, Shirley Weeks, let's make hay.'

The balm of sexual release carried her on a crest into Easter Monday. As the sparrow raced the blackbird to announce the dawn she slipped from Frank's bed and floated the half-mile home. Her head was slightly fizzy from last night's wine but just at that moment she didn't care. Even the thought that Maud might have discovered that she had stayed out all night couldn't destroy her sense of wellbeing.

As she boiled the kettle and made tea she wondered if at last she had turned a corner. She wasn't foolish enough to think that she could simply throw off her past. For nearly twenty years she had lived with the legacy of Guy. She would never escape the feeling that she was betraying him. Everything she had enjoyed since the moment of his disappearance had felt like a failing in her character. Good food, a spectacular sunset, a joke – what right had she to those pleasures when Guy might be anywhere, a prisoner, sick, down and out? Sobering, she realized that she would never get away that easily. Another thought niggled at her: was she fleeing the snare of Guy's memory only to become tangled up in a net of feelings about Frank? He hadn't promised anything. They hardly knew each other. With sour amusement she thought, One shag might not make a relationship but it could make you feel good.

Being the bank holiday, she visited Cartegena only briefly to prepare Lady Lamb's lunch. The old lady was tired but content.

'Yesterday was such a good day,' she repeated on several occasions.

A good day indeed.

Shirley hadn't been back at home long when Frank phoned.

'What are you doing today?'

'I – I thought I should take my mother out for a drive.'

'I could take you both.'

Her emotions flared and tumbled. In acknowledging her mother he had passed an unspecified test. At the same time, she and Maud had never been in the habit of talking about her social life. In the past she had been out with occasional men but none of the relationships had lasted long. They had never been significant enough to discuss at home.

At one time she had come to the conclusion that what she needed was a regular, once a week, no-commitments sexual encounter with a reliable male. She visualized them meeting in a quiet bar, a couple of drinks, then back to his place, or a hotel room, for good liberating sex with no complications. It sounded so civilized. It had never happened.

She went to find Maud. 'How do you fancy going out for a drive?'

'I don't think so. I'm too tired.' Her mother did indeed look worn out.

'I think I'll go then.'

'By yourself?'

76

'No. I bumped into Frank Agnew yesterday. He's home to sort out a few things. He invited us both out.'

Maud sniffed. 'Did he now? I've always thought there was something not right with that family.'

'What do you mean?'

'Something not right.'

Shirley knew what Maud was doing – warning her off. In spite of herself, alarm bells began to ring. 'How not right?'

'There were rumours.'

She grew impatient. 'What sort of rumours?'

'Just gossip.'

'What gossip? You can't just say that and then stop.'

Maud looked up stiffly. 'He was always wild, that one.'

'And what's that supposed to mean?' She felt her mother muddying the waters, making sure that she was put off-balance. It was what Maud would call 'nipping things in the bud'.

'You never want me to have any fun, do you?' She spat the words out.

'Don't be so silly. I only said he was a bit of a wayward boy. It doesn't mean he's still like that now. Where does he live these days?'

'In France.'

'France.' Maud's tone implied: 'What do you expect?'

In silence Shirley left the room and went to the kitchen. Her hands were trembling. Why did she always let her mother wind her up? She didn't know who she was most angry with, Maud or herself. Quietly fuming, she made her mother a sandwich and a cup of tea.

'Here's your lunch.'

Maud grunted. Her eyes were closed as if she had been dozing. Shirley was about to say, 'I won't be late,' but she thought better of it. Instead she said, 'I don't know when I'll be back.'

'Please yourself.'

I will, she thought. I most certainly will.

They went back to the cottage and made love.

'You are a beautiful woman.' Frank ran his hands over her breasts. She felt like some art object, something to be venerated and appreciated. Her earlier sense of being over the hill, gone to seed, was vanquished. Now she felt mature, ripe, at the height of her desirability. In turn she found Frank's body exciting. The skin tone, the taut musculature, the frizz of black hair across chest and belly held her entranced. His lovemaking was thoughtful, patient; his own sudden urgency exciting. This time, they had leisure to explore, to satisfy.

Afterwards, unease tugged at the edge of Shirley's thoughts: What will I do when he is gone? How can I go back to my nun's existence? She tried to push the uncertainties away. Live for the moment. Store up the pleasures.

'When are you leaving?' she asked, as they lay abandoned across the bed.

'Trying to get rid of me?'

She giggled. 'I only wondered.'

He stretched and leaned up on one elbow. With his other hand he traced the line of her jaw, twisted a strand of hair between his fingers.

'I have to go to London tomorrow. I've had a commission to photograph aspects of rural France. I'm taking the pictures up for them to pick and choose.'

'You've got them here?'

He nodded.

'May I see them?'

He shrugged as if they were of little importance, but slid off the bed and went to fetch a flat case. Sitting back on the bed, he opened it and lifted out a sheaf of photographs.

Shirley sat up and took a pile in her hand. One by one she turned them over. What she saw amazed her. In the first pictures, old, berry-brown men with squat bodies and gnarled sticks stood in patient conversation. He seemed to have captured their very 'Frenchness', the very essence of their lives. One close-up showed a square, weathered face with shrewd eyes, the soul of an old man looking out into his familiar world. In another, a woman with the light outlining her strong cheeks and jaw grasped an old wooden rake, staring confidently at the camera. Pictures of children followed, at play, at rest, a tot tumbled asleep beside an old dog. She stopped at several pictures of the same girl, probably in her early twenties with dark Romany eyes and full breasts, challenging the photographer, flaunting her body. An invitation? She felt suddenly confused.

'Who's this?'

'Juanita. She and her family come every year for the *vendage*. They pick the grapes then move on. Beautiful, isn't she?'

Shirley nodded. She wanted to ask, 'do you sleep with her?' She suffocated the jealousy.

'That's her husband.' He picked out another photograph of a rakish-looking gypsy, his features chiselled like those of an Indian chief. 'This is Yussef. He makes a living castrating the bulls. Bearing that in mind, I wouldn't mess with Juanita.' He grinned as if knowing her thoughts. His perception was comforting. Without meaning to, she put her arms around him and kissed him.

There were more pictures, landscapes, farm animals and buildings. Each one had a special quality as if here was something priceless, not to be ignored. She was lost for words.

'Are you going straight back to France?' She had to know. She had to get things sorted in her mind. This was – is – just a fling, she reminded herself. He doesn't live here. He's just passing through. It was up to her to fill the void when he left.

'I could pop back down again – just to say goodbye?' He kissed her then and his answering arousal pushed all other thoughts from their minds.

She arrived home at about seven. Maud was sitting where Shirley had left her, exuding an air of fortitude. She did not ask if Shirley had had a nice time.

'Do you want anything to eat?' Shirley dumped her bag and car keys on the table. She and Frank had showered before she left the cottage but she wondered if she still smelt of sex. His soap and shampoo teased her nostrils.

'I was going to open a tin of pilchards but I couldn't manage it.'

Shirley ignored the 'poor me' implied in Maud's answer. She went to the cupboard and took out the tin.

'It's too late now,' Maud said. 'They'll give me chronic indigestion eating oily fish at this time of night.'

'An omelette then?'

She didn't rise to the challenge. The day had been too good to spoil it with a row.

'Where did you go?' Maud was coming round and curiosity got the better of her.

'Just into town.'

'How long is he staying?'

'He leaves in the morning.' There was no need to say that he was coming back. Maud leaned back as if some anxiety had been suddenly removed.

The phone rang at that moment and Shirley answered it.

'Do you fancy coming out tonight for another one?'

Frank's voice produced a physical trickle of pleasure.

'Another what?'

'A drink, silly, although . . .' He didn't need to finish the sentence. Already the longing was there again.

'I don't think I should. Things are a little . . . frosty around here.'

'OK. Not sure I could stand the pace anyway. I'll call you from London.'

'Fine.'

'Good night then, Shirley Weeks.'

'Good night.'

'Who was that?' There was an edge of suspicion in Maud's voice.

'Only Agnes Selby asking if we wanted her to work this weekend.'

Her mother seemed satisfied and Shirley returned to the omelette. When it was cooked and eaten, Maud declared herself ready for bed. Shirley waited until she had made the long haul up the stairs and closed her bedroom door. The urge to see Frank was so strong she went as far as lifting the receiver, but then she thought better of it. It was never wise to seem too keen. This was a lesson she should have learnt by now – never let a man know you depended upon him. As she replaced the receiver, she wondered if she hadn't moved from the frying pan and into the fire.

Seven

The next morning, as she pulled into the driveway at Cartegena, Shirley saw a car travelling ahead of her. She frowned, slowing down as the driver slewed to a halt and parked on the gravel. A man and a woman got out, the girl hitching down the back of her skirt while he pulled at the back of his jacket. For a moment she wondered if they were Jehovah's Witnesses – but surely it was too early? Besides, they showed none of that zeal that went with a desire to preach light to the unconverted.

She realized then that they were probably something to do with the marketing company or the local council. Climbing out of her Mini, she followed them to the front door.

'Can I help you?'

'You are?' The man spoke. On closer inspection there was something world-weary about him. Probably in his mid-forties, she noticed that the edge of his collar was frayed in one place and his shoes looked as if they had never had much to do with polish. The woman was younger, with highlighted blonde hair, and the sort of mouth that implied pouting determination.

'I work here,' Shirley said. 'If you want to see Lady Lamb, she won't be up yet.'

The two visitors glanced at each other. The man said, 'Well, perhaps we can come in and wait.' He fumbled in his pocket and held something out to her. It was some sort of identity card.

'Police,' he said.

Shirley caught her breath. Carefully she unlocked the door, reminding herself that this might be about anything.

'Lady Lamb is elderly,' she started. 'She isn't very good in the mornings. Can't it wait?'

'I don't think so. You go ahead and do whatever you normally do. When her ladyship is up, perhaps you'll let us know.'

Shirley showed them into the library then went to the kitchen to prepare Florence's breakfast. She wondered whether to tell her that they were waiting to see her. The old lady would become flustered. She wished they would give her some hint as to why they had come but their demeanour defied her to ask. Her thoughts skirted round the obvious – that they had found Guy. Could he be in hospital somewhere, suffering from amnesia? That film, *Random Harvest*, had been about just such an event. A man remembering nothing, leading another life until something happened – a blow on the head, perhaps – that brought his old life flooding back. Perhaps somehow he had been carried back in the plane to Colombia, woken up there not knowing who he was – until now. She would not let herself consider the obvious. Even as she fought off the possibility, her legs threatened to buckle.

Closing her mind to everything, she laid up the breakfast tray and made coffee for the two visitors. As she set the cups on the table, she said, 'Lady Lamb has suffered several tragedies in her life. I hope you won't upset her.'

'We know about what has happened to Lady Lamb. If you could just hurry things up – we've got a lot to do.'

Suitably rebuked, she fetched the breakfast tray and took it upstairs. Her head seemed to be full of strange noises, a grey cloudy light affecting her vision.

Florence was sitting up in bed. She reminded Shirley of a nestling, waiting to be fed. Somehow she went through the routine of drawing back curtains, switching off the bedside lamp, placing the tray across her employer's knees.

'There's two people to see you,' she said.

'What about?'

'I don't know. There's no hurry. I've given them some coffee.'

Florence Lamb picked at her cereal, and lifted her teacup to her mouth with a shaking hand.

'What do you think they want?' she asked after taking a sip.

'I don't know.'

'Do you know who they are?'

'I don't recognize them.' She was not prepared to say that they were the police. The old lady had seen enough of the police to last her a lifetime.

Florence dressed with agonizing slowness, insisted on moisturising and powdering her face, pinning her hair up, putting on her pearls.

'Perhaps we should go downstairs?' Shirley resisted the urge to say, 'Come along! For God's sake, get a move on! Don't you want to find out what they want?'

She held Florence's elbow as they inched their way across the landing, settling her in the chair lift, pressing the button and watching it make its stately descent. At the bottom she helped her employer along the hall and into the sitting room. When she was settled she went across to the library and announced to the visitors that Lady Lamb would see them. They followed her to the sitting-room.

They both looked at her as if she should leave the room but she stood her ground. Something was very wrong here. She needed to be there. Her heart thundered but she did not move away.

Accepting her presence the man started. 'Lady Lamb, Detective Inspector Macmillan, WPC Nielson. I am afraid we have some news for you, madam.'

Florence leaned back in her chair and surveyed them with her fading blue eyes. She seemed to stiffen as if someone had wedged her back with a broomstick.

The inspector hesitated. 'I fear there has been a development, about your son.'

Shirley reached out and grabbed the edge of the table. From nowhere vomit hit the back of her throat. Her breath froze in her lungs. Blindly she felt for a chair and edged herself down, swallowing back the bile and shock and grief. The visitors had their backs to her as she struggled to regain control.

'You've found him.' Florence's voice was flat. It was not a question, just a statement, an acceptance of the inevitable.

'We – we think we've found him, ma'am, yes. I'm afraid—'

'Where? Where is he?'

The inspector said, 'It doesn't make a lot of sense. There was a funeral yesterday at Kingston. It was in a double plot. The wife died about eighteen years ago. Her husband was to be placed with her. When they opened the grave, they found a body on top of the coffin. It must have been placed there at, or soon after, the original burial, before the grave was properly turfed over and the headstone erected.'

'How do you know that it is my son?'

'We can't be absolutely certain. Not at this stage, but the age of the corpse, the time of the burial, certain items, suggest that it may be Guy Lamb.'

'What items?'

'In your original statement you said that he always wore a signet ring bearing the family motto?'

Shirley's hands flew to her mouth.

I want you to wear this while I'm away. When I come back I'll buy you a proper engagement ring.

No. Everyone will ask questions. Wait until you have told your parents. You keep it. Wait until you come back.

The inspector paused. 'We're getting the teeth checked with his last dental records.'

Lady Lamb was uncannily still. For a while she seemed to be gazing into space then, with an intake of breath, she said, 'Thank you for coming to tell me. Is there anything that you wish me to do?'

'No, madam. There is nothing at present. We will keep you informed of any developments.'

They prepared to take their leave.

Shirley was still fighting off the blackness.

'Are you all right?' The WPC frowned, noticing for the first time. She put out a hand to touch Shirley's shoulder.

A voice, not her own, said, 'I'm all right, thank you.' Shakily she got to her feet and tottered across the room like a tightrope walker trying to keep her balance.

'You knew him?' the inspector asked.

She nodded.

'Well?'

About as well as one person can know another. Aloud, she said, 'I knew him since we were children.'

'A shock then.'

A shock indeed. Her mouth seemed to have lost the ability to articulate words. Her mind had no concept of what was required of her. Before she opened the door, she managed to ask, 'Have you any idea what happened?'

'We think it is probably drug related,' the constable offered.

That couldn't be right, but then drugs, South America, Guy's smoking habit. She drew in her breath.

'Do you know how he died?'

'Not for certain.'

The inspector frowned, warning against giving out unnecessary information.

'Nothing is known for certain,' he reiterated. 'We'll be in touch when we know more. You'll stay with the old lady?'

She hardly heard his words. Images of Guy's struggle for survival, his fear, swallowed her up. She said, 'What will happen next?'

'A post mortem. There are shreds of clothing that someone might recognize, although they look like native, Indian cotton. He probably bought them while he was out there.'

The blast of light as she opened the door blinded her. She couldn't adjust from the dark tunnel of horror to the bright normality of life outside. Again she reached for the wall to steady herself, surreptitiously, not wanting the police to see. Amongst everything else was the need to protect herself from the knowledge that she, Guy's lover, the person she had thought was closer to him than any other, had not known what he was up to.

With promises to keep the family informed, the officers left and Shirley groped her way back along the corridor. Outside the sitting room she stopped. The actuality of his death engulfed her. Anger began to surge, mostly with herself. If she had been stronger, braver, she would have gone with him, not worried about taking her exams that got her nowhere, not worried about what her parents would think, or the might of the Lamb dynasty's disapproval. If she had been there she could have stopped him, protected him – somehow.

When she walked into the room, Lady Lamb did not appear to have moved. Shirley defended herself by thinking that his mother was in part to blame as well. The Lambs must have known about her. If they had accepted her instead of choosing to ignore their romance, he would never have gone off on his own. They all had a guilty part to play.

Suddenly aware of Shirley's presence, Florence Lamb leaned back in the chair.

'I – I think I should like a cup of tea, perhaps with a little brandy in it? My – my chest feels rather heavy.'

Shirley knew she should say how sorry she was but the words wouldn't come. Instead she did as the old lady suggested and went to the kitchen, made the tea, fetched the brandy from the dining-room cabinet and poured splashes into two cups. Back in the sitting room she sat down uninvited, waiting for Florence Lamb to say something, but she remained silent.

'Would you like me to stay?' Someone had to be with the old lady. She couldn't be on her own, not with a shock like this.

'It is kind of you, Shirley, but your mother needs you. Besides, I am sure you have had a shock of your own.'

Shirley looked up to find her employer looking at her. Her expression was ambivalent, perhaps asking not to be judged. She said, 'You were very fond of him, weren't you?'

'We were fond of each other.'

Lady Lamb nodded. 'I know. He . . . he wasn't ready to settle down, not then. We thought that going abroad, seeing a part of the world where people were so poor, it might help him to mature a bit. We didn't imagine . . .' She made a helpless gesture that conveyed her own sense of confusion.

Shirley thought of his idealism, his essential humanity. He had no need to mature.

'He asked me to marry him,' she blurted out.

It had to be said. Too late now, perhaps, but she owed it to Guy to let it be known that about some things he was very serious.

'The dream and the reality aren't always the same thing.' There was finality in Lady Lamb's words, the summing up of a life, her own perhaps, that had not turned out as she had hoped. Shirley thought of Lord Lamb with his roving eye, his breath that always smelt of spirits, his roguish, restless presence. Fair hair fading to colourless straw, once-sharp blue eyes turned watery; was this what Guy would have metamorphosed into?

As if knowing her thoughts, the old lady said, 'Sometimes it is better to live with what might have been, rather than face what actually is.'

Hard to believe that – not when the what might have been was her very reason for living.

The old lady refused the offer of lunch. Food was the last thing that she wanted. Shirley promised that she would return again in the afternoon. In a state of numbness, she drove home.

Letting herself into the cottage she struggled to find the words to tell her mother. She couldn't just say it, just blurt it out. *They've found Guy's body.* His body – the golden tan of his skin, the laughing brilliance of his eyes. What were they like now? Decayed, rotten. What happened to a body after all those years in the ground? She shied away from the images and hung up her jacket. How would her mother expect her to sound? Casual? Excited? Her parents had known too, of course, that she had been out with him, known that he wrote to her from university, from Colombia, but her mother had adopted a policy of ignoring it. She probably thought that if she pretended it wasn't happening then it would go away. Nice work, Mum. If you had acknowledged it, given me credit for what I felt, perhaps all these years wouldn't have been wasted. Another person to share the burden of guilt.

She did not consider that her mother might understand the intensity of her feelings. Even now she could not conceive of Maud ever feeling passion for a man, being prepared to risk everything to be with him. But neither could she see her father as the object of such desire.

'Is that you, Shirley? You're early.'

She couldn't put it off. Girding herself for the ordeal, she called out, 'Would you like a coffee?' Taking time to compose herself.

'Tea would be nice.'

87

As she boiled the kettle, rattled the cups in the kitchen, she called out: 'The police have been up to Cartegena. They've made a discovery. Guy Lamb is dead.'

Somehow she stumbled through the day, endured her mother's endless speculation. As soon as she could she escaped back up to Cartegena, going on foot, grasping the precious isolation of the long driveway to give vent at last to her mounting tears. As she trudged along, her thoughts conjured up Guy's ring, the heavy band on the third finger of his right hand. That same hand had caressed her, enfolded her breast, aroused in her such urgency, cupped her chin and filled her with a torrent of love. *I want him back. I want him back!* She beat her fists against her chest, flung her head this way and that to release the avalanche of pain and anguish. Only the distant crack of a branch in the wood stopped the flow, reminded her that even here she might be seen. The noise was probably only caused by a rook but somehow she subdued the ache, took back control.

Lady Lamb looked very frail. Defeated, that was the word that came to mind. Like Shirley, all these years she had lived in a state of limbo, knowing the truth and yet able to avoid it, able still to hold on to the possibility of some miracle, some explanation that would make everything all right. But now it was gone. Guy was dead. There was no going back.

Shirley made the old lady an egg custard, something light and yet nourishing that would slip down past her grief and give her the courage to carry on living.

'We'll have to close the house this Sunday.'

'I'll tell the tourist office, get some notices printed.'

Practical things saved the day. Shirley said, 'Mother and I feel that we should perhaps stay the night.'

'There is really no need.'

Shirley stared at Florence. 'You shouldn't be alone,' she said, dropping the pretence of an employer-servant relationship. 'You might not be able to sleep. You might want to get up in the night. I think we should stay.' As an afterthought she added, 'I can appreciate that you might want to be left alone. We wouldn't impinge on your privacy.' She thought of Maud's thoughtless monologues throughout the afternoon.

Florence nodded, accepting the wisdom of the words.

'Right. We'll come back after supper.'

Shirley stayed for two hours but afterwards she could barely remember anything that had happened and apart from the parting arrangements, nothing else that they had said. There weren't words to carry them through this. Silence was best.

When she reached home, Maud had the table laid and was at the stove, stirring something in a saucepan.

'I've opened a tin of soup. I don't suppose you feel like eating much.'

It was the first acknowledgement of Shirley's feelings. She sobbed back a sudden deluge of pain.

'Let it out,' Maud said. 'Grief eats away at you if you keep it in.'

'I loved him, Mum. I loved him!' The words wouldn't be held back any longer.

'I know you did, love.' Maud put the spoon aside and slid her arms around her daughter. It was a long time since they had touched. The old lady felt brittle, a stick insect, a shadow of her former self. For now Shirley sought refuge in her mother's arms, bending to be enfolded for the old woman was bowed by age. She was too big now for cuddles, not used to them, but it gave some temporary relief. Maud patted her awkwardly on her back.

She said, 'It wouldn't have worked out, you know, not really.' Shirley ignored the words as her mother continued, 'These things happen to all of us. You've been unlucky, stuck with the unknown all this time.' Before Shirley could wonder what her mother's tragedy might have been, Maud said, 'There was a phone call for you. That Frank Agnew.'

'What did he say?' Shirley wiped her eyes, her nose, put her hanky away and tried to grasp normality.

'He left his phone number.'

'Did you tell him what has happened?'

'I did.'

'What did he say?'

Maud shrugged, a small painful gesture that went with her arthritis. 'Just that he was sorry.'

What for? Shirley wondered. Sorry that Guy was dead? Sorry for Lady Lamb – even for her?

She took over the heating of the soup, cut some bread, fetched some cheese. It was a modest meal but she had no appetite.

Maud asked, 'Do you know when the funeral will be?'

Shirley hadn't thought that far ahead. Before that there would be the post mortem, a coroner's inquest, the press, speculation. She shivered.

'We'll go up to Cartegena at about seven.'

Just as she was finishing her soup, the phone rang.

'Hello?' The sound of Frank's voice jolted her into the present.

'Hello.'

'Are you OK? Your mother told me what has happened.'

'I'm all right.' The words came out sharp like pinpricks.

There was an awkward silence, then Frank said, 'Do you want me to come down?'

She shook her head into the silence. No, she didn't want Frank here, not now. Just at the moment he felt like the enemy; he hadn't liked Guy, had actually said that he couldn't stand him. He had even fought him. She needed to be with someone who understood how special he was, anyone who would understand.

'No thanks, it's all right.'

'In that case I'll come back down on Saturday then.'

'I—'

'Is that a problem?'

'No. I just—' She couldn't say that she didn't want him here. It didn't make sense but in a crazy way she now had Guy back. She needed time to be with him, with his memory. One day she would have to say goodbye, but not yet.

'Well, if you don't need me I'll go straight back home.'

Home, by which he meant France.

'All right.'

She didn't know what he wanted her to say. She was letting him go. She couldn't hold on to both of them at once. For the moment, Guy had come back, and now he was the one that mattered. Later, perhaps – but would there be a later? She didn't know.

'Right. Well, I'll wish you goodbye then.'

'Goodbye.'

After a second he put down the phone and Shirley was left with the emptiness of a new despair.

Eight

T hat night, by dint of two very large sherries and two Kalms, Shirley had a deep and dreamless sleep. When she awoke the unfamiliar light confused her. Opening her eyes, she gazed on the heavy alien curtains and as she remembered the events of the day before and that she and Maud were at Cartegena, a smothering pillow of misery pressed down on her. Blearily she glanced at her watch. It was 8.30. With a start she wondered if either of the old women had woken in the night and tried to call her. Hastily she slipped out of bed and hurried down the corridor in her nightie. Everything seemed calm and quiet. For a tormenting moment she thought that perhaps they were both lying dead beside their beds, having tumbled out and failed to wake her. She stumbled back to the bedroom and into her clothes, despising her own stupidity. Dragging a comb through her hair, she resisted the desire to check on the two women until she was properly up and dressed.

Shirley took them breakfast in bed. Even in her numbed state she was aware of the difference, something indefinable emanating from them that dictated who they were: Maud Weeks, wife of a council worker, Florence Lamb, wife of an aristocrat. Both women lay in large, old-fashioned beds covered with ancient but superior linen. Both women occupied tall panelled rooms that spoke of history, but those veneers of behaviour that seemed to have been imbibed with mother's milk shaped everything about them – deportment, language, dress, the essential soul. It was what Maud would call 'breeding'. If Florence had a word for it, Shirley didn't know what it was.

After they were up and dressed, the emptiness of the day

threatened like some desert. They needed to keep busy. Faced with the brutal truth of Guy's death Shirley knew that they needed something normal and yet special to help them hang on to the slippery surface of their lives, threatened as they were with chaos. It was decided that she should take them all for a drive.

In their different ways they must not succumb. As she helped Florence into her coat she thought that the old lady had a lifetime of tradition to maintain, not showing an unseemly display of emotion. Shirley had half a lifetime of keeping Guy's importance to herself. Now that he was gone and there was nothing to hide, she would not give way to the emptiness.

'You can drive us down to the village. Afterwards we'll have coffee at the Pantry.' Florence naturally dictated where they should go.

The village had once, in the mists of time, been the infrastructure for the grandeur of Cartegena. Outlying farms, workers' cottages, a huge duck pond that attracted the local children, St Bartholomew's church, pugnacious, stolid, losing its battle for importance to the Bull and Bishop. In a flurry of civic pride, the parish council had purchased sackloads of spring bulbs. This was the time of the year that they came into their own. Shirley slowed the car so that the two women could admire the blazon of colour along the banks.

They talked of trivia. The moment was all that interested them; no dwelling on the past, no speculating on a tormenting future. Coffee and cream cakes, a visit to the craft shop, a running commentary on minor changes in the neighbourhood supported them through the morning.

Shirley wondered if they shouldn't be at home in case the police called. Then she wondered whether Frank might phone again. Perversely, she wanted to speak to him with a sudden, engulfing hunger. The shadow of his body seemed to be close to her, his physical presence. An unforeseen surge of desire trickled its way across her lap. She had the strange sense that someone had cut her moorings, set her adrift, and she no longer knew what to think or feel. Mourning for Guy? Lusting for Frank? Where was she? Who was she?

'I think a sherry before luncheon.' Florence insisted on taking them to nearby Allenby, where an upmarket restaurant fronting the River Tweddle offered freshly caught trout and saddle of lamb.

Strange how they could still eat and drink, remark on the weather, feel the warmth of the sun.

The day continued in this fashion. Little treats, self-indulgences. The police did not call. Shirley suppressed her regret that she would not be there to receive any call from Frank. Maud flowered under the stimulation of so many unexpected pleasures.

That evening they had little appetite for more food so Shirley made what Florence referred to as a nursery tea: bread and butter, soft-boiled eggs, thin slices of Madeira cake. They looked to the television for distraction but diverse as their tastes were there seemed to be nothing that they could all enjoy. Florence, naturally, had first say but after half an hour of listlessly watching a nature programme she declared her intention of going to bed.

'Would you like something to drink?' Shirley put aside the book she was pretending to read.

'Nothing, thank you. Perhaps you will come and close the curtains. I have difficulty in reaching these days.'

As they left the room, Maud swiftly switched the television over to *Casualty*.

Shirley watched Florence settle herself in her stair lift, her bag clutched in her lap. The contraption made slow progress and Shirley took hesitating steps behind it. She waited as Florence extricated herself, holding her breath as her employer showed every sign of tumbling back down the stairs, but somehow she negotiated the exit and made her snail's progress along the corridor.

Shirley felt impatient to go ahead and sort out the bedroom but she held back. The last thing Florence needed was for someone to draw attention to the degree of her disability.

In the bedroom she placed her handbag on the bedside table and tottered in the direction of the adjoining dressing room that had been equipped with a hand basin, toilet and shower. She left the door ajar and while Shirley turned down the bedcovers and closed the curtains, she heard the sound of running water, and little creaks and gasps from her elderly employer.

Lady Florence was a long time but Shirley did not like to leave, uncertain as to whether she might require help to undress. Her eyes wandered round the room with its familiar trinkets and furniture. Certainly in the later stages of their marriage, Lord Lamb and Lady Florence had had separate rooms. Shirley suspected that it had always been so. She wondered whether it added spice to a marriage, those nocturnal visits, or whether in a marriage that was more or less agreed upon for convenience, Lady Florence might have listened with sinking heart as her husband crept along the corridor full of gin and lust. Unbidden, even unwelcome, the thought of the night shared with Frank came to haunt her. In the heat of remembering, she thought, I would never want separate beds.

The dressing-room door opened and Lady Florence felt her way out, leaning on the walls for support.

'Ah, Shirley, perhaps you will hang my things up for me?'

She now wore a voluminous nightgown. Her clothes were piled on a stool in the adjoining room.

'Of course.' Shirley went to fetch them.

She came back to find Florence gazing at a painting hanging beside her dressing table. Shirley recognized the sitter as the wife from the Tudor portrait in the long gallery.

'That was the very first Lady Lamb,' she said as she attached Florence's skirt to a hanger.

'It isn't, actually.' Florence sunk heavily on to the side of the bed. Shirley noticed that she still wore her shoes and stockings and without being asked she bent down to help the old lady remove them.

'It's not?' she asked, thinking that surely this was the same woman.

Florence dutifully lifted her feet one by one and then allowed Shirley to guide her legs under the covers.

'It's not. My family has been allied to the Lambs twice. Right back then, in fifteen something, Sir Francis Lamb married one of his neighbour's daughters, Elizabeth Knollys. Elizabeth had a twin sister, Catherine, and I am directly descended from Catherine.'

'Are you really?' The news surprised her. She hadn't considered Florence's pedigree.

'I am. Catherine Knollys married Sir Robert Charteris. I was a Charteris before I married.'

'How interesting.' Shirley hung the last of the garments up, swept up the satin underwear and prepared to take it away to be washed.

'Are you sure you wouldn't like anything else?'

'No, thank you, dear.'

Huddled into the pillows, Florence looked exactly what she was: an old, frail, defeated lady with regrets behind her and uncertainty ahead. On impulse, Shirley leaned forward and kissed her on the cheek.

'Good night, then. Don't be afraid to call me if you need anything.'

As she went back downstairs with the prospect of getting Maud to bed, she thought how strange it was that she could show affection to Guy's mother, who had blanked out her existence, and yet never forgive her own mother for the same thing.

'Ready for bed?' she asked as she went back into the parlour.

'Ready for bed. There's nothing on the telly, only rubbish.'

Shirley watched her struggle from the chair.

'Well, good night, then.'

'Good night.'

In spite of her arthritis, Maud did not permit help. She puffed her way up the stairs alone and Shirley waited until she reached the top and meandered off down the corridor.

Half an hour and two brandies later, as she climbed into bed Shirley thought, This is how it will be from now on. In spite of what has happened I'll continue to feel responsible for Florence and to resent my mother. For myself, I won't feel anything. The past is dead. I won't worry about the future. As from today I will live every moment in the present. Sedated by the brandy and more Kalms, she slipped away into limbo.

WPC Nielson called the following morning. This time she was

dressed in police uniform. There was something about the way she moved that made Shirley think of those parties where a stripper is hired as a surprise for the host. Claire Nielson's shirt was crisp, her skirt neatly tailored over her pert bottom and her flat, sensible shoes made her long legs look perversely tantalizing. At any moment Shirley expected her to rip open her blouse to reveal a frilly bra and begin to disrobe.

Instead, she said, 'This is just to let you know that the inquest has been set to open next Tuesday.'

'I'll just go and fetch Lady Lamb.'

Florence was sitting in the breakfast room, *The Times* crossword in front of her. It was a routine she observed every morning. Rarely did she solve more than one or two clues but the process seemed to give some sort of structure to the start of her day.

'That lady policeman is back. She's come to tell us about the inquest.'

Florence reached for her stick and propelled herself out of the chair, accepting Shirley's arm and making for the drawing room. As they entered, Claire Nielson hastily replaced a porcelain figure of a shepherdess on the mantelpiece.

'Good morning, ma'am. I've just come to tell you that the inquest will open on Tuesday.'

Florence nodded, sinking heavily into an armchair.

'It will only be a formality,' Claire continued. 'The coroner will seek to establish the identity of the deceased and hear any known details. After that he will decide whether there is a case to consider.'

'Is there any doubt – about the identification?' Shirley heard the hope in Florence's voice. Her blood gave an answering surge through her arteries. What if it wasn't him after all? Could she rekindle the hope, that loophole that had sustained her for so long? With a strange certainty, she realized that she no longer wished to do so. It had always been a false hope, holding her prisoner. Awful times were ahead but at the end of it she needed to be free. This would one day be the end of it.

'Is there a member of the family you would like to be present?' the constable asked.

Florence looked uncertain. There were no close relatives. Florence had no sisters, few friends. Lord Lamb's family was a shadowy muddle of distant cousins. They were hardly mentioned. Since his death, rumours had circulated about a growing dispute as to who the house should rightly pass to. Once Guy's death was confirmed, the knives would be out. Florence would certainly not wish for any of the protagonists to represent her.

'I'll go.' There was an edge of challenge in Shirley's voice.

'You are a relative?'

'I was his fiancée.' She was shaken by her own temerity. Would they ask her to prove it? Would they think that she had designs on the estate herself? She sniffed, thinking how little remained; just a beautiful old house falling into disrepair and crippled by debts.

'Thank you, Shirley. I should like you to be there.' Lady Lamb inclined her head.

It was settled.

The inquest was held at the magistrates' court in Allenby. On shopping trips into town, Shirley had sometimes noticed people coming and going from the grey monolith, formerly the old assize courts. She had even wondered what they might be thinking as they presumably gave evidence or were found guilty of some misdemeanour. She could not imagine what it must be like to be accused of a crime. Never had she been inside a court of law. Never had she imagined that one day she would.

A few years ago the outside of the building had received a facelift. As she climbed the steps she saw that the interior too had recently been modernized. Entering the courtroom, she was greeted by walls painted in a sunny buttercup colour. Was this an attempt to make the experience less stressful? If so, it wasn't working. The floor was carpeted with a muted grey and the furniture, mostly benches not unlike church pews, were in a light-coloured wood. Gratefully she slid into one.

It took her a while to regain her composure. On a raised platform at the end of the room there was a table and various chairs. Her anxiety surged as several persons entered from a door at the back and occupied the seats around the table.

The man at the centre was clearly the coroner. He had an air of quiet authority, a neat, dark suit, greying hair carefully cut and brushed back from his temples. He wore metal-framed glasses. As the proceedings started Shirley began to tremble.

Afterwards she couldn't decide whether she couldn't or wouldn't remember exactly what was said. Someone, presumably a clerk, read out the details. One of the gravediggers confirmed how he had found the body.

'We couldn't think what it was at first, just some old rags, then we saw the *skelington*.' He kept wiping a grubby handkerchief across his forehead as if the very memory made him sweat. Shirley in turn began to feel faint.

Vaguely, over the whooshing inside her head, she heard an officer explain details of how an identification had been arrived at. Guy's age, height, hair samples, a broken wrist sustained in childhood, his dental record, the ring, the clothing confirmed as having come from Colombia; each piece of information was notched up.

'Any details yet as to cause of death?' the coroner asked.

'A massive overdose of cocaine.'

Shirley struggled for breath. At her side, someone touched her arm. She shook her head vehemently, not looking at whoever it was. She had to see this through, had to.

A statement was read out from some person who had been on the flight with Guy all that time ago. It said that as they disembarked from the plane, the passenger noticed that the young man appeared to be feverish. When he asked him if he was ill he had shaken his head but hurried for what he presumed to be the bathroom. He did not see him again. Somebody else confirmed that when the luggage had been claimed, one bag remained, a rucksack. At first it was supposed that it was on the wrong flight but subsequent enquiries had established that it belonged to Guy Lamb, a passenger on the Colombia flight. He had definitely been on the plane but no one had seen him leave the airport. He had not been seen since.

At this point the hearing was adjourned for further investigations to be carried out.

Around Shirley people were leaving the court. She took great gulps of air, struggling with the threatening faintness. Somehow she had to get herself outside, back to the car, although she knew that she was in no fit state to drive. She realized that she felt in imminent danger of being sick. Please don't let me throw up, not here!

Wiping the cold sweat from her face, she felt her way along the edges of the pews and hurried for the door and the soothing coolness of an April breeze. There was a café just along the road and she made her way there, asking for a tea but before that, a drink of water. She put sugar in the tea because that was what you did for shock, wasn't it? Gradually the nightmare receded to manageable proportions.

When she felt strong enough she left the café and went back to the car park. Once inside the vehicle she felt safer. No one to stare at her now; no one to whisper and speculate about what she was doing there or what had happened to Guy. She turned on the engine and edged her way along the narrow street and out to the freedom of the countryside.

As she drove she anguished about what to say to Florence, how to explain what had happened without arousing the same agony in Guy's mother. She fell back on one simple statement.

'It was just a formality. The coroner asked for details then adjourned the case for enquiries to be made. We don't know how long that will take.' Mercifully nobody asked what those enquiries might be.

Later, as she lay in bed, she realized that the case would be reported in the local paper. Of course they would mention the drugs. Before then she must prepare Florence for the knowledge that Guy's death had been drug induced. She flew up in the bed and switched on the light. In spite of the peculiar circumstances of his burial, she had managed until now to hang on to the belief that there must have been an accident, for what other explanation could there be? For the first time the thought forced itself into her mind that the overdose could have been deliberately self-inflicted. Her chest heaved with fear. He could never have intended to take his life, never. But if it was neither an accident nor suicide then ... No, she wouldn't even consider an alternative. Something terrible had happened, an accident, it had to be an accident. For whatever reason, someone had buried him rather than contact the police. There must be a reason.

As she sat, her shoulders hunched, a terrible exhaustion swept over her. For the first time in decades she began to suck the end of her thumb. Curling up into a ball, with the light still on, she found escape in oblivion.

Since that first police visit, Shirley and Maud stayed almost continuously at Cartegena. Most days Shirley went home to check that the house hadn't been flooded or broken into and to see if there was any mail. In spite of herself, the prospect of a letter from Frank sustained her during these journeys. She did not have his address, so even if she wished to she could not write to him. Sometimes sentences would come into her head and she longed to sit down and scribble him a note, just something to hint that he should keep in touch. That feeling of anticipation took her back to those teenage days, watching for the postman, willing him to turn into their pathway with a letter from Guy. When he did so and she heard the satisfying clunk of mail on the mat, she would stop breathing, holding on to the moment before she discovered that he had only delivered bills and disappointment set in once again. Another twenty-four hours of waiting then had to be endured. The feeling was not so intense now. She had had practice in learning to shield herself against disappointment, but when she unlocked the front door and rescued the assorted letters, that same tension was there.

The days passed and Frank did not write. For a while she dreaded going back to the cottage and the inevitable disappointment, then gradually, in the way of things, she faced the truth. That brief, glorious interlude was simply that, an interlude. The relationship with Frank, such as it was, was over.

Nine

Somehow the succeeding weeks developed a self-perpetuating routine. Florence decided that the house should again be opened to the public on Sundays. She did not put it into words but Shirley knew that this weekly ritual would give a framework to lives otherwise crushed by uncertainty, her own included.

The tours proved surprisingly popular. Most places of entertainment in the neighbourhood had long since been explored so that something new was quickly seized upon. The tea and biscuits became more ambitious. Soon Maud was supervising the baking of Victoria sponges and rock cakes from her own secret recipe. A small collection of old farming artefacts was accumulated in one of the old barns to further divert the visitors.

As each week progressed, everything became geared towards the next Sunday visit. Mondays began to take on a sense of anti-climax. By Tuesday thoughts had again turned to anything that might be improved. Wednesday was marked by activity in the grounds. Ordering of supplies started on Thursday, baking commenced on Friday, and Saturday was taken up with cleaning and general tinkering. Soon it was difficult to imagine that things had ever been otherwise. As nothing was said about the inquest, like a bad dream it was laid to rest.

On a perfect Monday morning in the middle of May, Shirley cycled across to the cottage just to carry out her regular check. This was a time of year she regarded with almost religious awe. The muted greys and browns of winter were long since forgotten. The brave show of crocuses and daffodils had faded and suddenly, everywhere, the world was swathed in brilliant green and white. Leaves were so glossy they mirrored their neighbours while a froth of cow parsley edged every country lane with banks of lace. High in the hedgerows, hawthorn unfolded like a bride's veil. Here was the goddess of the pagans, timeless, immutable. Beneath her numbed surface, Shirley felt something approaching hope.

She was thinking of this as she unlocked the door. The usual mixture of junk mail and brown envelopes littered the doormat. Underneath was a larger envelope containing some sort of journal. Shirley turned it over, expecting it to be addressed 'To the occupier' but it bore her name. Putting the other envelopes aside, she slid her finger under the edge and tore it open. Out slipped a glossy magazine entitled *The Essential France*. Her heart notched up another beat. She flicked through the pages and was soon face to face with a series of photographs she instantly recognized as Frank's. Hastily she shook the magazine, waiting for a note to fall out but there was nothing. When she looked again at the envelope it had come direct from the publisher. Several emotions assailed her at once – relief and pleasure that he had made even tentative contact, disappointment that she could not in turn contact him. She began to read the article. It was written by someone called Yolanda Ferrier, a lively and nostalgic look at those French customs now under threat. From nowhere an unwelcome feeling of jealousy flooded her. This woman, this French woman, must have worked in conjunction with Frank. Did they hold comfortable conversations together in French? Was he interested in her? Did she have one of those delicious accented voices that would appeal to any man? Angry with herself, she put the magazine aside and scanned the usual offers for cheaper insurance or personal health care. Her fragile serenity was in pieces.

She cycled back to Cartegena, immune to the previous beauty of her surroundings. She hated to acknowledge it but the same sap that rose in those springtime plants, that flustered the birds and roused the farm bull, now also assailed her from all sides. Bugger you, Frank Agnew.

Later in the afternoon it occurred to her that she could write

103

to him care of the magazine publisher, but that smacked of keenness. Sourly she decided to do nothing.

Then, just as things were beginning to feel safe again, Lady Florence heard from the coroner's office. The examinations being complete, the body could now be released for burial. It was not, however, to be cremated. Shirley felt all the old confusion. The body, Guy's body, now so far removed from his living self that it was like an impostor, turning up uninvited, stirring up trouble.

In spite of the time that had elapsed since that fateful disappearance, Florence insisted that the proper formalities had to be gone through. The service must be in the village church, the burial in the family vault that lurked beneath St Bartholomew's. Rebellion rumbled in Shirley's heart. It was pointless, far too late, a piece of foolishness. What was really needed was to lay him to rest in the grounds, somewhere special with a quiet placing of flowers. She knew exactly where it should be, down behind the stables, Guy's favourite boyhood place where once he had studied the breeding habits of wood lice, where once they had made love thrillingly and urgently on the teasing grass that plucked at her bare skin. She shivered.

Leaving the old women together, she broke out of the house like an escaped prisoner. That same sacred place called to her to come and take refuge. In her haste to get there she stumbled over the uneven ground, slid down the shallow bank, reached out for comfort on that same patch of grass that had risen up and been cut down a thousand times since last they had been together.

'Where are you?' She tried to summon him up. Wasn't this the place he would come back to? *Next time we make love here I'm going to make you pregnant.* Shirley, bleeding, teetered on the chasm of despair. Suppose she had had a child, a new Guy, fulfilling her needs, doted upon by his bereaved grandmother Florence, quietly pleasing Maud, once she had got over the shock? How much that solitary child would have meant to so many women. She scrabbled in the earth with her bare fingers. Instead, a barren existence held her prisoner in every way.

Going back to the house she announced, 'I've got to go out.'

'All right.' Neither woman asked where she was going nor when she would be back. As she made for the door it occurred to her how things had changed. She no longer asked for permission or offered explanations. Young – well, younger – and more able bodied, she was in unspoken charge.

'Could you just check with the caterers about the food for after the funeral?' There was an edge of anxiety in Florence's voice.

Shirley nodded, resenting the smug and the curious who would make their way back here after the ceremony, offering platitudes, weighing up the value of everything in the house, speculating on who was next in line. Lord Lamb, refusing to believe that Guy would not return, had left everything to him. Now that he was definitely not coming back, the claims could begin in earnest.

She cycled down to the village. The wind was against her and the effort took all her strength. In the supermarket she wandered aimlessly along the aisles. For a moment she stopped and wondered at the logic of having Egyptian new potatoes. Long-forgotten lessons about the floodwater from the Nile made her wonder what possessed the Egyptians to sell their food half a world away.

'Hello.' She jerked out of her reverie, turning to see Margaret Whitton – Margaret Bryce as she was now.

'Oh, hi.' Margaret was one of the few girls who had stayed in the village, married a local man and settled happily into a humdrum existence.

Shirley forced an 'I'm all right' smile from somewhere.

They went through the 'What are you doing these days?' routine. Margaret had two boys at school and helped with school dinners.

Shirley noticed how stolid she had become. She wore clothes like her mother, which prompted her to ask, 'How are your parents?'

'They're both OK. Still in the same house. Dad's retired, of course, but he still does his garden.'

Shirley issued a bulletin on Maud then Margaret asked: 'You still at the town hall?'

'No. I haven't been there for three years now. I'm working up at Cartegena.' She immediately cursed herself.

She saw her old friend's eyes flare with interest. 'Must seem pretty strange there now, what with finding the body and everything.'

Margaret hadn't known Guy. He'd just been the son of the people up at the big house, away at university, leading a parallel existence. Even when they had been sort of friendly, Shirley had never confided in Margaret about her romance with the son of Lord and Lady Lamb. Now, though, the scandal of his disappearance and the discovery of his body, the mystery of how he had died, suddenly made him everybody's property.

'I must dash.' She avoided further conversation and made for the check- out. In the queue she remembered she had forgotten to get cheese but she didn't go back.

The funeral was arranged for Wednesday. Guy now lay in the chapel of rest at the undertakers. Nobody suggested going to see him. Florence had talked foolishly of having a horse-drawn hearse. In his youth Guy had been a rider, a showjumper. The hearse had been ordered for Lord Lamb's burial. Two handsome, black plumed horses had pulled the ornate carriage on which Lord Lamb's body had been drawn from Cartegena to the church. Like some re-enactment of a Victorian melodrama, villagers had lined the route to watch them pass, drawn by curiosity rather than servitude. Another horse had followed, saddled but with no rider, a pair of riding boots inserted backwards into the stirrups. In his youth, Lord Lamb had been the master of foxhounds. Shirley knew Guy's feelings about blood sports. This must not happen.

'I think the day should be as simple as possible,' she announced and Lady Florence, lost and defeated, did not argue.

Meanwhile, Shirley ordered Florence's wreath, and flowers from her mum. When it was all over she would buy a shrub and take it down to the meadow, plant it close to the hedge where it would not get mown down; something living to remember the dead.

Wednesday morning was crisp and bright, a yellow light suffusing everything. Not for the first time Shirley thought that a funeral should only ever be held in the rain, a grey day for a grey event.

Florence wore her traditional mourning clothes, including a veil. Maud wore her black skirt and coat. Shirley did not wear black. It was going to be a hot day. She had a simple dress in a petrol shade of blue, crisp lines that suited her shape. Guy would have liked it. She felt comfortable in it. No need for a jacket. She carried a small bag into which she pushed some tissues – please don't make me need them – and some money. Did they have collections at funerals? She couldn't remember.

At 12.30, the hearse followed by a Rolls-Royce drew up in front of the house. The sight of the coffin jolted through her. For the first time since he left for Colombia, Guy was here again, a few feet away from her and yet further away than eternity. Swallowing back her desperation, she helped Florence from her chair. Let me get through this, she prayed. Help me to go through the motions.

Earlier, Shirley had tentatively suggested that perhaps Lady Florence should travel with one of those distant cousins.

'Certainly not.' The matter of the heir to the estate was still under discussion. Invite any one of the contenders and there would be speculation. The subject was instantly closed.

At the last moment, Maud decided that she would not attend.

'It's no good, my screws are playing me up something rotten. Besides, it's not really my place.'

Shirley did not argue.

With agonizing slowness, Florence and Shirley made their way down the length of the church, behind Guy's coffin.

'Are you really in there?' Shirley tried to pluck him out of the air, to share with him the feeling that this ceremony was a piece of foolishness, a humbug, something that they would both have laughed about in other circumstances.

'I know you won't like it,' she told him, 'but your mother wants to do it. We'll tolerate it, shall we, just for her?'

Heads turned to watch their slow progress. The church was packed. Seats had been reserved at the front for those who counted. Men and women clothed in Bond Street and Savile Row prickled at the sight of her, taking her seat in the front pew.

Florence clutched her arm with unbelievable force for such a frail old woman. Only an unseemly tussle would release her from the grasp. Shirley did not try. The situation wasn't of her making. Somebody had to look after the old lady. As for Shirley, she closed her mind to everything but the thought that she would hold her own ceremony when this was all over.

The minister, replete in what she thought of as a frock, turned and began the service. Shirley found herself thinking of Mrs Agnew's funeral, the starkness of the occasion. Here, words now centuries old were delivered in the vicar's sepulchral voice. Readings from the King James' version of the Bible lent their own poetry. The minister pronounced on the cutting down of a young man in his prime, a mystery that the Lord no doubt understood and would make clear in the future.

Fat chance.

Three hymns, an anthem played on the organ, readings by those who thought they should be heard, lots of prayers and amens, it washed over Shirley like the aftermath of some deep dive she had made, waiting to break back through to the surface where everything was normal.

To the strains of organ music Guy was carried back down the aisle and outside, to be placed in the vault. Florence remained seated.

'You go,' she said to Shirley.

She shook her head. 'I'll stay here with you.'

When it was all over they made their way back to the Rolls-Royce. Just as Shirley was dipping her head to step inside, the periphery of her vision caused her to stop. There, standing on the grass verge, watching her progress, was Frank Agnew.

There was no time to respond. Those around were awaiting their departure, suddenly hungry for cold meat and caviar, thirsty for something stronger than tea or coffee.

As she sank on to the seat and the limo moved off, Shirley felt her heart rapping against her ribs. She hadn't even managed to catch Frank's expression, merely his steady eyes watching her. What was he doing back here and why now?

'That was all right, wasn't it?' Florence asked, seeking reassurance.

Shirley suppressed the chaos of her thoughts. 'Yes. It was fine.'

Frank did not come back to the house. As the various cars drew into the carriageway, Shirley could not stop herself from looking out for his old Capri but it was not there. She wondered if he might have got a lift with someone else but pretty soon she was sure that she had observed every arrival. He was not coming.

Telling herself that she was relieved, she turned her attention to those who were there. Mostly they were members of the Lamb clan, standing around with darting eyes, weighing up the opposition. None of them lived locally. One or two had flown in from abroad. Shirley, now in the role of servant once more, took coats and jackets and made sure that everyone had a welcoming drink.

Florence greeted them with cold dignity. She was under no illusion as to why most of them were there: either downright nosiness or self-interest. There was no will to be read out. Guy had died intestate. For as long as she lived, Florence held everything, but once she was gone it would revert to its natural masters – the Lambs.

A buffet was laid out in the dining room. Once everyone was furnished with a drink, the hungry ones retreated in that direction. Shirley went around with refills. Standing at the French windows, looking out across the lawn, was Edward Benningfield, the family solicitor. He was a short, plump man, what Maud would call dapper. A gold watch-chain looped across his paunch and he wore gold-framed glasses that glinted when he moved. As Shirley offered him a refill he turned to her and smiled. The pale blue eyes in his smooth face betrayed his weariness with such events.

'Miss Weeks, isn't it?' He accepted another sherry. Shirley nodded and went to move on but he continued. 'You shouldn't be working.'

'Why not?' She laughed uncertainly.

'If my memory serves me correctly, you were close to Guy Lamb?' Shirley felt her face grow hot. Why should this man know such a thing, and remember it after all this time? He gave her a gentle smile.

'I was fond of Guy Lamb. He used to talk to me sometimes. He was an unhappy young man, you know.'

'Why was he unhappy?' She was aware of the tension in her voice.

Edward Benningfield thought for a moment. 'He was born into a world of privilege. It did not sit easily with him. He said once that he would have been far happier to have been poor and to have something to strive for. He found it hard to live with the inequalities as he saw them.'

What the solicitor said was right. Shirley could hear Guy's voice, the inflexions, the way he would look apologetic for railing against the very privilege others coveted.

Edward said, 'He . . . hinted that you and he had an understanding.'

'He did?' The fog was beginning to blow in again. Shakily Shirley placed the tray on the nearest table, afraid that she would drop it.

'Go on, have a drink.' Mr Benningfield handed her one and guided her on to the brocade sofa nearby, sinking down next to her.

'A nice young man,' he repeated. 'I'm afraid he got himself mixed up in things he should have kept away from.'

Drugs. The sherry turned to acid in her mouth. She glanced round to see if they were being watched but the guests were busy with their own affairs.

'What will happen to the house, when Lady Florence—?' she stopped herself from using the D word.

Edward looked quizzical. 'Ah, there is the problem. There are two possible lines of descent, you see, one through Lord Lamb's great-aunt who was the eldest in her family and the other through his great-uncle. All in all there are seven living relatives but only two who could make a case for inheriting at least a part of the estate.' Glancing round he added, 'From the look of them they would each want it all.'

Shirley followed his gaze but was not sure who he was looking at. She asked, 'When will it be decided?'

110

'That really depends on getting Lady Florence to . . . partici-
pate. At the moment, understandably, she doesn't want to think
about it.'

They were both silent, mulling over the situation. Edward
Benningfield said, 'A pity you and Guy didn't marry before he
left – you didn't, by any chance, did you?'

Shirley shook her head, shocked by the suggestion.

'That's a shame.' Edward fetched more sherry, plonking
himself down with an out-rush of breath. 'It wouldn't be the
first time, you know – a secret marriage. Families like the Lambs
thrive on scandal, keeping the line pure and the young men
away from the servants— Oh, sorry.' He looked uncomfortable.

It wasn't like that, Shirley thought. It wasn't. Guy wouldn't
have come back and married some suitable society girl. She
heaved herself out of the depths of the sofa.

'I must get on,' she said.

'He was genuinely fond of you,' Edward offered as she
walked away but she pretended not to hear.

When the last stragglers left and the caterers had packed
everything away, Florence declared herself ready for bed. She
did not talk about the day, for which Shirley was grateful.

When she got back downstairs, Maud was sitting in the
breakfast room gazing into space.

'I think it's time we went back home,' she announced.

'Why? Why now?' Shirley wondered if something had
happened during the day to bring out this decision. Until now
Maud seemed to be blossoming under the roof of Cartegena.

'No particular reason. We can't stay here for ever. Besides, I
miss my own place.'

'All right. I'll talk to Lady Florence in the morning.
Meanwhile, I need some fresh air. I'm going to go out for a
while.'

Shirley retrieved her bike from the garage and pedalled
down the drive. She had no clear idea of where she was going.
On auto-pilot, she headed for home but beyond that, the
thought of Frank's cottage beckoned. With every turn of the
pedals she scolded herself. Even to think of going there was
ridiculous. He knew where to find her. As ever, Maud's words

111

intruded with advice: *Don't make yourself cheap.*

Anyway, if Maud wanted to go home, Shirley had better make up the beds, reinstate the order for milk. She leaned her bike against the wall and let herself into the cottage. A white envelope lay on the doormat. It had not come by post and she knew who it was from even before she retrieved it.

Inside was a scribbled note. *Called round but you were out. I'm here until Saturday. Give me a ring if you fancy a drink.* A phone number was scrawled at the bottom.

Shirley put the note into her pocket. She wouldn't do it tonight, but tomorrow, tomorrow, perhaps she would call.

Ten

Overnight, Shirley decided that she would call Frank once and if he didn't answer she would not do so again. He picked up the receiver at the third ring.

'Oh, hi!'

From his voice she couldn't decide what he was thinking.

'I was surprised to see you at the funeral,' she started.

'Not as surprised as I was to be there.'

'Oh?' she waited.

She heard him sniff before saying, 'Let's just say that something expected came up. Anyway, how are you?'

Predictably she said that she was fine.

'Do you fancy coming for a drink then? Tonight?'

'I could do. We're staying at Cartegena at the moment.'

'Are you now?' He seemed to find the idea amusing. 'OK. I'll pick you up there – seven o'clock? Don't eat, I've got something to celebrate.' He rang off.

For the rest of the day her thoughts were preoccupied with what it might be.

At teatime she said to Maud, 'I'm going out tonight for a meal with Frank Agnew.'

Maud snorted her distaste. 'I heard he was back sniffing around.'

'What do you mean by that?' Shirley's irritation flared.

'How come he hasn't been around for years and now, what with the inquest and the funeral and all, he keeps turning up?'

You're talking rubbish, Shirley thought. Aloud, she said, 'What are you talking about? He came back because his mother died. He's got legal things to settle.'

Maud gave her a disbelieving look. 'Covering his tracks, more like.'

'Mother, if you've got something to say, why don't you just come out with it?'

Maud licked her lips and swallowed in a way that was peculiarly hers. Her teeth did not fit very well and her mouth was almost permanently on the move. 'There's been something wrong with that family as long as I can remember, some bad blood between them and the Lambs. It wouldn't surprise me if he didn't know something about all this.'

'About all what? You're not suggesting that Frank murdered Guy, are you?'

'His father had a terrible temper.'

For a second Shirley remembered the fight at the birthday party, that feeling that she had to intervene before Frank, then bigger and bulkier, killed his adversary.

'You're mad,' she said.

'Well, don't come running to me if things go wrong.'

Hair wash, soak in a lavender-scented bath, shaved legs, attention to eyebrows – it was partly a reaction to Maud's outrageous hints. She wasn't going to let her mother's poison spoil things. Smothered in bubbles, she felt foolish about this teenage desire to please. Her face was a healthy brown so she moisturised it with jojoba from the Body Shop then applied mascara, a pale lipstick to accentuate the tan and a few dabs of perfume. She would have preferred to wear the dress she wore to the funeral but she didn't want Frank to see her in the same thing twice. Besides, she had worn the dress in memory of Guy. It would seem disloyal to wear it again to seduce Frank. Was that what she was doing? She smirked at herself in the mirror, despising her weakness. In any case, the timing was wrong. In spite of everything, the years of not knowing, Guy had only just been laid to rest in his grave. She still hadn't said goodbye to him properly. Any other relationship would feel like indecent haste, except that her living body was hungry for sex.

A tangle of undefined emotions, she dressed in a long burgundy skirt and sleek top. She was just putting on some earrings when she heard the strident jangle of the bell.

Frank's tan beat hers hands down. His white shirt only served to emphasize his brown arms, the tantalizing V at the neck. She wondered if it was deliberate. She thought he looked a perfect balance of casual yet smart, in his dark blue chinos. He kissed her on both cheeks and placed a hand at her waist to guide her to the car.

With an effort she pushed any misgivings away. 'Where are we going?' she asked.

'The Cavendish.'

She immediately wished she had worn something else. 'That's pretty posh, isn't it?'

'Posh enough.'

As they drove out of the gate they were silent. She wondered whether to ask what he was celebrating but decided against it. Instead she said, 'Thanks for the magazine. The photos look great.'

'Glad they sent you a copy.'

'Have you got any more commissions?' Perhaps this was his good news.

'A few. I'm flying out to Nigeria on Sunday to do some work on the Obi carvings.'

That must be it. She felt the too-familiar envy at the prospect of travel.

'Who is that for?' she asked, to keep the conversation going.

'The *Observer*.' He gave a deprecating grin.

No wonder he was pleased.

As they drove, Maud's insinuations hovered, like a wasp, persistent, making it impossible to ignore. Hating herself, the next moment there was a silence, she asked, 'Have you ever been to South America?'

He shook his head. 'I've been to North Africa and India, half of Europe. Why?'

'No reason.' The heat engulfed her, making the skirt cling to her limbs.

The Cavendish was ten minutes' drive away and when they arrived the car park was nearly full. A preponderance of BMWs and Mercedes were interspersed with the odd Porsche or Rolls-Royce, and several other upmarket saloons. Frank squeezed the old Capri into a space between a Saab and a vintage Spitfire, with aplomb. His disregard for the trimmings of success lifted Shirley's spirits. One of these days the Capri would be a collector's item anyway.

They made their way into what resembled a genteel sitting room for pre-dinner drinks. Shirley asked for Campari, savouring its bitter-sweet taste. Frank had a Guinness.

'The funeral went well?' It was the first time he had mentioned it.

'It did.' She chose her next words carefully. 'I was surprised to see you in the church.'

By way of response he shrugged. 'I was curious.'

'You didn't come back to the house?'

'I wasn't invited.'

She found herself telling him about the contenders for the estate.

'There's going to be a power struggle then, is there?'

In the face of his obvious amusement, Shirley said, 'It's not funny for Lady Florence.'

'No, I don't suppose it is.'

The waiter came to escort them to their table. It was by a window, a view of the herbaceous borders and ornamental ponds carrying the eye down to the parkland.

The handwritten menus in a script that would have done justice to a medieval monk listed the choices. When the dishes came they were in minute portions and displayed with all the attention given to a work of art. Nowhere were the prices mentioned.

'Well, what are you celebrating?' Soothed by good food and a heady red wine, Shirley relaxed into her chair.

Frank leaned forward and she realized how blue his eyes were.

'This, Shirley Weeks, is my way of saying thank you to you.'

'What for?' She couldn't think what she had done other than enjoy the delights of his body – and she hardly needed repayment for that!

'If it wasn't for you,' he said, 'I should never have known.'

'Known what?' She was getting impatient.

He gave a sigh of amusement, his grin spreading.

'You remember when you said you'd like the desk and I said to throw the contents away?'

She nodded, recalling how she had tipped them all into a carrier bag.

'Well, I nearly chucked the lot, but remembering what you said I thought perhaps I should go through them, just to tear them up in case there was anything my mother wouldn't have wanted made public.'

'Was there?'

'Yes and no.'

She thought he could be so annoying sometimes. 'What do you mean?'

He began to laugh. 'If what I think is true, you are looking at the next master of Cartegena.'

'You? How?' He must be mistaken. What he said didn't make sense.

Suddenly serious, he said, 'Promise you won't say anything to anyone for the moment.'

'I won't.'

He kept his eyes fixed on her.

'Well, apart from the usual invoices and bank statements and things in my mother's drawer, there was a large, linen envelope tied up with pink tape. It contained some love letters from an Algernon Francis Lamb to Ivy Davis – my great-grandmother. She was a housemaid at Cartegena.'

Shirley remembered what Edward Benningfield, the solicitor, had said about keeping the heirs away from the servants.

'You think she had a romance then, with Lord Lamb?'

'More than that.'

It took her a moment to realize what he meant. 'She had a child?'

'My grandfather.'

Shirley thought of the people at the funeral. She didn't know how to say it without disappointing him but there was one big difference – the ancestors of the next in line would not have been illegitimate. It might not matter now but back then it would have disbarred a child from inheriting unless he or she was specifically included in a will.

She raised her eyebrows questioningly.

'You don't believe it, do you? You're thinking that this was some illicit romance that was hushed up. Well, it was hushed up but it wasn't illicit.'

She looked uncomprehending.

His grin widened. 'I'll show you when we get home. There's a marriage certificate between Ivy Dorothy Davis, my great grandmother, and Algernon Francis Agneau.' He took out a pen and wrote on the napkin. When she looked uncertain he said, 'Don't you see the connection? Agneau, Agnew?'

Slowly it unfolded in her mind. Lord Lamb and his rhododendrons, *orientalis* subsp. *agnus*. Agnus, Latin for Lamb; Agneau, French for Lamb. Frank's family might not have understood the significance but they might well have spelt their daughter's new name phonetically – Agnew.

Frank added, 'They didn't get married locally. No doubt they didn't want anyone trying to stop them.'

'So you think—?'

'I know, my dear Shirley. Lord Algernon Lamb married my great-grandmother in Wells. I've got the marriage certificate to prove it. When his family got to hear of it they would have bought her off, had the whole thing hushed up. By then he too might have been having second thoughts, having had his fill of my grandmother's charms, and been pleased to step back into his own world. The fact remains, though, that the marriage was genuine and my grandfather Francis – Frank Agnew – was the legitimate first-born son.' His mouth twitched with wry amusement. 'That being so, it means that your Guy's grandfather, William George Lamb, was the illegitimate one.'

Shirley couldn't take it all in. There must be some mistake, but from what Frank said it seemed to be true.

He ordered coffee and liqueurs while she tried to find the flaw.

'What about your great-grandmother then? Wouldn't she have objected?'

She saw that gleam of anger in Frank's eyes again. 'She might have objected but in the face of the Lamb position and fortune she would have been powerless. They hushed her up, married her off to a nice obliging man who either didn't know or didn't mind that she was a bigamist, and left the cottage for her family to occupy as long as they wished. There was some money too, to educate young Frank Agnew, my grandfather, but he got himself killed in the Crimea. Fortunately he had married first.'

'How will you prove it?' Shirley asked. 'How will you prove that Algernon Agneau and Lord Algernon Lamb were the same person?'

'Handwriting? DNA?'

Shirley doubted if any of the current contenders would be willing to give DNA samples to disprove their own claim.

The significance of what he had just told her kept bubbling up. She wondered if he knew that the house was tumbling down and the estate was hopelessly in debt.

'Would you really want it?' she asked. 'Can you see yourself living there?'

He shrugged. 'When I was a kid I was so jealous of Guy Lamb, of everything that he had. I wanted it to be me. Perhaps subconsciously I knew that I belonged there. I think my dad knew something of it because he seemed to be guaranteed a job for life even though he was difficult and lazy and often down-right rude. He probably resented being the gardener instead of the lord of the manor.' He thought for a while. 'They must have been glad when he died and I simply went off, showing no desire to remain in the area.'

The Benedictine slithered effortlessly down her throat. She didn't know what to feel. Ruefully she thought of what Frank had said a moment before. He had been jealous of Guy and everything that he had had. Guy had had her – and now? She shivered.

'I think I should be getting back,' she said.

'Back to your old ladies?' There was an edge of sarcasm in his voice.

She felt angry with him although she didn't know why. They seemed to have reached that midway point when a balance swings from one extreme to another. A while ago she had been on the one side, enjoying herself, teetering on the brink of taking their relationship further, wanting it, wanting him. For no good reason she was now somewhere else, distrusting his motives, sensing that herein lay danger.

'What's the matter?' He paid the bill, then stepped back to let her precede him to the car.

'Nothing. You seem to find it funny that I look after my mother and old Lady Lamb.'

He shook his head. 'Why should I find it funny? It seems more to me that it's an excuse to run back home rather than letting yourself go. Why are you so afraid of taking a risk?'

'I'm not!'

'You aren't?' He didn't sound convinced.

They drove in silence and she tried to consider objectively whether what he said was true. Letting go of Guy, losing the protective shield behind which she had hidden for so long, was frightening.

She remained silent and the tension seeped up like some suffocating storm cloud. Shirley knew that she should be the one to say something. Earlier, Frank had said, actually said, 'I'll show you when we get home.' What did it mean? That he thought of the cottage as home? That she had a place there if she wanted it? She scrabbled round for some way to resolve things but nothing would come.

As they approached the village he said, 'Do you want to go straight home or—?'

'I—' She hesitated too long. He drove past the village and on towards Cartegena. The prospect of sharing his bed was snatched away and she longed to reach out and take it back. All the time her mother's words hung like some malevolent spirit over them.

As they got out of the car she said, 'Would you like to come in, for a nightcap?'

'No thanks. I don't qualify to step over the threshold, not yet.'

'Frank—'

He stood facing her. 'I don't know where I am with you, Shirley. One moment you are bright and bubbly and enthusiastic and the next you're like some timid snail, retreating back into your shell for no reason. Anyway, it's up to you. If you want to brick yourself up in this old house like some nun, that's your choice.' When she didn't answer, he said, 'Why don't you start living? Why don't you get away from here and these grasping old ladies? They'll survive without you, you know.' When she still didn't reply, he said, 'When do you ever take a holiday?'

'I—'

'Well, the next time that you do, why don't you come to France? Come and see where I live. Come and stay with me.'

She couldn't tell him that she didn't even have a passport. Instead, she said, 'If you inherit Cartegena you'll be able to throw me out.'

His eyes narrowed. 'I'd appreciate it if you would keep what I have told you this evening to yourself.'

'Of course.'

He stared at her, a man looking at a lost cause.

'Well, good night, then.'

'Good night. Thanks for the meal.' But even as she spoke, he turned away towards his car and perhaps out of her life for ever.

Eleven

'Whatever is the matter with you? You're so touchy these days.' Maud, scraping the last of the Weetabix from her bowl, grumbled into the mouthful of mush.

They had been back at Hawthorn Cottage for three weeks. Maud seemed happy to be back with her own things around her. Nearly every day she still went with Shirley to Cartegena to organize the catering for the following Sunday or to check up on Agnes Selby's cleaning. For Shirley, the solitary walks and sense of escaping from her mother were gone. Everything now seemed relentless, a treadmill upon which she sometimes felt doomed to spend the rest of her life.

'You've been like this ever since the funeral, ever since that Frank Agnew came back again. They were nothing but trouble, that family. Lady Florence never liked them. I can't think what makes him come back here. He didn't bother when his mother was alive and now she's dead he seems to be haunting the place.'

The familiar diatribe continued. Shirley walked from the room as an alternative to exploding. Once, long ago, Maud had pontificated about Guy in a similar vein: *That lad isn't going to make anything of himself. He's a wastrel. I don't know why you let him write to you. It's a disgrace, him just dropping off like that.* (Maud, trying to keep up with the current vernacular, meant 'dropping out'.)

Then, as now, Shirley didn't say anything. Her mother's flights of fancy were so unpredictable that she was left on quicksand, knowing that whatever she tried to say in response, the ground would have shifted and she would be wrong-footed again.

Maud called out after her, 'Anyway, I've rung Auntie Jean. She's going to come and stay for a few days. I think you should go away somewhere, sort yourself out.'

Shirley, halfway through the door, came back. She frowned, not quite believing what she had heard.

'I beg your pardon?'

'Jean. She's going to come and stay. You need to get away, young lady, sort yourself out.'

She was about to protest but the thought of a change, any change, began to present itself with all its possibilities. Where should she go? The prospect of just taking off into the unknown without any warning startled her.

'What about Lady Florence?' she asked.

'Jean and I are quite capable of looking after her.'

Whereas Maud was the eldest in her family, Jean was the youngest. Sixteen years separated the sisters, the same gap that separated Jean from Shirley. The last time Shirley had seen her aunt had been at her father's funeral. At the time she had been grateful for her presence. They seemed to have an unspoken rapport. Perhaps having Jean here now would liven things up.

Jean was Shirley's godmother but she often thought of her more as an older, though distant, sister. Her aunt lived in a cottage in Bridstow some thirty miles away and she had only been there once, in her middle teens. She remembered that that was just after she had started going out with Guy. Had Maud talked to her sister about her daughter's foolish romance? She wondered what Jean might have said. Instinctively she felt that her aunt would have been on her side.

Jean had not married. Shirley always thought of her as a liberal, easy-going, independent sort of woman in control of her life but really, when she analysed it, she knew very little about her.

'Why should she want to come here and look after Lady Florence?' she asked. What she really meant was, Why should she want to look after you? but she didn't say it. She was sick of the bickering; sick of everything.

'She won't mind. She hasn't got a job any more. She's just gone and thrown it up. Foolish, I call it. Anyway, there's nothing to keep her there. I don't know why she doesn't come back to the village to live.'

Shirley stopped listening, preoccupied with the possibility of escape. Where could she go? Who did she know? The idea of simply taking off on her own brought on an immediate rush of anxiety. The only person who came to mind was her old school-friend, Amy, who had left the village to go to university in Bristol and still lived there with her now teenage daughter. Their contact had been infrequent. Shirley wasn't even sure whether Amy had married the girl's father or simply lived with him. Casimera, the daughter was called. The exotic name, the thought of city life, stirred her.

She asked, 'When is she coming?'

'On the fourteenth.'

Going into the kitchen, Shirley refused to acknowledge the other possibility – that she could take up Frank's invitation and go to France. That would set her mother off! Besides, she still didn't have a passport, wouldn't want to admit that she had no idea how to get there – a ferry, a train to Dover, a flight to where? Anyway, it was academic because since they had parted on the evening of the dinner, she hadn't heard from him.

She decided that she would indeed write to Amy. Her mother was right to the extent that getting away anywhere would do her good. By the fourteenth the tours of Cartegena, scheduled to last only for the high summer, would be coming to a close. She had earned some extra money; could afford to splash out. She began to toy with the idea of booking herself on to a trip to somewhere exotic. The Caribbean, maybe? A scenario where she met somebody rich and sensual began to play out in her mind.

The possibility lasted for two days when the news arrived that the date for the inquest was set to commence on Monday, the seventeenth. Any idea of going away was immediately abandoned.

'You had better phone and tell Jean not to come,' she said to Maud.

'Why? You'll be next to useless while it is going on.' The invitation remained.

Shirley took herself for a long walk. That morning she had

been to the garden centre and bought a shrub. The choosing had been difficult. In her head the words *Rosemary for Remembrance* kept playing like a loop but there was already rosemary in the herb garden. She wanted something special. Wandering around, she noticed deep purple Bougainvillaea. That was not hardy, though, and she wanted something that would last. Some trees, she knew, lived to be thousands of years old, but then who would know in a hundred years that some growing plant was a memorial to a love that had ended with a kind of Shakespearean tragedy? She settled instead upon *Garrya elliptica*, a blue-green shrub that bore long catkins in winter, a symbol of hope in the darkest days. Clutching the tub and a trowel she headed towards Morton Down, a gently rising mound pushing its dome up through a fringe of hazels and willows. She found herself thinking about pilgrimages, how people needed to go to a geographical spot as if to make real their beliefs, to establish their contact with something outside themselves. This was what she was doing now; going back to the physical setting where she had lost her virginity as if to confirm that it had really happened.

That first summer Guy had written to say that he would be home for two weeks before going to Austria to visit friends. *Perhaps we'll get some time to ourselves at last!* She knew what he meant. The fumblings in the car had taken them nearly all the way. Since then a hunger for physical contact had plagued her, sometimes a fierce longing, sometimes a low, background discontent. Whichever, it was always there. Now was the time to complete the journey.

Guy's imminent arrival set her in a whirl. On the one hand she needed to keep their relationship a secret from Maud. At the same time she wanted to shout it from the rooftops: *I am the girl that Guy Lamb loves. Of all the women he could have, he has chosen me.*

The night before his arrival, she felt the same anticipation she had previously experienced at Christmas, a time for gifts and surprises. The next morning, in spite of not having slept, she was up ridiculously early, looking for excuses to go into town, hoping that by some miracle she would bump into him. Twice

125

she went to the Co-op. She changed her library books although she hadn't read them. She risked embarrassment and sat alone in the coffee bar, sipping espresso, watching the window with all the alertness of an Indian scout, then, just as she stepped back out into the High Street, there he was.

'Fancy seeing you.'

It took a moment for his features to mould into the vision she had been carrying round with her for weeks. He seemed a little thinner, a little fairer, his hair beginning to curl around the nape of his neck. His skin was darker than when last she had seen him, drawing attention to the blueness of his eyes.

She blushed, mumbled something, wished he had seen her coming from the library, where she would have had a legitimate excuse to be.

'Just had a coffee?'

She nodded, feeling that he had caught her out in something shameful.

'Fancy another one?'

'All right.'

He was talkative, which was just as well as she seemed to be tongue-tied. Eventually, after she forced down a second cup of strong, bitter coffee, he asked, 'What are you doing this afternoon?'

'Nothing.'

'Fancy coming for a walk?'

It was settled.

They set out in bright sunshine but armed with coats in case the disloyal weather should change. She told Maud she was going to visit Amy. Everything inside her seemed to be working faster: her pulse, the thump of her heart, the anxious flow of blood along her limbs. Her mouth was dry and several times when she went to say something the words would not come out.

'Where are we going?' she finally managed to ask.

'I know the perfect place.'

Cattle were regularly turned out to graze on the down and its slopes. They had worn their own streets and highways between the shelter of the trees and the summit. One such path led to a hollow eroded by time and the elements near the base of the down. Here, avoiding the cow pats, Guy spread out his coat for her to sit on. She felt tense and embarrassed. In all the films the characters' lovemaking, the surrendering to each other, was an impromptu act driven by sudden emotion. Even without actually saying it, she and Guy had set out with this in mind. Now it took away the spontaneity, the natural response. They were both awkward, laughing self-consciously as he made a clumsy attempt to kiss her, but then the tempo changed and Guy became intense, possessed of some inner drive she could only guess at. She hadn't enjoyed it. Unable to relax, it hurt. She had to fight the desire to push him away. When he finished he seemed ashamed, as if he had raped her.

'I'm so sorry. I should have known you were a virgin.'

She was shocked that he could even have doubted it.

There were unspoken disappointments in the air as they walked back. They parted at the point where one road led to the village and the other to Cartegena.

'I – I'll see you then.'

Two miserable days followed when he didn't get in touch. All Maud's predictions came to taunt her. Nice girls didn't. Boys only wanted one thing and once they had got it you wouldn't see them for dust.

When he rang she was so relieved, and so thankful that she had been the one to answer the phone.

'Sorry I haven't rung before. We've had visitors.'

She couldn't trust herself to speak for the relief and the longing.

Reaching the hollow, she picked a shady place where the shrub would be able to grow and spread. The ground was sandy and easy to dig. She hoped the plant wouldn't object to the spot. Easing it from its pot, she lowered it into the hole and tamped down the soil. She should have brought water but the ground was damp. She hoped it would survive.

Now that she had planted it she didn't know what to do. 'Here you are,' she called out in her head. 'This is for you. I hope you like it. Please look after it.' She wanted to share with him the remembrance of that first encounter and their innocence.

Where should she find him, though? In this hollow? At Cartegena? Where his physical body had lain for all those years or where it was now, inaccessible in the family vault? Perhaps the only place to find him was inside her. Unwillingly she stood up and ran her hand over the leaves of the plant in a kind of affectionate blessing.

As she started off down the slope, she found herself wondering whether Frank was still in Nigeria and whether the post from there was so slow that she still might get a card in the mail.

The next morning Edward Benningfield came to see Lady Lamb to explain about the inquest.

'You won't need to attend, dear lady. The coroner has all the statements and witnesses he requires. Once this is over you can begin to put this tragedy behind you. Please try not to distress yourself any more than can be helped.'

Shirley, now in her role as confidante and unofficial secretary, remained in the room. As they left, she said to the solicitor. 'Will I be permitted to attend?'

'But of course, if you wish to.' He added hesitantly, 'You should be prepared though. There will be details that you might find painful.'

She felt herself begin to close down inside. 'Do you know what they have discovered?'

'Not in any detail, no.'

She felt that he was avoiding the question. Did this mean that it was something bad? She saw him out and as she walked back along the hallway, she thought: Whatever it is, I'll face it, somehow.

The court was crowded. Guy Lamb's exalted position in society and the mysterious circumstances of his disappearance had aroused national curiosity. With misgivings it dawned on Shirley that the case might last for more than one day. What if it wasn't an open and shut case? As she sat there she could feel the memory of Guy creeping ever closer. *What happened to you? What had you been up to?* A precipice of uncertainty drew her closer, a fear that the Guy she knew and loved was about to be exposed as something different, alien.

Trying to hold on to the present, she wondered if he might be disappointed that recently it had been Frank Agnew and not he who had occupied so much of her time. In her head she tried to reach out for him. Sorry Guy, you know how much I loved you – I still do.

Reluctantly she recognized that neither of these men had brought her anything like lasting happiness, or even peace of mind, although perhaps that came to the same thing.

A few rows ahead and to her left she saw Annabelle Moorcroft, Guy's distant cousin through a great-great-aunt. She wore a very tailored suit, what Maud would call a costume. It didn't look as if it had come off the peg at Marks and Spencer's. As she turned her head, Shirley caught her rather chunky features, the matt finish of her make-up, plum-coloured lips that sat uncomfortably with her bottle-induced, straw hair. In spite of the obviously expensive outfit, she looked rather tawdry. Shirley guessed that as a contender for the inheritance she had felt it necessary to put in an appearance – that and of course curiosity.

About three seats away from Annabelle she picked out Auberon Lamb, the other main contender for the prize that was Cartegena. There was nothing to suggest a family likeness. Auberon was nearing forty, slight of build, a slim, foppish, still youthful-looking man with a prominent nose and softly waving hair that he had a habit of tossing like someone auditioning for a television shampoo advert. His claim to Cartegena came via Guy's great-great-uncle, the younger brother of Annabelle's great-great-aunt. Shirley wondered what their reaction would be when they learned about Frank's claim. Would they form a united front? At the moment they were studiously ignoring each other.

As the coroner took his seat, she glanced around again and everything seemed to lurch, for there, on one of the benches away to her right was Frank. Damn him! Her mother's words swirled around her: *haunting the place, sniffing around.* Was he like the rest, a vulture gathering to grab what he could of the carcass? She was so shaken by his presence that she missed the opening sentences. As his head began to turn in her direction she quickly looked away.

The formalities were long and intricate. Various witnesses were called with the purpose of establishing that Guy was who he was. Confirmation of his visit to Colombia, evidence of his presence on the flight home – home, somewhere he had never reached. Shirley tightened her grip on the strap of her bag and resisted the memories.

Next came the pathologist. He was a plump, pink man in his forties, his pale horn-rimmed glasses reflecting the tone of his thinning sandy hair. In a soft, slightly lisping voice he confirmed that the subject was a white male aged about twenty, who in his opinion had been dead for fifteen to twenty years. Forensic evidence confirmed without a doubt that he was the Honourable Guy Lamb.

'And have you been able to establish the cause of death?'

'I have.' The pathologist pulled at his tie as if it was choking him. 'The conditions in the grave were such that although the body had deteriorated with the passage of time, decomposition was not complete. At the time of his death the young man appeared to have been in good health.' The pathologist paused to clear his throat. 'Although there is insufficient evidence to establish whether he was a drug addict, there is no doubt that the cause of death was a massive overdose of cocaine.'

Shirley could feel the blood flood her face. Inside her head she denied it furiously, but the man was still talking. 'There is also evidence that he had been disembowelled.' A gasp whispered its way around the court.

Shirley felt the sickness again in her throat. Disembowelling – it couldn't be. For a wild moment she wondered if some animal had got to his body, eaten the soft tissue, but that image was as bad. A punishment? Everything began to fall apart. She thought of that other Guy, Guy Fawkes, hung, drawn, and quartered, his body broken on the rack. Was her Guy tortured? Who were these people? She couldn't bear it. She turned to get up but her legs wouldn't carry her. The man must be wrong. Guy had smoked pot but that was because he said it made everyone feel peaceful. *If everyone did it there would be no wars.* Not cocaine, though. Not hard drugs, not sticking needles in collapsing veins, if that was what you did. Not robbing banks to pay for an addiction that took you over. The pathologist must be wrong. Perhaps this wasn't Guy at all. Perhaps it was a nightmare, only she couldn't wake up.

The pathologist was still talking. 'Inside the stomach cavity there were tiny pieces of plastic, the sort used twenty years ago to make pellets that can be swallowed and passed through the body.'

'The sort used to smuggle drugs?' the coroner asked

'Exactly. My conclusion is that Guy Lamb was carrying cocaine into Britain. He ingested it then on the journey one of the capsules broke. The drug seeped into his system. He would not have been carrying just one item though. My contention is that when he began to feel ill he made for the people who had hired him but it was too late. Even if they wanted to, there was nothing they could do for him. At the same time they would not have been prepared to lose the whole consignment so when he died they cut him open and retrieved the rest of their haul.'

The coroner nodded, accepting the evidence. 'I think we'll break here for lunch.'

Shirley tried to claw back some control. Her mind flooded with butchery, soft tissue, the sickly smell of blood. People were filing out of the court. Like some radar she sensed Frank growing closer, felt the pulse of his attraction bouncing off her. She wanted to get out quickly, to pretend that she hadn't seen him, but there were people in front of her. As she waited impatiently to escape she picked up his approach, a dark blur bobbing his way through the assembly.

'Come on. You need a drink. Let's get out of here.' Leaning across he lifted her bodily over the rail of the bench and on to the aisle. Holding her arm he navigated their way to the exit. Outside he propelled her across the road and into the Bull and Bishop, depositing her in a niche by the window.

'Stay there, I'll get you a brandy.'

Shirley was silent. Inside her head tunnels of shadow and noise cut her off from the outside world. Numb, quiescent, she waited, and when he returned she sipped the drink like medicine.

He sat quietly next to her, not saying anything. When at last she put down her glass, he said, 'You were really involved with him, weren't you?'

She nodded, a guilty confession, guilty because she had wanted Frank to think that she was free.

She asked, 'Why have you come? Why do you keep coming back here?' She resisted adding, 'haunting the place.'

'I had to come back with the Nigerian photos. I – I guess I couldn't resist finding out what happened.'

'They must be wrong. He wasn't a drug addict. He went to Colombia to work in a children's home.'

'I'm surprised you didn't go with him.'

She looked angrily at him, cursing him for discovering her timidity. She said, 'I had my exams to finish. We—' It was none of his business. She picked up the empty glass and without asking he went to fetch her another drink.

When he returned he asked her if she wanted to eat. She shook her head.

'You don't mind if I do?' It was her turn to shake her head. He returned with a ploughman's lunch and proceeded to butter bread and cut cheese, which he held out to her as if she was a fledgling. At first she shook her head but then she opened her mouth and accepted the morsels.

'How did you get on in Nigeria?' She was calmer now, trying to put some normality into the day.

'It was good. I might even say great. Those artists out there are so skilled. They seem to have continuity in their lives. Their work, their art, it's all one.'

She tried to imagine the local women, supple, exuding warmth and sexual pleasure. Had he slept with any of them? What a question to be asking!

The brandy had soothed her. She began to feel sleepy but Frank was preparing to leave.

He asked, 'Are you going back for this afternoon's session?'

She nodded and did not resist when he took her arm.

When they entered the court most people seemed to have taken up their previous places. Annabelle Moorcroft and Auberon Lamb were still three places apart, not speaking. Frank sat down beside her. Shirley struggled to compose herself, to prepare for whatever happened next.

As the court reconvened a lugubrious man, no doubt marked out since birth to be an undertaker, took his place in the witness stand. He recounted the date and location of a burial where, eighteen years before, a Mrs Elizabeth Martin had been laid to rest, awaiting only the delivery of her husband Howard into the same soil. Her interment had taken place two days after the arrival of the flight that had brought Guy back from Colombia. The same undertaker confirmed the date upon which Mr Howard Martin was finally sent to join his wife, only to find an interloper in his place.

A court official next read out a statement made all those years before by Guy's father, confirming that as far as the family knew, his son had been travelling alone, intent on working in some distant school near Bogota. Subsequent letters sent to his parents had confirmed that this was the case. His father stated that from his last letter it had been clear that he was looking forward to coming home. Why he should have disappeared was a mystery. Kidnap was suggested, the waiting for a long over-due ransom note. Shirley could hear Lord Lamb's voice in the construction of the sentences, his blustering certainty. In spite of his conviction, he had not known that Guy smoked pot. He had not known that she and Guy were to marry. His parents did not know him as well as they thought they did. Did she? Her own certainty faltered.

The translation of a letter was read from a Father Ignatio Gonzales, head of the boys' home in Colombia. It described Guy as a quiet, devoted young man whose friendships had appeared to be conducted inside the mission. Guy had been a friendly, sociable person but had not appeared to have any contacts outside of the school. Father Gonzales found it difficult to believe that he might have been involved in drug smuggling.

A police officer then explained that he had re-examined the luggage left at the airport. There had been nothing present to indicate who Guy Lamb might have been carrying for: no address, no telephone number, not even a name. From the paucity of the contents it seemed likely that the deceased had left behind anything of any value, possibly for the use of the mission.

That was just what he would have done, Shirley thought. He would have given away anything of value. After all, once he got home he could replace it, although by then she knew that the family was struggling financially.

As the policeman finished his report, the coroner glanced at the large, round, old-fashioned clock on the wall that now looked incongruous in the newly refurbished surroundings.

'I think this is a good place to adjourn for today.' The assembly rose and shuffled out into the late afternoon sun.

'Another drink?' Frank was just behind her.

'No thanks. I think I really should be—'

'Getting home to your old ladies?' He shook his head and smiled before she could object. 'Of course you must. They'll be wanting to know what is happening.'

'Are you coming back tomorrow?' she asked.

'Yes.'

'I'll see you then?'

'You will.'

She would have liked him to touch her, even a pat on the arm, but he raised a hand in farewell and began to cross the road towards the Bull and Bishop. She was touched by the easy lope of his walk, the fluid movement of his hips. In his own way he was beautiful.

As she drove home she pushed him from her thoughts. There were other more pressing considerations, like how was she to tell Lady Lamb what had been said? Her instinct was to keep it from the old lady but she knew that the case would be reported in full in the papers. Maud and Jean were spending the day with Florence. Jean had arrived two days earlier but Shirley had seen very little of her. Now she was glad that her aunt was here, someone to share the burden of responsibility with.

As she turned into the drive she saw Edward Benningfield's car parked by the house. He had beaten her to it, taken on the responsibility of explaining the findings to Florence. Gratitude flooded over her.

Shirley went inside and followed the voices to the breakfast room, where the solicitor, along with the three women, was drinking tea. They all looked up as she came in.

'Are you all right?' It was Jean who asked.

Shirley warmed to her aunt. She hadn't talked to her about Guy but Jean was the type of person to put two and two together and, unlike her older sister, make four.

'I'm OK.'

Jean went to make more tea and Edward Benningfield said, 'I'm sorry if the revelations upset you.'

She shook her head. 'I shall go back tomorrow to hear the summing up.' As she said it, a treacherous glimmer of warmth touched her. She would be seeing Frank again. Tomorrow was all about Guy but she hung on to the memory of Frank Agnew. Perhaps all was not lost. He had seen her distress, acted in the very way that she needed. Perhaps he understood what she had been through. Perhaps, when this was all over, she could begin to repair the damage.

The next morning she managed to get the same seat in the courtroom. From this vantage point she could see both the clock and the door. People dribbled in and took their places. Annabelle Moorcroft arrived first, followed by Auberon Lamb shortly afterwards. They did not speak. The minutes ticked by and she could not stop from looking towards the door, waiting for the moment when Frank appeared. He did not. At the appointed time the coroner made his entrance and the proceedings began. Trying to ignore the disappointment, she struggled to pay attention.

The coroner's summing up was succinct. Here was a young man of good family but apparently without any particular aim in life. He appeared to be motivated by admirable humanitarian concerns and that was laudable. However, his lack of academic achievement and his apparent failure to want a career marked him out as someone perhaps unsure of the way forward. There was no evidence to confirm that he himself was a drug addict. It seemed clear, however, that he had been a willing carrier, for no one could swallow such a quantity of drugs by accident. If this sat strangely with his ideals, it was an all-too-familiar story. Carriers were frequently recruited for the money, the payment being considerable. The contents of one man's stomach would be a valuable consignment.

Whilst the Lamb family might be aristocratic, it was confirmed that at the time of their son's return they were short of funds. No doubt the young man saw this as a way of making easy money. Perhaps he did not fully realize, or perhaps he had managed to ignore, the misery his burden could cause to those who would pay dearly for it on the streets of London or Leeds or Liverpool. Sadly it had ended with tragic consequences for himself.

Who those miscreants were who had commissioned him, there was no way of discovering after all this time. Having considered all the evidence, therefore, he felt that this was a case of accidental death and he thus recorded it as 'death by misadventure'.

Outside, the sun was behind angry, smoke-coloured cloud. Shirley felt the chill of the day touch her. She stood among the dispersing crowd and surveyed the streets, the entrance to the pub. There was no sign of Frank.

The inquest was over. This was the time, as so many people had implied, when she should begin to put the past behind her. The thought of Guy's life in Colombia, the friendships he had shared at the mission, his reasons for carrying drugs into Britain, all separated him from her. Suddenly he felt like a stranger. Standing there alone in the crowded street she looked one last time for Frank but he was not there. With a heavy heart, she thought that perhaps not one but two chapters were closing in her life.

Twelve

That evening, Shirley and Jean went out for a drink. Shirley needed to get away. The stress of the final verdict, the reality of the loss of Guy and the disappointment that Frank had not kept his promise reduced her to numb despair. Once again they were staying at Cartegena for at this perhaps the worst of times, Florence could not be left alone.

Taking one look at her niece, Jean said, 'Come along, you and I are going to go out and get blotto.' In the face of her sister's firmness, Maud made no objection.

They walked into the village so that neither of them would need to drive back.

As they traversed the gravel driveway, Shirley was aware how fit her aunt appeared to be: straight backed, walking out briskly, her still brown hair neatly shaped to her head, her clothes fashionable and yet timeless. Shirley felt the increase in her heart rate as she hurried to keep pace. Those extra pounds around her waist caused her body to complain of the effort. When she could be bothered, she must do something about it.

They went to the village inn where it was not unusual for women to drink without the company of men. Inside, the place was well lit and gave the impression of a social centre rather than somewhere devoted to serious drinking. The first person Shirley saw was Frank's cousin Douglas Kirk. He raised his hand in acknowledgement then continued his conversation with two friends at the bar. From his manner she wondered if he was talking about her. Ignoring him, she went in search of a table. As she put down her bag she glanced across at the bar and Douglas quickly looked away.

'What are you having?'

With an effort she turned her attention back to Jean. 'Wine, please. Red.' Her aunt headed to the bar and she watched as Douglas turned his attention to the older woman, taking in her appearance with an easy, practised eye. Something about his expression told her that he was waiting for her aunt to move out of earshot so that he could continue with his saga.

After the drama of the day, Shirley felt drained. In place of the raw pain of the revelations in court was a continuing sense of defeat. The inquest was over. For a while she would like to crawl away and hide but common sense told her that what was needed was some normality, something to put her life back on an even keel. Where to find it was a different matter.

They settled themselves with their wine at a small table in an alcove by the chimney breast. A real wood fire burned in winter, making the pub a haven of comfort. Now it was pleasantly cool.

Shirley had mixed feelings about this outing. She could not bear the prospect of spending the evening at Cartegena with the oppressive ghost of Guy's inquest still invading every room. In their very attempts to behave with some normality, both Florence and Maud only underlined the fact that there was something they were trying to ignore. Everywhere Shirley looked the tragedy of Guy's death shouted loud into the silence.

It was a long time since she had had a conversation with her aunt and she was not sure that they would have much to say to each other. She already felt as she did at home – that if the subject of Guy was avoided, it was more than likely to intrude and yet it was the last thing she wanted to talk about.

As they both took their initial sips of wine, Shirley asked, 'What are you going to do now that you have given up your job?'

She wasn't even sure exactly what it was that Jean had done but as far as she was aware, she had been at the same place for several years. Jean wasn't old enough for a pension so she wondered how her aunt would manage.

Jean shrugged and took another speculative sip. 'To tell the truth, I haven't decided. I have seven weeks' paid holiday so I'm holding off, waiting to see what happens.'

'I don't suppose you planned to spend it here.' Shirley thought of the exotic holidays she had conjured up for herself.

'Not exactly, but I was glad to get out of the village. Sometimes the horizons can shrink so much that you can't imagine a world outside your tiny circle.'

Was this Jean's way of telling her that she was in a rut?

She asked, 'What would you like to do?'

She needed to keep the focus away from herself.

Jean raised her shoulders in a who-knows gesture. 'Perhaps I've left it a bit late to be a backpacker but I fancy escaping, seeing the world, all the things you should do when you're twenty, not fifty.'

'I don't think there's a right time to do anything.' Even as she said it, Shirley wondered if she shouldn't heed her own advice.

'Perhaps not. It gets harder though. I've got a house to sell and material possessions. The dear old dog died a couple of months ago so there aren't any dependants, unless you count the visitors to the bird table.'

'Where would you like to go?' She warmed to the possibilities.

Both glasses were already empty and Shirley went to refill them. Before she could pay, however, Douglas Kirk had done so.

'Heard from my cousin?' he asked. Surely there was innuendo in the question? Shirley felt an answering blush.

Annoyed with herself she said, 'Not lately.' With a brief nod she picked up the glasses and moved away.

Other people had noticed then; had seen her with Frank. The knowledge disturbed her.

'Who's that?' Jean nodded towards the bar.

'Oh, he does some work in the garden at Cartegena. He's a bit of a gossip.'

Shirley tried to dismiss him quickly, but Jean said, 'He seems to be interested in you.'

Lost for an answer, Shirley shrugged.

'What about you then?' It was Jean's turn to ask the questions.

'No particular plans.'

'Maud felt that you needed to get away. Is it to do with the inquest?'

How to answer? Of course it was, in part, but it was more than that: an admission that the doors were fast closing on her life. She glanced at Jean, who was watching her with her intelligent brown eyes.

'Don't do what I have done,' she said gently. 'Don't leave it too late.'

'Too late for what?'

'Adventure, family, fulfilment, whatever it is that you want. Life goes faster than you imagine.'

Shirley guessed that her aunt was right. Just because Jean still looked good didn't mean that time wasn't catching up with her. With something approaching alarm, she thought that where children were concerned, Jean's body clock had probably already ceased ticking. Too late for her – that is, if she ever wanted kids. Her own emptiness touched her like a chill.

Jean took another gulp of the wine and placed the glass carefully on the table. 'I – I've been instructed to have a talk to you. By your mother.' She smiled apologetically.

'What about?' Shirley smiled back but her face felt taut with resentment.

'Your mother's worried about this chap you've been seeing – Frank someone?'

'She would be.'

She hesitated, wondering whether to say how her mother had always tried to scupper her friendships. Would Jean believe her? Before she came up with an answer, Jean said, 'She seems to think there's something sinister about him, that he has an ulterior motive in coming back now.'

The words began to curl around them like unwelcome smoke. *'You're looking at the next master of Cartegena.'*

Shirley could feel Frank's triumph. Was he simply amused by the discovery or was there more? Did his smile hide revenge? Was it true that if she hadn't insisted that he kept the papers in the drawer of his mother's desk, he might never have known? She shook her head to drive the thoughts away. She wanted to share her uncertainties with someone and her aunt seemed the obvious person but she had promised Frank that she wouldn't say anything about his claim to Cartegena. Besides, her own feelings were so confused she did not know how to put them into words.

'If it's personal, don't feel you have to talk about it.' Jean shadowed her thoughts.

'It's simply that . . .' She couldn't articulate what she felt; the attraction for this man, the knowledge that they were living in unnatural times. If Guy had not disappeared and Frank had returned to the village on his mother's death, surely no one, not even Maud, would have come to such conclusions. She wondered why she even gave them a second thought but there was something about Frank, his passion, that raw anger of so long ago, that stirred her unease.

'My mother has always been the same,' she started. 'When I was young, very young, I became . . . friends with Guy Lamb. I know with hindsight that Mum must have thought that such a romance couldn't lead anywhere and she was probably trying to protect me, but the way that she went about it was to blacken Guy's character. Now . . . now she's doing the same with Frank Agnew.'

'You think he's OK then?'

Again Shirley shrugged. 'I don't know what I think about anything any more. Guy – Guy and I were going to get married. I know everyone thinks it was all in my mind but I know that he was serious. I have his last letter, just before he left Bogota. He was talking about marriage. I don't know what happened on the journey home, after he arrived at the airport, but what-ever it was I can't believe that he was running drugs.'

Jean looked thoughtful. 'Your mother said he was doing missionary work or something. The two don't seem to go together very well. What did he plan to do when he came back?'

'Missionary work? It was nothing like that. He helped out at a mission school because he was driven by a sense of injustice that he should have so much, all those advantages, whereas others had nothing. He simply took an unpaid job in a home for orphaned children. I think it was a Catholic-run place – well, it probably would be in South America. He simply wanted to give something back.'

Carefully, Jean said, 'You don't think he might have chosen an ordinary girl like you as some sort of rebellion against his family?'

'He loved me.' She was about to protest but there was just enough doubt to make her hesitate. Perhaps he had seen her as a way of showing that he was nothing special, that like her, he belonged in the ordinary world. There were no truths any more, nothing that you could rely on.

'What about this Frank?' Jean asked. 'Do you like him?'

What could she say? Like wasn't a word that fitted the situation. After a moment's thought, she said, 'For all I know he has been using me as a way to get at the Lambs, to find out what is going on.'

'And why should he do that? What is going on?'

'I don't know. Now that Guy is officially dead, there are all those vultures waiting to make a claim on the house. It's hopelessly in debt and yet the kudos of ownership remains. Even if it were sold there wouldn't be any money although there are treasures in the house that must be worth something.' She paused. 'No one seems to love the place, not for itself.'

'And you do?'

'It's been there all my life. I don't want to see it sold off, turned into a conference centre, or even worse, pulled down.'

Jean nodded her understanding. 'Would Frank have a claim on the house then?'

With dismay Shirley realized that she had hinted as much. 'Please, please promise that you won't say anything, but it seems that he might be the descendant from an earlier marriage, one that no one knew about.'

'He's got proof?'

Shirley looked uncertain. 'He claims to have.'

Jean looked amused. 'Then if he's after you, you could still end up as mistress of Cartegena.'

'It's not funny. It's not like that.'

'I'm sorry.' Jean looked chastened. 'It just seems that one way or the other, if you have designs on the house – and on him –

you could fulfil them.'

'I don't want the house. I just want to see it safe.'

Like cats when they lose face and seek refuge by washing, they both turned their attentions to their glasses, sipping with unnatural focus.

'What does this Frank do?' Jean asked.

'He's a freelance photographer. He lives in France, does casual work, drifts, I suppose.'

'Where is he now?'

'In Nigeria the last I heard, doing some photographic work for the *Observer*.' She did not mention that she had seen him only yesterday. To do so would be to bring questions she could not answer.

'He's successful then?'

'I suppose he is.'

'What does he look like?'

'Tall, dark haired . . .' The tension eased and as the wine began to do its work, she suddenly softened as the thought of him poured warmth into her. In an attempt to be light-hearted, she said, 'He's not the sort of man you'd kick out of bed.'

'Have you been in his bed?'

She knew that her look answered the question.

Jean took a deep breath. 'He sounds like a pretty good distraction to me.'

Again they were both silent. For something to say, Shirley offered, 'His father worked at Cartegena, as a gardener.'

'A sort of Mellors figure?'

Shirley tried to remember what Frank's father had been like. As a child she had seen him simply as an old man. Had he too had some of that charisma that existed in his son?

'Anyway, your Frank must have an interesting life,' Jean mused, interrupting her train of thought.

'He's not my Frank.' He did have an interesting life, fascinating in comparison with her own. In that case, why should he have any sinister interest in an old house in England? Perhaps she was being drawn into Maud's fantasies.

'You've never thought of marriage?' Shirley asked the question to change the subject. It felt clumsy, intrusive, but she needed to switch the attention away from herself.

Jean smiled wryly. 'I thought of it once when I was in my teens. He was a roustabout with the fair. It stayed in the village for two weeks and we – I fell madly in love. I was going to go with them but my father found out and that was the end of that.' Her eyes began to dance with mirth. 'It hurt so much at the time but just imagine – where would I be now?'

'Where are you now?' She was turning the tables, being the challenger. Her aunt was at a crossroads. She wanted to know more.

Jean shrugged, tapping the side of her glass with a neat, shiny fingernail. 'For the past God knows how long I have worked as a receptionist for a dentist. Hardly cutting-edge stuff but then, you see, I've been having an affair – with the dentist.' She looked abashed. 'It's been going on for years but he's married, of course, and he has three children.'

Shirley crushed all those objections that immediately came to mind – the why doesn't he leave her and the why don't you leave him questions. As she waited, Jean provided her own answers.

'His wife has been ill for the last seven years – multiple sclerosis. She's practically bedridden. Until now I've been convincing myself that she needs him and that he needs me to help him cope with the strains at home. Just recently I had a scare of my own and I thought that perhaps it was time that I got out, looked around.' She tapped her lower lip thoughtfully. 'It's probably an empty gesture. His children are grown up now. The youngest will be eighteen soon. She'll be away to university in October. Their mother is on borrowed time really. Soon there will be no reason for us not to get together.' She stopped talking as if to consider the implications of what she had just said.

'I don't know, perhaps it has become a habit. Perhaps the romance is over before the relationship even starts officially. I'm just taking time out, really, leaving them to wind down their affairs, to say their last goodbyes.' She sighed. 'I'll probably go back. In fact, I know that I will. You see, he might be a habit but it isn't one that I want to break.' Behind her smile was the hint of tears.

They were both silent, absorbing information, trying to put into context each other's lives.

Of Frank, Jean suddenly asked, 'Does he come back often?'

'He's asked me to go to France and visit.'

'So why don't you?'

'I don't have a passport.'

'Easily resolved.'

'I can't leave Maud, or Lady Florence.'

'I'm sure Florence could afford help. Maud could come back with me for a bit.'

'I—' I haven't got the courage, she thought. I can't really believe that he means what he says. Aloud, she said, 'I don't even have a proper address for him.'

'But you've got his phone number?'

Shirley gave a single shake of her head. 'Only one for the cottage here in the village.' As she said it she thought that he might be there at this very minute. She felt an almost unbearable desire to go straight away and find him.

Jean frowned. 'So although he's invited you to stay, you don't know where it is?'

'No.' She felt foolish.

Gently, Jean asked, 'Why do you think that is? Don't you keep in touch between his visits?'

Shirley didn't know how to explain. 'We always seem to part on bad terms,' she started, then realized that painted their relationship in a worse light than it really was – or was it?

'You don't think that perhaps he's married?' Jean's voice was gentle, the way you might break bad news to a child.

'No. He's been married but he's divorced.' She knew with a kind of certainty that in this respect Frank was straightforward. He would have no trouble with telling the truth on that score.

'So you believe him?'

'Yes, I believe him.'

'In that case you'll just have to wait until he comes back.'

'If he comes back.' Shirley drained her glass. Why had Frank not come to hear the summing up at the inquest? She had taken his words as a promise, thought he understood at that moment how much she needed his support, taken it for granted that he

145

would keep his word and be there. In this state of uncertainty she couldn't even begin to guess at his reasons. Anyway, she didn't want to think about him any more, not at the moment.

Two glasses of wine were usually her limit, but that much-needed feeling of numbness had not yet been achieved.

'Another?' she said to Jean.

'I most certainly do.'

Thirteen

Shirley and Jean left the pub just before closing time. In the last half an hour, their serious thoughts were swallowed up by a sudden, inexplicable discovery that everything was really very funny. When their giggles began to attract attention they decided that it was time to go. Rising unsteadily, they made for the door, accidentally nudging against each other, jostling for the narrow path between tables. Shirley was aware of the indulgent, cynical, amused eyes that watched their progress, including those of Douglas Kirk. She wondered if he ever kept in touch with his cousin and whether they talked about her. Stupid thought: Frank had probably forgotten her existence.

Outside, the evening was balmy. A navy blue sky shimmered with stars, brief moments of light that flared and extinguished only to reappear elsewhere.

'What a wonderful evening.'

Companionably they linked arms, leaned against each other for mutual support and continued an unconnected stream of comments that for some reason reduced them both to helpless laughter.

As they passed through the gates into the drive leading to Cartegena a barn owl swooped low over the pathway. Something about its silence halted them both and they stood very still, watching it land in one of the beeches that lined the drive, where it magically blended with the branch and the leaves.

'Beautiful,' Jean whispered.

They both listened, trying to pick up the slightest rustle, or scampering of feet around them. Shirley imagined she could hear the very earth breathing, a gentle rise and fall of minute movements. Her own chest rose and fell in rhythm with the world around her then gradually she became aware of something else, an up-and-down pattern of sound, growing louder.

'What's that?'

'A police car?'

'Fire engine?'

They both turned in the direction where, along the road outside the gates, a pattern of flashing blue marked out the vehicle's route. As it came closer the siren stopped but the light continued to flash, its progress growing suddenly slower. Seconds later an ambulance slewed through the gates and began to come up the drive.

Shirley and Jean stepped back quickly from the path.

'Come on!' As the significance hit them they began to hurry in the vehicle's wake, hearts pumping now, quickly sober.

They broke from the cover of the trees as the ambulance men were just entering the front door, carrying a stretcher.

Maud, or Lady Florence? The question gnawed at Shirley as she stumbled up the steps in her haste to find out. The first person she saw was her mother, standing in the hallway, looking small and lost as the two men mounted the staircase to the floor above.

'Mum?'

'Oh Shirley, I'm so glad you're back. I didn't know where you were. I didn't know what to do.'

'What happened?' Shirley guided Maud towards a chair, lowering her into it.

'It was about an hour after you had gone. We had been watching the telly. Lady Florence said that she felt tired and would go on up. She went up the stairs in that thing of hers and I heard her go into the bathroom and then all of a sudden there was a crash. I called out but she didn't answer. At least—' Maud's face crumpled at the memory. 'She was making a queer noise, like an animal. I kept calling but she didn't answer. I – I tried to get that lift thing but it wouldn't come back down the stairs so I had to climb up. It took me ages and I was afraid I might fall.'

Shirley glanced up to where the lift still stood, the seat neatly folded up, at the top of the stairs. 'You only had to push the switch down,' she said, but Maud wasn't listening.

'Stay there.' She went across to the stairs herself and hurried up, turning in the direction of the bathroom where the light shone and the two ambulance men were crouching down beside the figure of Florence Lamb. One of them looked up as she appeared in the doorway.

'Is she all right?' Shirley asked.

'She's had a stroke. You are?'

Shirley told them. 'We've been living in since her son died,' she said.

'The other old lady phoned us.'

'She's my mother. Is she all right?' She meant Florence. She couldn't see much of her in the cramped space of the bathroom but she wore an oxygen mask and one of the men was massaging her hand as if to help her blood make the journey from her extremities.

'We'll get her to hospital at once.'

'I'll come.'

The elder of the two men shook his head. 'Better to stay here with the other old lady. She's had a shock.'

'My aunt is here.'

'Nothing you can do if you come. They'll phone if there is any change.'

'Shall I pack her some night things?'

'I shouldn't worry, not for the moment. See how things seem tomorrow.'

Defeated, Shirley left the room and made her way downstairs.

Jean and Maud were in the kitchen. Jean had made tea and was just pouring it out.

'If only I'd known where to find you,' Maud was saying. There was a certain exultation in her voice, the knowledge that she had discovered a new cause for complaint that could be dragged out whenever she felt like it.

'If you had been here you would have known what to do. Me, what with my legs . . .'

149

Shirley accepted a cup of tea and sat down.

'Is she going to be all right?' Jean asked quietly, across her sister's head.

Shirley gave the smallest shrug. Florence had looked so small and ashen lying there. The limpness of her head, supported on a folded bath towel, made her think of a rag doll. Even if the old lady began to get over this, it would be a long road to recovery.

Her hand was trembling as she put the cup and saucer back on the table. It seemed as if the battle to inherit Cartegena might be starting quicker than she thought.

Shirley awoke from a troubled sleep and realized several things all at the same time. It was the middle of the night, her mouth felt like the Sahara and an insistent throbbing bored into her head, just above her right eyebrow. An answering jumble of thoughts immediately assailed her. She needed a drink of water, she should never have had that fourth glass of wine, and Lady Florence was in hospital. Immediately she was wide awake, facing that staring void that comes when sleep is suddenly snatched away by worries about the waking world. Peering at the clock, she saw that it was nearly ten minutes to four. Shakily she felt her way to the bathroom and ran the cold tap, cupping her palm and drinking like some explorer stumbling on a water hole. She reached up to the cupboard above the basin and fished out a packet of paracetamol, clumsy in her haste to release the tablets from their foil casing. As soon as she swallowed them she felt some of the tension begin to leave her. The headache at least could easily be dealt with.

Knowing that sleep was impossible, she collected her dressing gown and went quietly down the stairs to the kitchen. A cup of tea beckoned like some first aid post. She tried to think of something positive, some anchor that would hold her fast to her present existence, but there didn't seem to be anything. Lady Florence was ill, very ill, and Cartegena, the focus of her existence, would shortly be snatched away, thrust into the grasping hands of one of Lord Lamb's distant relatives or, if they couldn't afford the death duties, into the maws of a finance company. For a second she thought of Frank's claim. As she raised her teacup to her lips she found that her hand was trembling.

She tried to keep calm. Perhaps the situation could turn into a sort of liberation. What Jean had said was true. Maud could go and stay with her, at least in the short term and at last she, Shirley, would be free to – do what? The blank wall of the future confronted her once more. When she finished the tea she washed her cup and saucer at the sink, emptied the teapot and on auto-pilot climbed back up the stairs. She must sleep. Who knew what demands the next day would make on her?

For a long time she lay in the dark trying to create a series of scenarios that might permit her to escape. Eventually she must have been successful for she awoke to the insistent though distant ringing of the phone. Somehow she scrambled from her bed, dragged on her dressing gown and was about to descend the stairs when she heard Jean's voice.

'I see. Well, thank you for letting us know.'

As Shirley reached the bottom of the stairs, her aunt saw her. From her expression the news was clear.

'She's dead?'

'She died at ten to four this morning.'

Just when I woke up, thought Shirley. She had no idea what, if anything, it signified.

Jean boiled the kettle and Shirley took her mother a drink and broke the news. To her surprise, Maud began to cry, a passive weeping that touched her all the more because her mother was usually so acid.

'The poor old lady. She didn't have anyone, only us.'

It was true. Florence was an only child and a widow, whose only son was dead. Her only friends were two old ladies, like her, products of a bygone age, who lived miles away and to whom she wrote dutifully once a week. The thought of the gathering storm reminded Shirley once more of her own uncertain future. Now that her employer was deceased she had no role any more, not here at Cartegena. Who should take interim responsibility for the house she didn't know. Anyway, it was really nothing to do with her. Best not to worry about it.

'After breakfast I think perhaps we should go home,' she said to Maud.

'I think perhaps we should.'

They made a half-hearted attempt to eat some toast but before they could think of leaving, the front bell rang. Shirley opened the old oak door to find Edward Benningfield, the solicitor, on the step.

'You've heard the news?' he asked.

'The hospital phoned.'

'I have really come to make sure that you knew and to ask if you wouldn't mind hanging on here, just for the present?'

'We were thinking that we should leave.' Her words sounded stubborn and she felt awkward, not knowing how to explain what she felt. She added, 'I don't know what the usual procedure is – I've never been in this situation before.'

'I don't suppose that you have.' He gave her a tight little smile and followed her inside.

'Would you like a drink?' she asked.

'I'll come into the kitchen.'

Jean and Maud had both gone upstairs to dress so Shirley boiled the kettle once again and made some coffee.

'Have you any idea what is going to happen?' she asked as she carried two cups to the kitchen table.

'As far as Lady Florence goes, I'm the executor of her will. There will be a post mortem because she died so suddenly but there's no reason to suppose that there is anything untoward about her death. She was an elderly woman who had been under a lot of stress. In the circumstances a stroke seems likely.'

It had not occurred to Shirley that the manner of Lady Florence's death might even cause speculation. For a wild moment, thoughts of foul play formed in her mind. She and Jean had left two defenceless old women and been cavorting in the pub. She could just see the newspaper headlines: *Carers cavort while elderly victims face death*. Could they be accused of neglect?

'I feel bad,' she started. 'My aunt and I went out last night. My mother and Lady Lamb were here alone.'

'Why should you feel bad? You aren't a nursemaid to either of them.' His expression was kind and Shirley warmed to his understanding. His hands rested around his teacup and she noticed how clean they were, the nails neatly trimmed, fingers that must surely be so smooth to the touch. The thought of touching his hand sent an embarrassing thrill through her and she quickly stood up.

'Is it all right for my mother and my aunt to stay here as well?' she asked. 'Or would it be better if we went home and I came up every day?'

'That is entirely up to you. You do whichever suits you best.'

'I think I would rather go home.'

'Then that is what you must do.'

Placing his cup carefully back on the table, Edward said, 'Don't be alarmed if the police call round, just to check out the circumstances before your mother called the ambulance. It really is purely a routine enquiry but I'm sure you'll agree that all deaths should be treated with seriousness.'

She gave him a brief smile and waited for him to leave. As he rose from the table, he said, 'I hope I'm not speaking out of turn when I say that you must think about your own future. In my humble view you have given more than enough to this house and the Lamb family.'

Shirley looked away.

'Sorry if I'm poking my nose in,' he added.

'No. I have been thinking the same myself.'

'Any plans, dreams, ambitions?'

'Nothing concrete.'

He halted by the hallstand, his head tilted to one side, his gaze resting somewhere level with her mouth.

'You are still a young woman. A very attractive one.' His face flared with sudden colour and, retrieving his hat, he made an awkward bow. 'Goodbye, then. I will let you know when arrangements for the funeral have been made.'

As he hurried down the steps, Shirley was left with the strange feeling that she had just been propositioned. Walking thoughtfully back along the hall, she tried to untangle her muddled thoughts. Although she had always thought of Edward Benningfield as old, in truth he was only somewhere in his middle forties. Was he married? She didn't know. In fact, she knew nothing about him other than that he had always been a calm, rational figure against which the various dramas in the house had been played out. A trickle of amusement at the thought of his diffident flirtation warmed her. The next drama would surely be the one deciding Cartegena's future.

The police called later that morning, two uniformed men. The elder, overweight, hair thinning at the crown and greying at the temples, did all the talking.

'Nothing for you to worry yourself about, my dear. We just need to be clear about what happened yesterday evening, before poor Mrs Lamb died.' As he stepped closer she smelt that cloying scent of stale tobacco. When he raised his hand she saw that his fingers were nicotine yellow.

'My aunt and I went out,' she started. 'It had been a difficult day – you probably know all about Lady Lamb's son.'

'Lady Lamb, yes. So you went out, leaving Lady Lamb with another elderly lady?'

'My mother. We have been staying here while the inquest and everything has been going on.'

'So the two old ladies were together?'

Shirley nodded. Did she detect some surprise, some disbelief, that any sane woman would go out and leave two such frail beings to cope alone?

'I don't usually go out,' she started. 'It was just that the trial and everything has been hard and—'

'Of course. Nothing to worry about. Don't look so anxious. If I could just see where Lady Lamb collapsed?'

Shirley escorted them up the stairs, explained about the lift and assured them that Florence had always worn the pendant with which to summon help. The younger policeman, yellow thatch, an apology for a moustache, haunted the background like some elusive shadow.

'Normally she lives alone,' Shirley added, just to underline the point.

Both men gave a cursory glance around the bathroom. 'Do you know what time she actually collapsed?'

'Around 9.30, I think – I'm really not sure.'

'Could we perhaps have a word with your mother as she was

the only other one here?'

'My mother is very upset.' Shirley felt all the old guilt again, the sense that somehow she, or even Maud, was about to be blamed for something no one could have foreseen. 'She heard the crash but she couldn't operate the lift – she suffers from arthritis so it took her a while to climb the stairs, then she had to go down again to phone.'

Oh God, was there a time lapse here? She tried to remember what time she and Jean had arrived home, what time the ambulance had reached the house. Were they going to say that if they had been summoned earlier then Lady F would have lived?

'We've been trying to help out as much as possible,' she said.

'I'm sure you have. Can we just have a word with your mum then?'

Shirley led them to the parlour where Maud and Jean were now sitting. Jean was reading Lady Florence's *Times* while Maud was staring into infinity. They both transferred their attention with some effort.

'Mum, the policeman just wants to ask you about what happened last night. Nothing to worry about.'

She watched the older man approach Maud's chair. He pulled up a stool and sat down close to her, a little grunt as his back protested. Leaning forward and speaking slowly and clearly he said, 'Just one or two questions, darling.'

'Don't shout, and I'm not your darling.' Maud leaned back to put more distance between herself and the arm of the law.

Abashed, he straightened up. 'Can you tell me what time Lady Lamb collapsed last night?'

'I don't know. We'd been watching the telly and she said she felt tired. I thought I'd wait up for the young ones.'

'What programme were you watching? Can you remember?'

'Of course I can remember. I'm not daft. It was that detective fellow, Frost.'

'And what time did it finish?'

'It didn't finish. Lady Florence went up during one of the intervals. She'd been gone about ten minutes when I heard the crash.'

'What did you think had happened?'

155

'I thought she had fallen over. I went out as fast as I could and called up to her but she didn't answer, just moaned in a queer way. I had to go up to see what was wrong and when I saw her I knew she'd had a stroke.'

'How did you know that?'

'Because that's how my husband went.'

'So what did you do?'

'You know very well what I did. I went back down the stairs and found the telephone and dialled nine, nine, nine.'

'And they sent an ambulance?'

'You know they did. Why are you asking such silly questions?'

'Right, my dear.' The officer stood up, glancing at his mate as if to say, 'Let's get out of here.'

Shirley went with them to the door. 'Bit of a character, your mum,' the older man observed. 'No flies on her.'

'What will happen now?'

'Happen? Nothing. We'll file our report and when the PM is over the old lady will be released for burial. Thank you for your time.'

As the two men retreated towards their car, Shirley, thinking of her mother's acid response, found herself smiling.

Fourteen

Shirley, Maud and Jean went home to Hawthorn Cottage that afternoon. It was a relief to be back in a world uncluttered with death and mystery. As Shirley opened the front door she scooped up the mail, that tormenting hope edging at her as always, but there was nothing of interest.

'Put the kettle on,' Maud called, struggling for the comfort of her own chair.

'I'll have to pop out and get some milk first.'

Leaving her aunt and mother to settle in, Shirley went back out to the car then drove to the corner shop for bread and milk and other necessities. As she packed them on to the back seat she had a guilty sense of being let off the leash. Now was a chance to grasp some brief freedom. She scrabbled in her mind as to what to do with it. Perhaps she should go to the post office and get an application form for a passport but then she would need to have her photograph taken, find someone in authority to sign the copies as a true likeness, dig out her birth certificate. She abandoned the idea. In any case, she knew what she wanted to do. Glancing around as if she expected someone to be spying on her she slipped into the driving seat and set off away from the village. After about half a mile she stopped and parked the car, crossing the road and wandering casually down the other side, stopping by a tree. From here she could clearly see Frank's cottage. Immediately she registered two things: that the Capri was not there and the place had a deserted look. Restless, frustrated, she went back to the car and drove home.

The next morning, Jean offered to go with her to Cartegena but she preferred to be alone. Besides, supposing Maud had an accident? One dead old lady might be excusable, but two . . . ? She suppressed the thought as unworthy as she set out on her bike.

As she approached the house it was in shadow. Now that it was empty it seemed to have taken on a new persona. For the first time it looked sulky, even hostile. Childlike fears of ghosts gnawed at her. Could Lady Florence's spirit have come back to blame her for going out that evening? Might she and Lord Lamb even Guy all be there, pointing out her failings, expressing their various disappointments? She could see them posed like a Victorian portrait, Florence sitting upright in a chair, the two men behind her, ramrod stiff backs, Lord Lamb nursing one of those Gilbert and Sullivan hats with feathers worn by admirals or ambassadors or something. Guy would have his head tilted to one side, his eyebrows slightly raised to gauge her response to their presence. She derided herself for her stupidity and unlocked the front door but already her blood was hammering in her temples and it took all her willpower to step over the threshold.

Inside it seemed more cavernous than ever, as if the solid flesh of even one resident normally absorbed the echoing emptiness. Now that there was no one, every room seemed bottomless, waiting to suck her in, hold her prisoner.

She tried to shake off the sense of menace and wondered if old Moses or even Douglas Kirk might be around to take away the sense of isolation. She looked out of the ancient, latticed window but with the thick distorted glass, it was like staring from a fish tank, the world outside wavy and distant. Nobody seemed to be about.

With a deep intake of breath Shirley knew that she must strip the beds, in particular Lady Florence's. This sudden fear was ridiculous. She was not afraid of the dead. Besides, Florence's body had been moved to the morgue awaiting the post mortem. Maud had already suggested that once she was released to the chapel of rest, perhaps Shirley should go to view her, an idea she quickly quashed.

Dragging the vacuum cleaner up the stairs, she made her way to Florence's room, leaving the door open as she went inside. Quickly she drew back the curtains, opened the casement windows and welcomed in the daylight.

It was clear that the night before Florence had not got as far as the bed. It was still neatly made from that morning. Her handbag, however, had been placed on the stool by the dressing table. Shirley stared at it with increasing sadness, seeing the old lady's blue veined hands clutched around the tortoiseshell handles. In the bag she carried her purse, an antique powder compact and gold lipstick case, a lace hanky, tortoiseshell spectacle case, leather-covered notebook and fountain pen. Shirley had seen them all before, had a vision of Florence scrabbling amongst the contents for some tiny item hiding in the bottom. The bag also contained the keys to the other rooms, one for Lord Lamb's study, one for Guy's bedroom. For a second, she held her breath. She was alone. For once she could enter these rooms and any other without fear of interruption. Quickly she plunged her hand into the bag and fished around for the keys. As her hand closed round them she started to withdraw them and in the same moment she knew that she couldn't do it. Whatever secrets the rooms might hold, for the moment they must remain so. Driving herself to work, she heaved the voluminous eiderdown off the bed, folded the blankets, piled the sheets and pillowcases and retreated with them downstairs. Soon the mumble of the washing machine made a companionable background to her isolation.

With the same sense of mission, she turned her attention to the bathroom where Florence had had her fall. Here indeed was evidence of the drama: a broken tumbler, a wooden towel rail turned over. The folded towel that the ambulance men had placed under Florence's head still lay on the carpet. Could she see the indentation of the old lady's head? Was she already dead when they carried her by stretcher to the ambulance? In that case, her spirit might have left her body in this very room. Her heart beating unnaturally fast, Shirley began to clear up. She had the distinct impression that Florence was watching her, accusing her of interfering with a scene of crime, destroying evidence although of what she had no clear notion. No crime had happened here, just an unfortunate accident, or perhaps even the naturally, pre-ordained death of an old body that had used up its allotted life span. Picking up the shards of glass, hoovering up the splinters, she cleared the mess and hurried back down the stairs. The washing machine was now quiet and she couldn't decide whether to hang the laundry on the line or put it on a clothes horse indoors. If she hung it outside she ought to come back later to take it in. She left it indoors.

She was glad to leave at lunchtime. As she cycled home her fears seemed pathetic. They were based on some primeval darkness which, as a rational woman, she should long ago have overcome, but even as she parked the bike at the back of the cottage she knew that those feelings would come again and again.

Maud had a dental appointment the following morning so Shirley made only a brief visit to Cartegena to check that all was well. The following morning however, she returned to finish off the cleaning. She was in the process of ironing the sheets when the clang of the doorbell resonated through the house. Turning off the iron, a precaution in case she forgot to come back, she went to answer the door. Edward Benningfield was on the doorstep. He smiled at her and wiped his dry, impeccably clean shoes on the doormat before stepping into the hall.

'I've just come to let you know that the coroner is satisfied with the circumstances of Lady Lamb's death. The post mortem has taken place and she will be released for burial.'

'Do you know when?' Automatically Shirley placed the kettle on the hob, preparing to make him coffee. She had brought milk with her, stored it in the fridge that she had left on because soon there would be the funeral to cater for.

'Friday.' He pressed his lips together then the pink edge of his tongue moistened his lower lip. 'I – I think it might be better if the mourners met up afterwards at the Cavendish. They lay on a good spread there and personally I think it would be better if they didn't all troop back here. Besides' – he gave her a quick, sideways glance – 'you would end up working and I don't think that is a good idea.'

'I don't mind,' she started but something about his manner

made her acquiesce. 'Do you know what is going to happen next?' she asked. 'About the house?'

'First things first. Let's get the funeral out of the way.' He accepted the coffee and settled down at the table.

After a rather uncomfortable silence, he asked, 'Have you decided what you are going to do, after the funeral?'

Shirley shrugged her uncertainty. 'I've still got my mother to think about,' she started, knowing that she was already counting on Jean to invite her home for at least a week or two.

'You should get away. Besides, things change.'

When Shirley looked sceptical, he added, 'The only thing we can be certain of is that life is uncertain.'

Shirley did not reply and they both drank their coffee in silence.

'Where do you go for your holidays?' she asked when the void grew too great.

He took another gulp of coffee and placed the cup on the saucer.

'Sometimes I go up north to see my mother. I'm rather interested in paintings so I like to visit art galleries every chance I get.'

I, Shirley thought, he said I, not we. Perhaps he isn't married. Forty-something bachelors were unusual. If men were single at that age there must be a reason: the death of a loved one, some personality defect that frightened women off, some physical deformity that made them unappealing. None of these appeared to apply to Edward Benningfield. The other obvious thought of course was that he was gay. She wanted to ask him, 'Do you have a partner?', to show that if he was gay, she was comfortable with that, but supposing she was wrong? The other day she had had the feeling that he was flirting with her. Surely gay men did not do that, not unless they were trying to give the impression that they were straight? Edward seemed at peace with himself. She did not think that he would choose to act out a role. Anyway, who would he be trying to impress?

For a moment she wondered how people viewed her, a woman also heading for forty, also unmarried. Surely no one would conclude that she was a lesbian? Thoughts of sex with

Frank intruded, making her feel hot and embarrassed under Edward's covert surveillance. When she looked at him he quickly picked up his cup and drained the contents, standing up as he replaced it on the table.

'Well, I must be going. The funeral will be at eleven. I'll see you then.'

'Is there anything you want me to do?'

He smiled. 'No, nothing. Everything is in hand.'

As he walked to his Mercedes, she wondered who was now taking responsibility for running things. The thought that it was no longer her was painful indeed.

On Thursday night Shirley dreamt that she was in the church in the front pew. Everyone else was crowded at the back. Immediately behind her the pews were empty and she knew that everyone was staring at her, whispering, asking who did she think she was? When she turned round, the first person she saw was Frank and he too was staring, questioning.

'It's not my fault,' she said to him. 'I didn't ask to sit here.'

He gave her a disbelieving grin and she felt betrayed, so betrayed that she awoke, disorientated in the dark. The thought of this second funeral filled her with dread. The last time, she had sat with Florence and held her hand as they both mourned Guy. Now Florence had left her, gone to join him, to become one of the ranks of ghosts that haunted her life. She had never felt so lonely. The thought that Frank might perhaps be there stirred both hope and fear. His only reason for coming would be to make his presence felt. The next step would be to stake his claim to Cartegena. She despised him then. In that moment she knew that as soon as the funeral was over she would go away. Perhaps she and Maud could move somewhere near to Jean. Shirley could find a new job, start a new life. That was what she must do.

Unlike the unseemly sunshine on the day of Guy's funeral, the weather was appropriately grey and misty as Shirley, Jean and Maud set out for the village church. Shirley drove. Jean said she would come to keep Maud company. The three of them found seats in the already crowded church somewhere near the back. It was a good place from which to view the rest of the congregation.

Shirley noticed that the front row of pews remained empty. Lord Lamb's relatives were in evidence, seated in the second rank, spread right across three rows of seats separated by the two aisles. She supposed that they felt they had to come to show some sort of family solidarity. Florence wouldn't have wanted them there. She had no love for any of her in-laws.

People continued to drift in. Others shifted up closer to make room for the latecomers. She saw Edward Benningfield make his way along the opposite aisle and seat himself next to Doctor Braxton, the family physician. Moments later the organ music, which until that moment she had hardly noticed, stopped then struck up a doleful air and the congregation rose to their feet. Slowly, the funeral cortège walked the length of the aisle, the vicar preceding four men who held Lady Florence aloft in an oak coffin.

The reality of the occasion hit Shirley for the first time. Beside her, Maud gave a little sniff. Standing next to Shirley she seemed so small, a shrunken wraith, the merest shadow of what she had once been. Shirley thought that soon it must be her mother's turn. She tried hard not to wish that it would happen before too long.

The ceremony was almost a re-run of Guy's, except the vicar, who knew Florence, was able to give vent to his narrative on her life and good works. A member of the church choir sang a haunting solo, prayers were offered up for Florence's new life with her maker. Shirley knew that the old lady had hung on to some rather ill-defined belief. She hoped that she would not be disappointed.

When it was all over, they stepped back out into the mist. As Shirley went to make for her car, the solicitor came over.

'People are going to the Cavendish,' he started, 'but before that the will is being read at my office. I think you should come along.'

'I don't think—'

'You should.' He glanced at Jean and Maud.

Jean said, 'I'll drive your car.'

Edward added, 'You can come with me.'

Surprised, Shirley agreed. It had not occurred to her that perhaps Florence had left her some memento. She wondered what it might be. She had always had a particular fondness for a small Staffordshire dog that stood on the writing desk in Florence's room. She had admired it several times. Perhaps Florence had remembered and left it to her. She felt a glow of warmth for the old lady and hoped that she was right. As she climbed into the car she warned herself not to be disappointed if it turned out otherwise.

Edward's office was only two minutes' drive away and apart from general conversation about the appropriateness of the funeral, they did not speak. When they arrived, Shirley realized that with the exception of Moses Jenkins, all those others who were present were Lord Lamb's family and those with a direct claim to Cartegena. That, of course, was a different issue, for Florence had no claim on the house. Having no family of her own, though, it was likely that as in-laws, they qualified as the next of kin.

With fellow feeling she could see that Moses looked even more uncomfortable than she felt. As she nodded towards him he hastily removed his bicycle clips and slipped them into his jacket pocket.

Edward's office was large enough to accommodate them all and two rows of chairs had been laid out for their comfort. Shirley sat at the back, feeling uncomfortable in this company. She looked around, taking in the large desk, the rich golden velvet curtains, the bookshelves filled with formidable-looking legal books. On the desk there was a telephone, an inkstand and a wooden box containing paper and pens. There was also a photograph but it was facing away from her so she couldn't see who it might be.

Edward bustled forward, businesslike, welcoming those who were present.

'Please, make yourselves comfortable, ladies and gentlemen. I will read the last will and testament of Lady Florence Lamb. It is not a long document.'

He seated himself at his desk, pulled back his sleeves a fraction so that the white cuffs of his shirt were exposed, each held by a gold cufflink. Picking up the paper laid out on his desk, he cleared his throat.

'I, Florence Elizabeth Lamb of Cartegena, in the village of Astley, Somerset, being of sound mind, do hereby make my last will and testament. I appoint my solicitor Edward Giles Benningfield as my executor and bequeath to him the responsibility for honouring any debts or expenses that remain after my death. I also bequeath to him the sum of five hundred pounds.'

Edward glanced quickly at the assembly. Shirley wondered if he expected someone to object. For the first time she also wondered how much money Florence might have had. She knew that when Lord Lamb died he had left her various annuities but the main concern then had been that Cartegena was in desperate need of repair, that sooner or later there would be crippling death duties, and that the family was broke.

Edward continued. 'To Moses Jenkins who has faithfully served the family for most of his life I give the sum of four hundred pounds.' Shirley heard the old man let out his breath in a whistle of surprise. She glanced at him and nodded her approval.

Edward continued. 'To the Red Cross I award the sum of one thousand pounds and my pearl earrings and necklace, to be auctioned or sold as they see fit.'

Around her, people stirred uneasily. Shirley vaguely remembered the pearls. Lord Lamb had purchased them for their pearl wedding anniversary. Lady Florence had once confessed to never having liked them. 'Pearls are for tears,' she insisted. Although she had worn them on one or two occasions they had then been deposited in the bank. Shirley was surprised that they were still in the family's possession.

'I, being of sound mind, do hereby leave the rest of my estate, including my bonds, monies, paintings and jewellery and all my other earthly possessions to my friend and loyal support for many years, Shirley Alice Weeks, in recognition of her selfless devotion and long association with my family.'

Shirley had not been listening. After a moment she realized

that there was a scandalized silence in the room. Looking round she felt the eyes dart away from her. Only Edward gazed steadfastly at her. Gently, he said, 'You are the main beneficiary of Lady Lamb's estate.'

Shirley frowned. This couldn't be so. Around her, hostility bristled in the air like an angry porcupine.

'Thank you, ladies and gentlemen.'

The reading being at an end, the others got to their feet, mouths set in disapproval, eyes flinty with anger.

Edward said to Shirley, 'Perhaps you'll wait behind a moment. I'll run you up to the reception when we have gone through a few papers.' Bemused, numbed, Shirley rose to her feet. She couldn't take in what was happening. She hadn't been listening and now she thought that she must have misunderstood, but Edward smiled and said, 'Congratulations.'

Still disbelieving, she wondered if she might be responsible for the death duties that would be incurred when Cartegena was finally handed on to the next in line.

'Come and sit here.' Edward went to a cabinet in the corner of his room, taking out two rather fine antique glasses and a decanter of sherry. 'I think you need a drink.'

'I can't believe it,' she started. 'Surely whatever there is should go to the family?'

'That was up to Lady Florence.' He handed her a glass and shakily she raised it to her lips. As she replaced it on the desk she shook her head, still not believing what she had heard.

Edward sat down. 'I don't suppose you want to hear all the details now but you have actually been left a fair sum of money.'

'But I thought the family was broke.'

'Lord Lamb was certainly in financial difficulties when he died but he had had the foresight to transfer various investments into his wife's name. Therefore those could not be touched.'

'They aren't part of the Cartegena estate then?'

'No. Lady Florence had no claim on the estate and the estate had no claim on her own assets.'

Shirley took a deep breath, breathing out slowly. 'I—'

'You don't believe it.' Edward smiled. 'She didn't want you to know in advance. She appreciated your kindness so much. She also understood how much you had been involved with her son, what pain his disappearance and death had caused you. I think she wanted to compensate you for that as well.' He paused. 'After all, if you had married him, you would now be in the same position as Lady Florence, entitled to stay at Cartegena for the rest of your life.'

Shirley nodded slowly, not really being able to think of anything.

'So what happens now?' she asked.

'I'll get you to come in and sign some papers, then the will can go to probate and you'll get your inheritance.'

With some embarrassment she asked, 'What are we actually talking about?'

Edward smiled. 'We're talking about roughly twenty thousand pounds in cash plus about half a dozen paintings, some rather splendid vases and furniture that came from the Charteris family and some pieces of jewellery.'

Inconsequentially she thought, Good, I can have the Staffordshire dog after all.

'I— Will there be any death duties?'

He shook his head. 'No death duties. There could be an inheritance tax but I think the total will fall just below the threshold.'

As Shirley absorbed this, he added, 'You, Miss Weeks, will be quite a comfortably off young lady.'

As she rose from the chair she realized that she was now able to see the photograph on the desk. Glancing casually down at it she saw that it was the portrait of a large, handsome, dewy-eyed Great Dane.

Fifteen

The reception at the Cavendish passed in a haze. When Shirley arrived, Maud was seated near to the food and Jean was filling, or perhaps refilling, their glasses for Shirley had no idea how much time had elapsed. Edward escorted her into the room, holding her elbow as if she was now his property and as such he had to protect her against the curiosity or even the wrath of the disinherited.

'What happened?' asked Maud.

Shirley shook her head, still not believing what she had just experienced.

'Who has she left her things to?'

She continued to shake her head. 'You won't believe it. I don't. She – she's left nearly everything to me.'

'You?' Maud's expression reflected her own. After a moment her mouth tightened and she said, 'I worked there all my life, long before you were even born.'

With shock Shirley realized that her mother was jealous. She thought quickly, before saying, 'Whatever comes to me comes to you too.' Maud looked slightly mollified, like a disgruntled hen whose feathers gradually sink back into place.

With the speed of a bush fire, news of the contents of the will were relayed around the room. Shirley could feel the glances, sense the speculation.

'Let's go,' she said.

'Not yet.' Maud was enjoying the free food, the sense of occasion.

As Jean came to join them, Shirley said, 'I don't want to stay here.'

'You go then,' said Maud. 'Someone will run me home.'

To her aunt, Shirley said, 'I've just had a bit of a shock. I'm going to walk home. Will you drive Mum back?'

'Of course. What's happened?'

She told her.

'Good God,' said Jean. 'No wonder you're in shock. Are you sure you want to go off on your own?'

'I do. I need to think about it.'

'We'll see you later then.'

As she moved away, Shirley came face to face with Douglas Kirk. He stepped into her path so that she could not avoid him. 'Congratulations. Bit of a surprise, was it?'

She didn't know what to say. For the first time she realized that she had been hoping, fearing, wondering if Frank would be here. He wasn't. Now she felt mostly relief. Just at the moment she could not have coped with the complicated feelings his physical presence aroused.

'You'll be mistress of the house now then?' Douglas observed.

'No.' She explained to him that the house and Lady Lamb's estate were two different things. 'She's left me the things that belonged to her, that's all. When Lord Lamb died the house should have gone to their son. Now that he is dead the solicitors have to decide who is the next in line.'

He gave a single nod to show that he understood. 'You disappointed then, that you didn't cop the lot?'

Her anger stirred. 'No. I'm not disappointed. If you want to find out about the house, you had better ask your cousin.'

Pointedly she turned her back on him, leaving him to work out the implications of what she had said. Before anyone else could approach her she made for the door.

She was just leaving when Edward caught sight of her and hurried over.

'You're leaving?'

'I must. I feel . . . uncomfortable.'

'Would you like me to give you a lift?'

'No thanks.' He was being so kind but she wondered if perhaps it was purely in a professional capacity. With dawning unease she also thought that now she was about to be wealthy, perhaps his interest in her had a more personal motive. After all, he must have known for some time that she was the beneficiary to the will. She wondered how long ago Lady Florence had made her decision.

To Edward, she said, 'You had better have the keys to the house back.'

He shook his head, his expression questioning. 'There's no need for that. Apart from anything else you might like to have a look around and see what you have inherited. I'll come with you if you like, to show you which items are yours. I've got an inventory.' When she hesitated, he added, 'Is something wrong?'

Weighing her words, she said, 'I guess I shall have to be careful from now on. If I'm an heiress there will be plenty of gold diggers after me.'

Did he get the message, realize that she was telling him she knew what he was up to? In response, he smiled. 'Twenty thousand isn't exactly a million.' He looked embarrassed, perhaps realizing he was belittling her inheritance. His eyes flickered with some unspoken discomfort then he said, 'It beats me why you haven't been courted by every single man in the village, although until now I know that you haven't been free, not from Guy Lamb.'

What he said was true. Guy might have been absent for eighteen years but his claim to Shirley had still held her as securely as if he had been present.

'Well, I'd better be going,' she said.

'I'll give you a ring to arrange an appointment at the office. In the meantime, you go up to Cartegena whenever you want.'

'I will. Thank you.'

She gave him a tight little smile, feeling embarrassed. His face was open and honest. It was unworthy to hint that he was only interested in her money. After all, didn't solicitors charge an obscene hourly rate? He wasn't short of cash so what would he want with hers?

As she went to move away he raised his hand in farewell and went back inside. Left to herself, Shirley thought, This is like some nineteenth-century woman's romance, the governess inheriting a fortune, the servant winning the heart of the hero – only who the hero was in this case she wasn't sure.

Maud came back from the reception full of it. The knowledge that her daughter had inherited Lady Florence Lamb's estate gave her a new sense of privilege. Shirley was now an heiress. Their social status had soared. As Maud slumped into her chair, her face was a heated red. Shirley thought that perhaps she was tiddly.

She went into the kitchen to begin cooking a meal although there had been so much food at the Cavendish both Maud and Jean said that they weren't hungry. After a few minutes Jean came to join her.

'Anything I can do?'

Shirley shook her head. 'I thought I'd make an omelette.'

Jean seated herself on the edge of the table. 'How are you feeling?'

Shirley could not find the right words. Her life had taken such an unexpected turn that she felt like a small boat loosed from its moorings, buffeted, drifting according to the mood of the tide. She didn't know if she was headed for a treasure island or a desert island.

Jean said, 'What are we talking about here? What sort of things has she left you?'

'Some money, some bonds – I think. Then there are her personal possessions. I suppose that means I get her clothes.'

'What will you do with them?'

'Take them to the charity shop. Some of them should be in a fashion museum, really – they are antiques.' She remembered the Minton vases that Frank had given her to take to the Red Cross. They had gone to the head office to be sent on to an auction. Thinking of Frank's claim to Cartegena, she guessed that perhaps the notorious Algernon Lamb had bequeathed them to his erstwhile wife, Ivy Davis. She glanced at Jean before adding, 'She's also left me some pieces of furniture and some ornaments.'

'Any idea of value?'

'Not the individual items. In cash there would be about

twenty thousand pounds.'

'Phew! No more worries about what you do next then?'

'I don't know. I really don't know. For the moment Edward has left me a key. I can go and gloat over my possessions.'

After a moment, Jean said, 'I've been thinking that perhaps I'll go home soon – that is, if it's all right with you.'

'Of course it is.' She felt that sinking feeling of abandonment. Having her aunt around was such a bonus. She asked, 'Are you going back to your dentist?'

'Rodney. His name's Rodney – a bit naff, isn't it? Everyone calls him Rod.'

'Have you been in touch with him?'

'I phoned him this morning. Jenny, his wife, is going into hospital. I – I want to be there.'

'Of course you do.' Shirley put down the bowl she was nursing. 'You go now if you want to.'

'What about Maud?'

'She's not your responsibility.' In the words she heard the echo of Edward's voice and behind him, the slightly mocking tones of Frank. She asked, 'What was my mother like when she was young?'

Jean thought for a moment. 'She was sixteen when I was born. Our mother, your grandmother, was then in her forties. She always seemed very old to me. Some widows still wore black in those days. Maud, though, she was young and glamorous and I always thought she was wonderful. She was very pretty, you know.'

Shirley thought of the bowed, hatchet-faced old woman in the other room and could not imagine her otherwise.

'How did she meet my dad?' she asked. As she said the words she wondered why she had never asked Maud. It was a sad reflection of their relationship that they never talked about anything personal.

'I think she knew him during the war. I was still a child but I was aware of the excitement that women seemed to feel about young men in uniform. I can understand it now, the not knowing if you would ever see them again. I don't remember your dad as being particularly dashing or anything but I think they made promises to each other – if he came back – and of course he did.'

'She wasn't in love with him, then?'

'I never got any hint of wild passion, and I think I would have recognized it even then.'

Shirley thought that perhaps what Maud was suffering from was terminal disappointment. Perhaps life, marriage, hadn't come up to her expectations. Perhaps if Shirley had followed the traditional line and married a local boy and had children, Maud would have found fulfilment in her grandchildren. Anyway, there was nothing anyone could do about it. What was past and all that.

She glanced at the clock. It was nearly six. The evenings were beginning to draw in now. By eight it would be dark. She wondered whether to go back to Cartegena and look at her acquisitions, explore Florence's bedroom in a new light, then she changed her mind. She would go tomorrow.

'When are you going to go?' she asked Jean.

'I'll hang on for a day or two longer.'

Two days – perhaps she could get her life in order by then.

The next morning she approached Cartegena with a completely new expectation. Once inside she placed her bag on the hall-stand and stood looking around. Not all of Lady Florence's things were confined to her bedroom. As she took in every statue and ornament, she wondered, Does that now belong to me?

It was a bright morning and the house no longer felt menacing. Idly she thought that perhaps by publicly putting her seal of approval on Shirley, Lady Florence had sent a message that she was still welcome.

She made her way around the ground floor, opening doors and windows to keep the house aired. It made her feel she had a purpose in being there, other than gloating over her new possessions. By the time she was upstairs, though, she couldn't resist the tremor of pleasure at the thought of seeing the things that would now be hers. As she pushed open the door of Florence's room, she spoke silently to the old lady. 'Thank you,

I really appreciate what you've done. I'll take care of your things.' Would she? Would she want to keep pieces of china or paintings that were valuable but which she didn't personally like? Would Florence feel let down if she sold them?

Her eyes scanned the room. The bed, now stripped, was Victorian with an elaborately carved bed head and unfashionably high legs. She thought of her own divan and knew that the idea of fitting this into the cottage was ludicrous. In any case, surely it was part of the Cartegena estate?

She turned her attention to the dressing table, walnut, with heavy bevelled mirrors. As a piece of furniture it was beautiful. Again, as an item in a small cottage it would be a liability. Cautiously she opened the door of the matching wardrobe. Lady F's clothes hung in a neat row, muted colours, silks and georgettes, tweeds and linens. On the top shelf there was something resembling a hatbox. She took it down and opened it, to be met with an unblinking stare, for inside was a fox fur. Shirley stared back with a mixture of distaste and compassion at the amber button eyes. Probably the only place it could find a home would be a theatrical wardrobe. Crocodile shoes and handbags, a seal-skin jacket all bore witness to a vanished and less compassionate age. Quickly she shut the door.

With pleasure she picked up the Staffordshire dog that sat on the mantelpiece. I'm glad you're mine, she thought, knowing that in reality it would have been enough. Behind the initial excitement was a sense of discomfort. She had never had any money to speak of before. Its possession might prove as much of a liability as a blessing. Carefully she replaced the dog on the shelf. As she did so her eyes rested on the portrait of Florence's ancestor, the dark woman whose twin's portrait hung in the long gallery. She wished now that she had asked Florence if, like Lord Lamb, she could trace her ancestry in a direct line from this woman, Catherine. Again this sense of history, this awareness of knowing your place in the great scale of things left her feeling adrift.

At that moment she heard the distant clang of the doorbell. As she stepped into the corridor a voice called out, 'It's Edward Benningfield. Are you upstairs?'

'I'm coming.'

As she reached the staircase he was already halfway up. He looked up and waved.

'Thought I would find you here.' She noticed that he was breathing heavily. Like her he needed to lose some weight. As he reached her, he added, 'I've got a copy of the inventory here. I thought you'd like one.'

'Thank you.' She took it awkwardly, saying, 'I've just been opening up the house to air it.' She couldn't admit that she had been nosing in the cupboards.

Somehow they drifted along to Florence's bedroom and Shirley hurried across to open the old casement windows. The curtains stirred under the influence of a mild breeze.

Edward looked around curiously and Florence thought that he had probably never been upstairs in the house before.

'How many rooms are there?' he asked.

'Eleven on this floor, the same downstairs.'

'A lot of cleaning then.'

'Enough.' She smiled at him.

'Well . . .' He looked embarrassed. 'Shall I leave you to check out the list?'

Before she could answer his eyes alighted on the portrait of the dark lady.

'The first Lady Lamb,' he said, revealing that he had indeed seen more of the house than the drawing room.

'Actually it's not. She is the ancestor of Lady Florence. She was married to the first Sir Francis Lamb's younger brother.'

When he looked uncertain, she added, 'She and the first Lady Lamb were twins.'

Hesitating for a moment, she said, 'Have you seen the long gallery?'

'Many years ago.'

'Would you like to have a look?'

He nodded. Shirley fiddled in her bag to find the right key and he followed her along the corridor to the door. She inserted the key and tried to force it to turn.

'Here, let me.' Edward wrenched it round and pushed the door hard. It gave way with a satisfying, ghost-story creaking.

A greenish yellow light filtered the length of the gallery.

'It's not very safe,' she started.

'You think I might be too heavy?'

'No.' She glanced at him to discover that he was smiling and her response mirrored his own.

Together they wandered the length of the gallery, stopping to study each portrait. They were interspersed with an occasional painting of the house, a likeness of a favourite hunter, several pictures of dogs.

'I like this.' Shirley stopped in front of a large picture of a chestnut horse beneath which was the caption, '*Glencoe, 1766,*' and beneath, '*After Stubbs.*'

'The artist's name is not known,' Edward said. 'The picture is in the style of Stubbs.' He studied it closely. 'It is very well commissioned but sadly, it is part of the Cartegena estate, not the property of Lady Lamb.'

'I didn't mean I wanted it.' Shirley felt embarrassed, as if everything she saw she wanted to claim for herself.

By now Edward was in front of the first portrait of Sir Frances and Lady Elizabeth Lamb. He stared at it for a long while.

'It says in the guidebook that Lady Lamb might be the Dark Lady of Shakespeare's sonnets,' Shirley offered.

He shrugged. 'Who can tell after all this time? She does look exactly like the woman in the other painting.'

'They were twins,' Shirley repeated.

He nodded. The atmosphere was in danger of growing awkward again, so Shirley asked, 'Would you like a coffee?'

'I would. Thank you.' Together they left the long gallery, locking the door behind them, and went to the kitchen. North facing, now that the Aga had gone out, the room seemed dark and damp.

'Perhaps we'll drink it in the breakfast room?' Shirley switched on the electric kettle and fetched the milk from the fridge.

'One sugar, isn't it?'

'None, thanks. I'm er, trying to cut down.' His smile was boyish, conspiratorial.

In the breakfast room they made small talk. As he drained his cup, Edward said, 'I was wondering if you might like to come out to dinner, perhaps tomorrow night?' The words came out in a rush.

His face had grown red and Shirley scrabbled round to put the suggestion into context. This must be a date, not an official meeting. Did she want to go? Before she said yes she wanted to know what she was agreeing to. Did he see this as the beginning of some sort of courtship? Or was he merely carrying his official responsibilities to the extreme?

The next evening would be Jean's last night with them. She couldn't very well go out and leave her. 'I'm afraid I can't, tomorrow,' she said.

'Saturday, perhaps?'

By then Maud would be on her own. She would miss the company of her sister. Perhaps she should stay home, at least for a few nights until things settled down again.

'I, er . . .'

'I'm sorry, I've embarrassed you.'

'No. It's not that. My aunt goes home the day after tomorrow. That means my mother will be alone.' She trailed off. 'Perhaps we could meet for lunch?' She was amazed that she had suggested it.

'That would be very nice.' He looked worryingly relieved. Straightening his tie, a nervous habit she had noticed before, he said, 'There are some papers and things at the office you should see. Perhaps you could come in afterwards and we'll go through them?'

'Of course.'

It was settled.

Sixteen

Saying goodbye to Jean was harder than Shirley had ever imagined. Her aunt had been with them for only a short time but now that she was leaving Shirley realized how much she had come to rely on her.

'We'll see you again soon?' she asked as they embraced.

'Of course. You and Maud must come and visit me.' Jean smiled encouragement but behind her cheerful expression was the anxiety of an uncertain future. Shirley felt her own precipice of unease. Uncomfortably she thought that if she took her mother with her she and Jean would never be free to go out on their own. Besides, Jean would have her dentist to consider. Shamefaced, Shirley realized that whatever she did she yearned for freedom, a chance to behave spontaneously without having to think of anyone else. She silently prayed that Jean would not retract her offer to have Maud to stay on her own.

'Good luck,' she whispered, kissing her aunt and thinking of Rod the dentist. 'I hope that everything works out well.'

They moved a little further away and Jean gave her a doubtful smile. 'I guess after all this time, we're really like a married couple. You learn to take the rough with the smooth. When . . . when he's free, we'll see what happens.'

Shirley joined Maud in the doorway as Jean climbed into her car and drove away. Maud gave a small sniff and guiltily Shirley realized that she wasn't the only one who would miss Jean's presence. She gave her mother's shoulder a gentle squeeze.

'Come on, let's go and make a drink.'

She had arranged to meet Edward Benningfield the following

lunchtime. Feeling suddenly embarrassed, she said to Maud, 'I'm having lunch with the solicitor tomorrow, just to talk over the will and everything.'

Maud raised her eyebrows. 'I didn't think solicitors took people to lunch, not without charging them for the privilege.'

'He was very fond of Lady Florence.' Shirley spoke in his defence but Maud's expression remained sceptical.

She said, 'You'd better watch it, he's probably after your money.'

'Twenty thousand isn't that much.' Shirley echoed Edward's own comment.

'Well, it's a lot to me.'

'Well, perhaps it's not just my money he's after.' Shirley grinned to show that she wasn't taking the invitation too seriously.

After a moment, Maud replied, 'Perhaps not,' then she paused. 'But you could do worse.'

On that note the subject was dropped.

Edward had arranged to meet her at the Country Kitchen, a chintzy, well-established restaurant that fell somewhere between the refinement of the Cavendish and the everyday pub image of the Bull and Bishop.

As Shirley walked in he was already sitting at a window table that was a sufficient distance from the other seats for their conversation not to be overheard. She thought he looked mild and comfortable, a man very much at home in these surroundings.

'How are you?' He stood up and bowed his head in a rather old-fashioned gesture. Shirley guessed that if he had been wearing a hat he would have raised it.

'I'm well, thank you.' She allowed him to pull out the chair for her and was relieved when he asked her if she would like wine. She needed it. She noticed that he was nursing what looked like a half of lager.

'Your aunt has departed?'

'She has.'

'You will miss her.'

'I will.'

She hoped that soon one of them would think of something interesting to discuss. This polite froth felt uncomfortable.

To help things along, Shirley said, 'You mentioned an interest in paintings the other day. Do you paint yourself?'

Edward shook his head. 'I have few talents and painting certainly isn't one of them. Besides, I don't have much time.'

'I – I couldn't help noticing the photograph of the dog on your desk the other day. He is a beautiful animal.' She wasn't sure whether it was appropriate to admit that she had been nosing around his office but Edward warmed to the subject.

'That's Biggles. I've had him for three years. When I'm not at work he takes up a lot of my time – probably not unlike a dependent relative?' He laughed in embarrassment.

'He's probably better company.' Shirley realized as she said it that he would know she was comparing the dog with her mother. It sounded a tasteless thing to say. She had no idea why she had agreed to come and she feared that it was going to go badly.

The waitress came with the wine and also to take their order. Shirley began to scan the menu, not sure what she should select.

'What are you having?' she asked.

'The lasagne – it's good. I come here quite often, it saves cooking.'

'You live alone?'

'Apart from Biggles.'

This question too felt inappropriate. Surely it was bad manners to ask such direct questions, to probe into someone's private life? With this man she felt wrong-footed, not sure how to behave. It reminded her of those early days at Cartegena, before Lady Florence had become ill and alone and they had lapsed into a comfortable everyday relationship.

Edward took a drink of lager and she noticed that his hand trembled very slightly. Was he nervous, too?

To be on the safe side, Shirley also ordered lasagne, and when it came they ate with concentration.

Edward finished first and sat back with an air of contentment. The unease had taken away Shirley's appetite. She didn't feel hungry but felt that it would be impolite not to eat it all. That sense again of doing the right thing. It was foolish really. Edward knew who she was, where she came from. Putting on what Maud would call airs and graces would serve no purpose, but she could not relax. After another mouthful she put her knife and fork down.

'I'm so sorry. We had a late breakfast. I'm not very hungry.'

'No pudding then?'

She shook her head.

'Would you mind if I did?'

'Of course not.'

He gave a boyish grin, suddenly a youngster caught out raiding the biscuit tin. She warmed to him. After that, the conversation grew easier.

When they had finished the meal Edward paid and, leaving Shirley's car in the car park, they walked the short distance to his office.

'There are just one or two papers,' he explained, making a point of walking on the outside, between her and the traffic. 'I need your signature and then my secretary will witness it. It won't be painful.' She thought he sounded like the dentist.

His office was on the first floor of a four-storey building that was part of a Georgian terrace. It fronted the main street. Once these would have been desirable town houses but now the road outside was too narrow to cope with the volume of traffic, the noise through the huge sash windows too intrusive for gracious living.

Climbing the stairs, Edward told her a story about a client who had once tried to impersonate his wife by dressing in her clothes and calling at the office. The deception, although painfully obvious, was compounded when he signed his first name as George. Laughing, they reached the landing and Edward opened the office door. His secretary sat at a desk, surrounded by filing cabinets. She looked up sharply as they came in and they both stopped laughing. She was a woman somewhere between fifty and sixty, her large features framed by grey hair stretched back into a tight bun. Shirley thought of the mothers-in-law in comedy films, harridans who ruled the men in the family. Edward looked suitably subdued.

'Mrs Etheridge, please will you bring in the papers for Miss Weeks to sign?' He led Shirley to his office and she had the urge to giggle. Edward kept his back to her and she suspected that he was trying to resurrect some dignity and assert his role as employer.

Mrs Etheridge rapped on the door and strode to his desk, placing a sheaf of papers in front of his seat.

'Thank you. I'll just explain them to Miss Weeks then perhaps you will come back and witness her signature.'

She gave a single, regal nod of her head and retreated.

Edward invited Shirley to take a seat and sat down himself in front of his desk.

'As you will appreciate,' he started, 'by law we have to establish that you are the person you claim to be. It is a formality, of course, but if I did not know you, I would only have your word for it that you were Shirley . . . Alice Weeks.' He pronounced her second name as if it came as a surprise. 'I should by rights ask you to produce proof of identity – your passport, perhaps, but on this occasion it will not be necessary.'

Shirley thought uncomfortably that it really was time she got a passport, if only to wave it as proof of who she was.

When the explanation was complete, Edward walked to the door and asked Mrs Etheridge to join them. She stomped in and stood like a warder by the desk, her sharp eye following the stroke of Shirley's pen. When the document was signed, Edward added his signature and the secretary did likewise.

'Thank you, Pamela.' She was dismissed, taking the documents with her.

Shirley wondered if she should go but Edward had now leant back comfortably in his chair. As she waited for him to say something, he smiled briefly and clasped his hands together.

'Right, that is that little formality out of the way.'

When he lapsed into silence, she asked, 'Have you any idea of the timescale, before all this is settled?'

'Perhaps a couple of months. In spite of the size of the Cartegena estate, Lady Florence's own affairs are quite straightforward. Unless someone challenges the validity of her will, it shouldn't take too long.'

Might someone do so? Shirley thought of the disgruntled faces on the day the will was read. Would one of the contenders for the estate decide to try to add Lady Lamb's inheritance to their own?

While she was thinking, she could see that Edward was preparing himself to say something. She thought that maybe he was going to ask her to dine with him again. As she was scrabbling around in her mind for an answer, he said, 'I hope you don't mind my asking, but you say that you and Guy Lamb were engaged?'

'Yes. He had asked me to marry him. We were going to get married as soon as he came back from Colombia.' The question embarrassed her, as if he doubted the validity of her statement. She refused to think of the events leading up to or following Guy's disappearance.

'Was it general knowledge?' Edward asked, forming a steeple with his fingers then lowering his hands to the desk, where he picked up a pen and began to rotate it.

Shirley's face reddened. She shook her head. 'He – we were waiting until he returned. I don't think people would have thought we were serious if we had talked about it before. We were very young.' She glanced at him to see if she could see disbelief written on his face. His gaze was steady, yet expressionless.

'So, it would perhaps be difficult to prove that you were his fiancée?'

'I – I suppose so, yes.'

'He didn't buy you a ring?'

'He was going to do that when he returned.' She began to feel angry at the implication she might be lying. In spite of herself she visualized the signet ring by which Guy had been identified, wondering what difference it would have made if she had agreed to wear it while he was away. She said, 'I have his last letter. In it he mentions our wedding.'

'He does?' Edward looked suddenly expectant. He must have seen the confusion of Shirley's face for he added, 'Please, treat whatever I tell you this afternoon in confidence. An idea occurred to me only as I was waiting for you at lunchtime. Now that Lady Lamb is dead and the inquest is out of the way, I have to start the procedure for finding the heir to Cartegena. Having looked at what I know so far, the path is unclear. I need to go back two generations to where the descendants of Lord Lamb's great-aunt and great-uncle trace their roots. At first glance it would seem that any descendant from the great-uncle would be the beneficiary. Although he was the youngest, the heir has traditionally come through the male line. There is a problem here, however, for it turns out that the great-uncle, Benedict Lamb was in fact born out of wedlock. His father had him brought up with his other children but at the time, his illegitimacy would have debarred him from inheriting. He has a great-grandson but effectively he is not the next in line.' He smiled briefly before continuing. 'The only other line still extant is that of a younger sister and she has a great-niece now living – you will have seen her at the funeral.' Shirley thought of Annabelle Moorcroft and Auberon Lamb, the two contenders at the church and also at the inquest. Clearly they viewed each other as rivals. Thinking of Frank, she wondered if there might be anyone else who had a claim.

When she put the question to Edward, he said, 'Not to my knowledge but my next step is to place a notice in appropriate newspapers asking for anyone who thinks they might have a claim to come forward. There might of course be somebody but I have been thinking.' He licked his lower lip in a way she recognized as habitual whenever he was uncertain. He began to speak slowly as if explaining things to himself. 'If your betrothal to Guy Lamb was official, then there might be a case to be made for allowing you, as his intended next of kin, to live in the house in much the same way as Lady Lamb was permitted to stay after her husband's death.'

Shirley frowned. 'You don't mean . . . ?'

'I'm not clear on this, but in law, an engagement is a legally binding statement of intent. In the absence of any other obvious contender, your claim as the fiancée might be equally valid.'

'Surely not?' It was too much to take in.

Edward looked embarrassed. 'Please forgive me if it turns

out not to be the case. I haven't dealt with a situation quite like this before. If no one else presents themselves, then your claim might be as valid as that of the others.'

She immediately thought again of Frank and his revelation. For a moment she imagined being in direct conflict with him for ownership of the house. Clearly he had not yet made his discovery public, but as soon as he did . . . ? She began to shake her head.

'This is foolish,' she said. 'I could have no claim on the house at all. It is impossible. Now, I really should go.'

Quickly she stood up, seeing the surprise and then pain on Edward's face. He too rose to his feet.

'I'm so sorry if I have upset you. I was simply exploring some possibilities. If you don't want to pursue this line then of course we will not do so. It is just that—' He looked shamefaced. 'To be honest, I don't have much respect for either of the people who have already come forward. I know that my duty is to see that the right person in law inherits. My feelings do not come into it but . . . you obviously have so much feeling for the house and Lady Lamb was so fond of you. Please, forget that I even suggested it.' As an afterthought, he added, 'It was probably a mad idea anyway.'

Slightly calmed, Shirley acquiesced to his request that she should sit down once more. He rang the bell on his desk and Mrs Etheridge promptly responded. 'Could we have some tea?' he asked.

She withdrew without comment.

As they waited, Shirley tried to think of something to defuse the situation. She could think of nothing and it seemed clear that Edward was having the same trouble.

Eventually he said, 'As soon as the probate is complete you will need to think what you intend to do with the bonds and shares you have inherited.'

When she looked uncertain he said, 'I am no expert but I would be pleased to go through them with you and see if I can help.'

'Thank you.'

Again they relapsed into silence, thankfully broken when

Mrs Etheridge brought in the tea. It was on a tray with a cloth and neat, floral, china cups.

For a moment they sipped in silence, then Edward asked, 'I suppose you don't like the ballet?'

'I—' She had never actually been to a ballet. Several times she had watched performances on TV, been mesmerized by the skill and formality, uplifted by the music, but there were no theatres within easy distance, unless you went to a matinée, and no one had actually suggested going before.

'I do like ballet,' she started, torn by the desire to say that she didn't and thereby get out of any impending invitation. On the other hand she didn't want him to think that she was some sort of ignoramus.

'I – I have tickets for a new ballet being performed in Bristol in a couple of weeks. It is very modern. I don't know what you think?'

What did she think? That she would like to go? That she would enjoy his company sufficiently to spend an evening with him? Then she began to wonder whether they would be able to get home the same evening and what Maud would say. As she looked at Edward she saw the apprehension on his face. She found herself saying, 'The other day you suggested that as long as Guy was alive, I wasn't free. What makes you think that things have changed?'

He looked bemused by the question, the links she seemed to be making. Carefully he said, 'Only you know whether you feel "free", as you call it. I just thought that perhaps you would enjoy an evening at the ballet.'

She was making assumptions that he had designs on her. Was this his way of telling her that she was wrong? Crushed by embarrassment, she said, 'I do like the ballet. It would be very nice indeed.'

'Then perhaps you would like to come with me?'

It was decided.

Seventeen

Shirley did not of course tell Maud that Edward Benningfield had suggested she might have a claim to Cartegena. To do so would mean admitting that she had been talking about her engagement to Guy and that others at least had taken it seriously. It was stupid, really. Since Guy's body had been found, Lady Lamb would no doubt have talked about it. She could imagine the two women together, poring over the legacy of sadness and failure their children had brought them. As for Shirley and Maud, though, they had never discussed it and probably never would. In fact, now that Jean was gone, they said very little to each other at all.

Shirley realized how ill suited as housemates she and her mother were. Jean had acted as a sort of catalyst, enabling them to interact. Now she was gone they reverted to their usual pattern of separate and monosyllabic existence.

Shirley continued to visit Cartegena. Twice a week she opened the windows to air the place and redirected any post to Edward's chambers. She could of course have dropped it in but she did not do so. Neither did she look at the items in the house that were soon to be hers. She did not want even to think of a future when she would be faced with the reality of having an inheritance to deal with. Meanwhile, she was technically unemployed. She wondered whether she should not look for another job or sign on. She wasn't sure how you were supposed to do it but she definitely needed an income. Not knowing what to do, she did nothing.

The following weekend the local paper carried an advert in the Public Notices asking anyone having anything to do with the estate of Lord Lamb to contact E. Benningfield. She wondered how many people might do so. Foremost was the thought that by now Frank must surely have put forward his own claim. What would Edward think? What would people say? She felt curiously disloyal to Frank, suspecting that his revelation would be regarded with suspicion not to mention disbelief in the village. Indeed, had she not regarded it so herself? By now she was getting good at shutting out thoughts she didn't want to face up to. She turned her mind to other things.

Too quickly the time passed. On the Friday before the Saturday visit to the ballet, Edward phoned to say that if it was all right he would pick her up at about four. They would then drive to Bristol and perhaps stop on the way for a bite of tea then afterwards, if she was willing, they could have a late supper.

'That's fine.' She still hadn't mentioned the outing to Maud. As she put the phone down she knew that her mother was listening.

'That was the solicitor. He's got some tickets for the ballet tomorrow night and he wondered if I might like to go.'

'And you said yes.'

'Well, it would be rude to refuse.'

Maud gave a grunt. 'You could have said it was too short a notice – that is, if you didn't want to go.'

'I've never been to the ballet before.'

'What time will you be back?'

'Er . . . quite late.'

Maud gave another sniff of disapproval. 'There's something not quite right about that man. He must be fifty if he's a day and to my knowledge he's never so much as had a girlfriend. You want to be careful. Don't go getting ideas about him because you'll probably be disappointed.'

'He's nowhere near fifty and anyway, what do you mean by that?' In a strange way, Shirley was relieved at her mother's response. It was so predictable. There was nothing bad that one could say about Edward Benningfield but Maud had managed to think of something. Her earlier condemnation of Frank now seemed exactly what it was, a reflex action by a bitter old lady who was afraid of being left alone. Unaccountably, Shirley felt a sudden surge of affection for her mother, almost tenderly sorry for her.

'Oh Mum, why do you always have to find something bad to say about people?'

'I don't.'

'You do, especially men. I'm not planning on leaving you, if that's what you think.'

'I don't think anything of the sort. If you want to go you must go.'

'Go where?'

Maud was nonplussed. Shirley shook her head.

'You really are an old dope,' she said. 'I'll probably be back before midnight.'

In this fairly positive state of mind she set off the following afternoon. She wasn't quite sure what to wear. The weather was beginning to turn cool so the things in her summer wardrobe were no longer suitable. She did have a dark blue skirt that fell somewhere between formal and casual and she settled for this, with an almost identical blue over-shirt with silver, oriental swirls woven into the fabric. As she came down the stairs, Maud was waiting for her.

'All dressed up, aren't you?'

'Don't want to look like the poor relation.' As she saw Edward's silhouette on the glass of the front door, she gave Maud a quick peck on the cheek.

'You take care.'

Edward was wearing a lightweight navy suit and an unexpected pink shirt. He also sported a bow tie that made her think of a theatrical magician. His eyes behind his gold-rimmed glasses looked clear and alive.

They exchanged greetings and Shirley slid into the front seat of the BMW. She thought briefly of Frank's old Capri but switched her mind determinedly to the present.

'A lovely day.'

'It is.'

As they pulled out into the main street, Shirley asked after the dog. It was something to say.

'He's fine. I took him for a long walk this morning. He'll sleep for several hours now.' Briefly she wondered whether Edward too might fall asleep – hopefully not at the wheel but perhaps later in the darkness of the theatre.

'Who looks after Biggles when you are at work?' she asked. Surely he didn't leave the dog shut in all day?

Edward leaned back in his seat as they left the village and started along the deserted country road that would suddenly, alarmingly, hit the frenzy of the motorway. 'My neighbour pops in and lets him out. Sometimes she takes him for a walk.'

She. Shirley wondered who and what but did not ask. After a couple of miles Edward turned off the road and along a country lane, coming eventually to a small village, little more than a hamlet really, where a stone, thatched cottage doubled as a tea garden.

'I thought perhaps we could stop here for something to keep us going until after the performance?'

'Fine.'

The cottage was old and quaint and the tearoom the type of place where you might find Miss Marple. They were the only visitors and the proprietor – plump, crisp and wearing a frilly apron – served them the sort of tea that might have been in fashion fifty years ago. She arrived with thinly sliced bread and butter, apricot jam and an assortment of cakes arranged on a glass plate mounted on a silver stand. It was so twee that Shirley wanted to laugh.

'Do you come here often?' she asked, chiding herself for asking such a hackneyed question.

'Occasionally. I hope you don't think it's too ... old fashioned?'

'No. It's fun.'

After a few moments she realized that it was down to her to pour the tea. Immediately she felt clumsy. Should she put milk in the cups and if so, first or last and how much? The teapot was accompanied by a tea strainer for this was no place for teabags. Awkwardly she picked up the teapot, cursing herself for being so gauche.

'Milk?'

'Please.'

She tipped a small amount into the bottom of the delicate, flowered cups, thinking, I must remember to crook my little finger when I drink!

Edward looked abashed. 'I'm sorry if you don't like this place but I love the cakes. They are the best I have ever tasted. I hope you aren't on a diet or anything – not that you need to be.'

She laughed at his embarrassment, suddenly relaxing. This was ridiculous. Why did she let herself feel on edge when clearly he was equally at a loss?

They ate slivers of bread and then had two cakes each followed by more tea. The cakes were so light that she could easily have managed a third.

Back in the car, Edward turned the radio on: Radio 3 of course. There was a jazz recital and she noticed how he seemed to be reading the music in his head.

'You like jazz?'

'Love it.'

She tried to hide her surprise, which increased when he added, 'I still play double bass with a group sometimes.'

Neat, portly Edward and a solid, beefy double bass. She could not imagine it. They were back on the main road and the traffic was increasing. Tentatively she asked, 'Have you had any response to your adverts in the papers – about the estate?'

'I've had one.' He did not elaborate and she couldn't ask. It must be Frank, she thought. It must be. She wondered how he knew what was going on in the village. Did Douglas Kirk keep him informed, or perhaps he had the local paper shipped out to France? Remembering his sudden absence from the inquest she felt again the sense of loss and disappointment. Not a man to be relied on, Frank Agnew. Glancing to her side she tried to interpret what Edward was thinking but he would have made a good poker player.

'Is there a deadline for responding?' she asked, again for something to fill the void.

'We'll give it a while.'

She sat back and licked a stray grain of sugar from her lower lip. The jazz piece scrambled to a cacophonous end. There was nothing more to say.

The ballet was not exactly what Shirley expected. In stark contrast to the fussy Victorian interior of the theatre, the stage was bare. The dancers wore not tutus and tights but loose-fitting jackets and trousers that might belong to kung fu fighters. The dance routines smacked of martial regimentation and the music was strident and challenging. After the initial surprise, the gymnastic skills of the performers sucked her into a fascinated awe at the liquid qualities of their bodies. She began to wonder about their relationships. Were these lithe, muscular, beautiful young men all gay? The intimacy of contact between male and female, the apparent domination of the man over his imploring, subservient partner aroused a sense of hunger, a wish to be in some physical relationship with a virile Adonis. She glanced quickly at Edward. In the semi-darkness, the light glinted on his glasses. He leaned slightly forward, his face intent on the activity on the stage. What was he thinking or feeling? Shirley sat back. It was no good. Whatever she might feel about him, it was not sexual attraction. She began to feel uneasy at the thought of the journey back, a possible – nay, probable – proposition. She began to sift through the various sexual encounters she had experienced. If she was honest, apart from Frank the best sex had not always been with the men she most fancied. She and Guy had been too young and inexperienced. Their relationship was more to do with commitment and belonging than with sexual pleasure. She realized now that skill and experience were probably more important than looking like Michelangelo's David. Perhaps kindness rated way above sex appeal. Perhaps a few glasses of wine would blur the difference.

The performance came to an abrupt end and the audience obligingly gave the cast a standing ovation. Shirley joined in. She had enjoyed the experience. Now she wanted to get home but the journey and a meal came first.

'What did you think?' Edward held her elbow as they jostled their way through the crowd.

'I thought they were very good.'

'What about the music?'

'It was . . . interesting.'

'You didn't really like it?'

'I think you would need to hear it more than once.'

He nodded. 'That's the case with any piece of serious music. You need to absorb the light and shade, the patterns.'

It was nearly dark as they set off.

'We'll stop at the Crown in Shorningham,' he said. 'I think you'll like it.'

What cannot be cured must be endured – she didn't know why the phrase came into her mind.

To her surprise the Crown was a lively roadhouse fronting the street and vivid with lights. The car park was almost full and a raucous hubbub greeted them as they pushed their way inside. At the back was a dining area but that too was busy. Edward found them a table and went to the bar. She had time to look around thinking again that this wasn't the sort of place she would have thought he would like. Perhaps he thought it was more her sort of place, a bit common? She smiled to herself.

He returned with a bottle of red wine. 'You'll have to drink most of this. I'm driving.'

'Are you trying to get me drunk?' She said it in jest but he looked uncomfortable so she added, 'I'm only joking.' He gave a tight smile and sat down.

'Do you come here often?' She grinned to show again that it was a joke, but he answered her seriously.

'My father used to run this pub. We spent part of our childhood here.'

'You? In a pub?' She could not hide her disbelief.

'I haven't always been a solicitor,' he said. 'I started off life as a child.' They both laughed at the ludicrousness of their situation, simultaneously relaxing and taking slow, large mouthfuls of wine.

The conversation began to flow easily. Edward talked about his childhood in the Crown, how his poor mother had endured the long hours, the rowdy behaviour and a growing family of three boys and two girls.

'My father drank himself to death,' he said. 'When he became too "indisposed" to run the place we were thrown out. My mother's sister took us in, all of us. Now I think of it she must have been a saint.' He was silent for a moment, absorbed by his own thoughts. Remembering where he was, he looked up and smiled. 'Perhaps it was her husband who was the saint. He was a carpenter. He took one of my brothers on as an apprentice. The second one, David, joined the army. I haven't seen him for years. My eldest sister Beth took up nursing and Becky, the baby of the family, married a surveyor from Banbury.'

'And you studied law?'

'I did. I was lucky. My aunt didn't have any children of her own but she had ambition. I was the bright one in the family so they gave me all the chances.'

Shirley felt those nagging regrets but only for a moment. The wine was doing its work. She felt warm, cosy, no longer ill at ease with a man whose roots were as modest as her own.

'You didn't marry?' She had to ask. Would he after all tell her that he was gay? She didn't think so. In unguarded moments she saw his interest, felt his stirring awareness.

He looked down at the tablecloth. 'Let's say that like you I met someone who got so far under my skin there was no going back, not for a long time anyway.'

'But you are . . . free, now?'

'I suppose I am. She married a professional footballer. When that went wrong she married some actor. He's on television sometimes but I haven't seen her for years.'

She was about to say something about getting over things, then she thought of Guy. He had been way beyond reach, far more elusive than a woman married to a sportsman and then a TV star. He had been so far away, in fact, that she was separated first by half a world and then by his almost certain death – but that hadn't stopped her. She tried to detach herself from her own feelings. What had Guy really been like? What had he really felt for her? When she saw that disbelief on other faces, were they right? She didn't know. Anyway, what did it matter? Those years were beyond recall. If she had wasted them on some foolish, unrealizable dream then that was her bad luck.

'You look very thoughtful.' Edward interrupted her soul searching.

'I was just wondering ... how do you really know who anyone is? How do you know if what you feel and what they feel is the same thing?'

'You don't. You have to go with the laws of probability.'

Probability: she was no further forward.

Their food arrived. Switching to the present and emboldened by the wine, she said, 'I do know who has come forward, about the estate.'

'You do?' He looked first surprised and then, she thought, relieved. After a pause, he said, 'It must have come as a shock.'

She pondered the statement. 'Well, not exactly a shock, but I was surprised.'

'You had no idea?'

'No.' She wondered why he should think that she had.

After a moment he said, 'There will have to be a blood test. She seems a very nice girl.'

'She?' The word escaped her.

'Isabella Garcia.' He smiled at some secret thought. 'It will come as a bit of a shock to several people.'

Seeing her expression he stopped. 'You haven't met her? I thought that, as she's staying with the photographer, Agnew, you might have ... ?'

Shirley could not hide the shock. Edward frowned.

'We are talking about the same person?'

'Frank Agnew, yes.' She grasped at his name, trying to make sense of what he was saying.

Who was Isabella Garcia? How come she was championing Frank's claim? How come she was staying with him? She thought of French women, slim, dark, confident, sexy. Her blood began pounding. She only knew one disturbing, agonizing thing – that she was instantly, totally and humiliatingly jealous.

'Are you all right?' Edward looked concerned.

'I'm – I think perhaps ...'

'Come along, I think I should get you home.'

Hurriedly Edward paid the bill. He was solicitous, guiding

195

her gently to the car, lowering her into the seat, offering her a blanket from the boot, which she declined.

They drove in silence except for the occasional request for a progress report on how she was feeling.

'I'm fine, really.' She felt irritated with him, with herself. Thoughts of Frank Agnew roamed around the periphery of her brain like some hungry, marauding tiger. One moment's carelessness and they would engulf her.

At the house he saw her up the path and waited while she fiddled with the key, praying that he would not notice how her hand trembled. As the lock eventually turned, he said, 'I hope your mother won't think I haven't been looking after you properly.'

'I'm not a child!' she snapped, then managed a tight smile. 'Thank you, really, for a lovely evening.'

'I hope you enjoyed it. Is it all right if I ring tomorrow, just to see how you are?'

'I'll phone you.'

Gratefully she closed the door. Even more gratefully she realized that Maud had gone to bed.

Releasing her breath with a huge outpouring of tension, she went into the living room. This feeling was terrible, stupid. She'd had a couple of drinks with Frank, a meal, briefly shared his bed. In his terms this sort of thing probably happened all the time. At the thought of his physical presence, her longing, like some great tidal wave, threatened to burst free.

She wanted him. She wanted him so much and yet there was nothing that she could do. And now he was in the village with another woman staying under his roof. As she searched in the cupboard for Maud's medicinal brandy, her one consolation was that she had been forewarned. At least she would be able to save face. She took a swig from the bottle. As someone, somewhere had said, tomorrow was another day.

Eighteen

T hree times Shirley was sick in the night. The physical discomfort had the minimal benefit of distracting her from her mental pain. In the morning she dragged herself from bed, her mouth like acid and her ribs aching. As she stumbled her way to the kitchen it was to find Maud sitting at the table eating porridge. Shirley registered instant dismay to find her mother there, followed by a second's surprise that she had gone to the trouble and effort of making breakfast.

Maud said, 'What happened to you then? Did he get you drunk or were you eating some Chinese or Indian rubbish last night?'

'Neither. It was Italian rubbish.'

She made tea, drawing some slight comfort in its liquid warmth. She wanted to get out quickly before the cross-examination started but Maud had lapsed into a reverie of her own. As soon as she could, Shirley escaped upstairs to dress and then set out for Cartegena. It would have done her good to walk but the effort was too great. She took the car.

As she got out into the indecently cheerful sunshine, the sound of voices echoed from somewhere behind the house. Frowning, she hesitated before starting in their direction, reminding herself that the front gate really should be kept locked.

Before she had walked more than a few steps, a woman appeared around the side of the house. On seeing Shirley she stopped and smiled uncertainly. She looked about Shirley's age. Shirley noticed that she had a nice figure although with a rather sallow skin and large near-black eyes. Her long, thick black hair was tied back in a plait, making her look modest and unworldly.

Shirley felt a gathering unease. As she was about to question the trespasser, someone else came round the corner of the building. It was Frank Agnew.

Shirley's stomach jolted with shock. She tried to think of something to say, some way to hide the instant, visible redness of her face but she could only swallow back the paralysis and wait for him to speak. He looked consolingly abashed to see her.

'Hi. I thought perhaps you didn't work here any more.'

'Did you?' She tried hard to keep her voice from wavering. She asked, 'Is there something you want?'

'This is Isabella Garcia. She's—'

'I know who she is.'

'Ah.' He gave a little shrug. 'Well, I was just showing her the gardens.'

Shirley wanted to shout at him for daring to bring the woman here. Some small corner of reason warned her that she must not take on the role of guardian of the house. It was not her place to ban them. Covertly she noticed how tanned he looked, how lithe and healthy. Bitterly she thought that this woman, whoever she was, must be good for him.

Awkwardly, Frank said, 'Someone has told you then, about what has happened?'

She did not answer. What had happened? This woman was not French as she had expected but Spanish. Briefly she spoke to Frank in Spanish and he replied. Their easy communication left her feeling excluded.

He said, 'Isabella says she is pleased to meet you. She had been hoping to do so. It might seem strange but she has heard a lot about you.'

Strange indeed. Shirley was at a loss as to why this woman should even have heard of her and who had been talking to her anyway? Surely not Frank?

Isabella smiled uncertainly. Shirley said, 'I can't let you in. Until the estate is settled I don't think it would be right.'

'No. I understand.' Frank thrust his hands in the pocket of his jeans and the curve of his neat bum sent a wave of undiluted hunger through her. Pointedly she fished the house keys from her pocket and turned to let herself in. Frank came closer.

'We've got to have a talk,' he said.

'What about?' He was close enough to smell the soap he used. Her senses wavered dangerously.

'About what's happened. Look, we've got to go to London tomorrow but I'll call you the next day.'

We – he and Isabella? Aloud, she said, 'I don't see . . .' She was shaking her head but he ignored her.

'It's important. I knew you'd be upset. Who told you, the solicitor?'

She didn't answer.

Nodding towards Isabella, he said, 'She speaks some English. She wants to explain. Perhaps later you'll be able to have a chat.'

Shirley kept her back to him and unlocked the door. Her breath was coming fast and deep and she had to get away.

'I'll call you then.' The rest of his sentence was cut off as she closed the door.

Inside she leaned back against the panel and took long, deep gasps of oxygen. Damn him. She didn't know what he was up to. How could he bring his wife or mistress or whatever she was and openly flaunt her? Her disappointment in him, in her own judgement, was oceans deep. She wanted to cry but a sudden thought distracted her. She wondered if Frank was treating this woman in the same thoughtless way. After all, who did she think that Shirley was? It was a crazy mess.

After a while she peered cautiously through the window but there was no sign of them. They must be walking back to the village. She would have to wait otherwise she would overtake them. Seeking refuge she climbed the stairs to Florence's bedroom. Inside it was calm and orderly. She picked up the little Staffordshire dog and smoothed it, finding comfort in its cool lines. She tried to imagine packing up the things in the room and transporting them to the cottage but she didn't want to think about a time where she spent the foreseeable future with Maud in the village. Looking up she caught the button eyes of the lady in the portrait, Catherine Charteris. She wondered what her life must have been like. Had she loved that first Sir

Francis's younger brother or had the marriage been merely for convenience? Had she dreamed of escape, longed for another lover? She moved closer and gazed at her, trying to pick up something of her life. 'I hope you were happier than I am,' she said aloud.

When she thought that sufficient time had elapsed, she went down to the car and drove slowly home. There was no sign of Frank or his lover.

As she poked her head into the kitchen, Maud announced, 'That solicitor rang. He asked if you were all right. I told him you weren't used to drinking and eating rich food.'

Shirley's mood sank even deeper. Now she would have to ring him back and apologize for her mother's rudeness. She didn't want to see him. She didn't want to see anyone. She went back to the hall and dialled Edward's number.

He answered the phone himself.

'It's Shirley.'

'How are you?'

'I'm fine.' Her tone challenged him to think otherwise.

He hesitated and she guessed he was trying to decide how to respond to her tone. After a moment he said, 'Look, I've been doing some poking around and I've discovered something quite exciting. It might not mean anything but would you like to come round to the office?'

'When?'

'Now?'

She thought for a moment. It would mean escaping from Maud. It was the lesser of two evils. She said, 'All right, I'll be there in half an hour.'

She was greeted not by Mrs Etheridge but a large, amber-coloured dog that wandered politely over to the door and languidly wagged its tale. Biggles.

In its wake Edward emerged from his office. He looked slightly distracted as if what really interested him was still on his desk.

'Come and have a look,' he said by way of greeting. 'It might not mean anything but I'd like to see what you think.'

She followed him through the door. His desk was littered with papers. A magnifying glass rested on the top sheet.

He said, 'I have been going through the box that Florence left with me. It contains certificates and various bits and pieces. At the bottom, though, I found this.' He indicated the brown, brittle-looking document on top.

'I don't know exactly what it is but it appears to be a sonnet. The writing is hard to decipher. Take a look.'

Shirley walked around the desk and gave the paper her attention. In places the brown of the paper had darkened and the brown of the ink had faded to the point where they nearly blended. The writing itself was extremely ornate, a series of swirls and squiggles that were almost impossible to interpret as individual letters. She glanced briefly at Edward for a comment.

'You remember what you said about the guidebook, how it was suggested that the first Lady Lamb might be the Dark Lady of Shakespeare's sonnets?'

She nodded doubtfully. 'It doesn't say why they should think that.'

'Well, I'm probably barking up the wrong tree and all that but this is definitely a poem of some sort and it contains fourteen lines which, I believe, makes it a sonnet.'

'You don't think this is—?'

He shrugged. 'It looks about the right period, but there's something else. You know you said that the first Lady Lamb was a twin and that the painting in Florence's bedroom was of her own ancestor, that other twin?'

Shirley nodded cautiously.

'Well, perhaps if Shakespeare did write sonnets to an unknown Dark Lady, it could just as easily have been Lady Lamb's twin.'

Shirley didn't answer. This was purely speculation with nothing to back it up.

Sitting on the edge of the desk, Edward said, 'I have managed to read the first line. Look at these opening words.'

He pushed a sheet of paper towards her on which he had transcribed what he could read of the sonnet. She read, 'Come Again Temptress, fill (?) this empty heart . . .'

She glanced up at him and impatiently he said, 'Don't you see? It's a code. Look at the first letters of the words in capitals

201

– CAT. I think it might be short for Catherine.'

As Shirley hesitated he added, 'It would explain why it is in Florence's possession and not part of Sir Edward's estate.'

'So you really believe that William Shakespeare wrote a sonnet to Lady Florence's ancestor and this is the original?'

'I don't know. He wrote numerous sonnets. I've checked the first lines and this isn't one of the published ones but if this is what I think it is, it might be a new discovery!'

'Surely not?' She couldn't take it in.

Edward said, 'I'm probably wrong but it is such an exciting thought that I wanted to share it with you.' He sat back and whistled softly at the enormity of his revelation. 'Apart from anything else, if this is genuine then not only will every museum in the world be bidding for it, you will also own a portrait that is absolutely priceless!'

He was right. It was like thinking you had the winning numbers for the lottery. If you did, thousands, no, millions of pounds were about to be showered on you. She shook her head to clear her thoughts.

'Supposing it isn't?' she asked. 'Supposing this is just some old poem by no one in particular?'

'Then it is still an interesting artefact. If it dates back to Tudor times, the museums may still be interested – although not of course as much as they would be if it was really by the Bard.' Absently, Edward was playing with Biggles' ear. The dog gave his hand a tender lick.

Edward said, 'I'm going to go out to eat and then take this boy for a long walk. Why don't you come?'

'All right.' She didn't stop to think. Maud was at home waiting for her lunch but Shirley was caught up in his euphoria. 'I'll just phone my mother,' she said, 'to tell her that I won't be home to eat.'

He nodded towards the phone. 'Do that and then, Miss Shirley, let's go out and celebrate.'

They went to the Bull and Bishop where dogs were permitted. Biggles curled up under the table although his bulk left little room for their feet. The occasional feel of his warm head against her leg sent a comfortable sensation through Shirley.

Edward said, 'How about champagne?' She had never seen him like this before – excited, carefree – but she shook her head, the excesses of last night still taking their revenge. 'Just mineral water, please.'

'You didn't drink that much last night,' he observed.

She did not enlighten him about the brandy.

They were just contemplating the pudding menu when more guests arrived. Shirley glanced up and to her dismay Frank and the Spanish woman had just come into the dining room. She immediately felt sick.

Aware of her sudden tension, Edward dragged his eyes from the menu and looked at the couple. They were settling themselves at a table in an alcove. It looked private, intimate.

'You know him,' Edward said. It was a statement rather than a question.

She gave a single nod of her head.

He said, 'Clever chap, apparently. Very artistic.'

She wanted to leave but without making a fuss it was impossible to do so. She said, 'It looks as if it might rain. Don't you think we should go now, if we are going to take the dog out?'

He glanced again longingly at the menu. 'You're probably right. I'm supposed to be cutting down. Coffee?'

'No thanks.'

'All right then, I'll go and pay the bill.'

He stood up and went across to the bar. Frank, who had been showing the menu to his companion, also wandered over, stopping by Shirley's table. His very shadow emanated sexual magnetism and she found her hands were trembling.

'New friend?' he asked and she couldn't answer him. Biggles, stirring himself, licked Frank's hand in greeting and he smoothed the dog on the head.

'Nice dog.'

Shirley stood up and grabbed her bag. 'We were just going.'

He gave her a quizzical look and followed her as far as the bar. Edward was just putting his wallet away. He held out his hand to Frank.

'Good to see you again. We have an appointment on Thursday, isn't it?'

'That's right.' Frank inclined his head, bidding them farewell. To Shirley's chagrin, Edward rested his hand in a proprietorial manner on her arm. She wanted to shake him off but some remnant of pride prevented her. She felt dizzy with emotion. Biggles walked close to their heels and she knew that Frank was watching them. She would have given anything to know what he was thinking.

She longed to go straight home but instead she followed behind Edward, her eyes fixed on the path, wishing only for solitude. They walked like this for several minutes.

It was a perfect day, clear and bright but with a whispering southerly breeze that fanned them. The dog was not on a lead but he walked companionably at Edward's side. After a while they waited for her to catch up.

He said, 'Nice chap, Agnew. Do you know him well?'

She shook her head. 'Only as someone local.'

She thought he looked surprised and prayed that he would let the subject drop. The last thing she wanted was to hear about Frank and his woman.

They started to climb and as the path grew steeper, some of her tension evaporated. Eventually they came to a standing stone looking out over a panorama of fields, some ploughed, others still green with pasture.

'Just think,' said Edward. 'This landscape must have been the same for centuries; the same pattern of reaping and sowing.'

Shirley nodded, thinking that it must have been all woodland once and then later, miles of open land, before the enclosures.

'History interests you, doesn't it?' Edward asked. 'That was why I felt you should be the one to live at Cartegena.' He gave a little sniff. 'Things have changed now, of course.'

For a while the fantasy of Shakespeare and Edward's discovery had distracted her but now the reality was that Frank was back.

'It must be hard for you,' Edward said.

'Not really.'

She didn't want to talk about it. They had reached a point where the track led down to the hollow where she and Guy had first made love. She wondered how the shrub was doing. From somewhere a mood of defiance claimed her. She turned to Edward, his face pink from his exertions. 'That would be the perfect place to make love,' she said, looking down into the hollow.

He looked predictably surprised. 'Perhaps it would.' She waited but he merely said, 'I suppose we should get back.'

She wondered what he would do if she suddenly grabbed his hand and placed it on her breast, or flung herself down and lifted her skirt – except that she wasn't wearing a skirt. It must have been easier when girls wore skirts and no knickers, she thought.

'Have you ever made love in the open?' she asked him.

'Not really.' She could see that he was uncomfortable with the conversation. He was the sort of man who would always do the right thing. Wryly she thought that if he had acted rashly at that moment, asserted himself, shown some abandon, she would have had sex with him there on the grass. With his reticence, his sense of propriety, she could never attach herself to him.

Aloud she said, 'Come along then, let's go home.'

He left her at the front gate with a promise to let her know as soon as he had discovered anything further about the sonnet. He did not suggest that they go out to dinner or the theatre, for which she was grateful.

'Well . . .' she bent forward to pat Biggles' head and smiled stiffly at Edward.

He gave her an answering smile. He said, 'I'm sorry about the way that things have turned out but I do understand your wish not to talk about it.'

She bowed her head, acknowledging his words. He continued: 'You must never think that there was anything that you could have done differently. From what I have heard, you always behaved with courage and loyalty.'

As he turned to go, she thought, I wonder what the hell he is talking about?

Nineteen

T he next day Shirley took Maud into town. For a long time
they pottered in Gilchrists, the department store. It catered
largely for the older generation and Maud felt comfortable here.
This was where she had shopped before she was married.
Shirley persuaded her to buy a skirt.

'Winter's coming,' she urged. 'You could do with something
new.'

Maud settled on a tweed skirt and in a moment of reckless-
ness also bought a jumper. Shirley could see that she was
pleased with herself, almost excited by her own daring.

Afterwards they stocked up in the supermarket and then had
lunch in a small café. Several times Maud looked into the carrier
bags holding her new purchases. 'I don't know when I think I'm
going to wear them,' she said.

'We'll find some occasion.'

Shirley found herself looking round, wondering if at any
moment Frank might appear, then she reminded herself that he
had gone away for the day – with the Spanish woman. The
bitterness soured her – she would not even grace her with a
name.

As soon as they got home she found an excuse to go out
again. Maud was tired and happy to sit in front of the telly and
doze for which Shirley was grateful. She felt so restless that only
physical activity could assuage the discontent.

Whether by accident or design she found herself taking the
same path she had walked with Edward the day before. She
carried on in the same way, using it as an excuse to go and see
how Guy's shrub was faring. As she walked she tried to concen-

trate on her relationship with Guy. For years she had talked to him inside her head. There was really no need to stop now. In reality she was probably talking to herself but in the end, it didn't matter. If he wasn't there then no harm was done. If he heard her, so much the better. As she trudged up the hill she knew that he would understand her dilemmas. Now the petty jealousies of life were banished, perhaps death gave the deceased a certain wisdom. I know you'll understand, she thought. After all, haven't I been virtually alone and in limbo for eighteen years?

Puffing from the exertion she laid out the problem for him in her mind. Here I am, thirty-five years old, nearly thirty-six. I am in such a rut that something has to happen. Your mother has been so kind to me. Whatever the outcome of the Shakespeare sonnet, I will not need to work, so what should I do? She paused to let the question germinate. I know you don't like Frank. You never did. He was aggressive as a boy and he disliked you. I don't like him either – not actually like him. He's disloyal, not to be trusted. Anyway, he's no longer even in the picture. He's trying to steal Cartegena from you by the way – from your family. She waited a few moments before carrying on. That leaves Edward. He's respectable, kind, trustworthy – and free. How would you feel, I wonder, if I were to marry him?

She mulled over the idea, seeing Edward plodding up the hill ahead of her, hearing his voice. He's a nice man. We could probably have a good life together, that is assuming that's what he's looking for – but it might not be. I'm such crap at reading the signals. She didn't even allow herself to consider that he wasn't what she wanted. To Guy she confessed, All my life my head has been full of rebellious thoughts but I've never acted on them. What should I do?

Something else occurred to her. If she could survive without working then she could begin to study again. Maud was still a problem but something could be arranged. They could sell Hawthorn Cottage and rent or even buy a flat in a university town and Shirley could study whatever she wanted. What did she want? A degree in English? In history? Something esoteric that had not yet occurred to her? She made up her mind to get hold of some syllabuses.

For a while these distractions helped to ease the emptiness then as she arrived at the hollow she saw that the shrub was wilting. She cursed herself for not bringing water. It seemed symbolic, as if her relationship with Guy was withering and dying. Hopelessly she sank on to the damp grass and moaned quietly to herself. This won't do. This will not do.

The telephone rang at 8.30 the next morning. Having had a rotten night, Shirley had dozed off after sunrise and was now deeply asleep. The bell dragged her back to the daylight and she hurried into her dressing gown and stumbled down the stairs.

'Hello?'

'It's Frank.'

The sound of his voice startled her awake and she held the phone away from her as if it might bite her.

When she didn't respond he said, 'I'm coming over to pick you up. I need to know that you are all right about what has happened.'

'I don't—' She didn't want even to think about it. Didn't he understand that trying to explain his new relationship was worse than simply going away without saying goodbye? She felt sick at the thought that he must take some sadistic pleasure in parading it all before her in detail.

'I'll be over in half an hour.'

Before she could object he put the phone down. Dragging herself into wakefulness she went into the bathroom and showered. Some vestige of self-respect demanded that she try to look her best. She wondered whether to invite him in so that she could conduct this meeting under her own roof but then there would be Maud to contend with. She thought that once again she would have to let him take the lead.

She waited until he actually rang the doorbell before she called out to Maud, 'I'm just popping out. Won't be long.' She did not give her mother a chance to reply.

As she opened the door the physical presence of Frank destroyed any residual self-control. She barely acknowledged his greeting but brushed past him and strode ahead down the path. He loped along behind.

'Where are we going then?' she snapped.

The Capri was outside the gate and he opened the door. 'Get in.'

She obeyed.

As he eased himself in beside her she thought his long legs breathtakingly desirable.

'Where's your girlfriend?' she asked.

He went to turn the key in the ignition but stopped to look at her.

'There's something you're not understanding here. How much has Edward Benningfield told you?'

She did not reply. He started the engine and drove in silence along the road that led towards Cartegena. She didn't know why but it seemed the obvious place to go for here was the source of so many of their problems.

At the gateway he pulled up and turned off the engine. Shirley remembered that this was the spot where she had first seen him all those months ago.

He leaned back in his seat and tapped his fingers against the steering wheel. 'This,' he said, 'is very difficult.'

Shirley stared ahead, closing down all her feelings, ready to be hurt.

Suddenly businesslike, Frank said, 'I'd been thinking a long time about Guy Lamb and what had become of him. I like mysteries. They are there to be solved. On the day of the inquest I received a very interesting letter – so interesting in fact that I was on the next available plane to Bogota. I'm sorry I didn't say goodbye but I hope you'll understand.'

This wasn't exactly what Shirley was expecting. She began to listen more closely.

Frank said, 'I wanted to know what Guy Lamb had been up to while he was away, to see if I could find out something concrete about the drug connection. I rang one of the papers I have been doing some work for and they agreed to pay my fare.' He glanced at her before adding, 'The misdeeds of the nobs always make a good story.'

Shirley felt her face redden, wanting from habit to defend Guy, but she remained silent. Frank stretched his shoulders in a now familiar way and said, 'What I did find out wasn't what we could have foreseen.'

Turning towards Shirley he said, 'I wrote in the first instance to the children's home where Guy worked. The man in charge, Father Gonzales, was reticent to begin with but I bunged him a few bob to help the funds and he became more helpful.' Frank stopped as if he didn't quite know how to continue his story. 'You are going to find this hard to take, Shirley. From what you said the other day I thought you already knew, but it seems that you don't.' He sat back and stared ahead. When he spoke he seemed to be feeling his way.

'While Guy was out there in Colombia he formed a close relationship with a local girl. I don't know how serious he was about her but she was certainly serious about him. It might not have meant a lot to him. In fact, too late, he told her about you.' He leaned forward and spoke quietly and slowly. 'It was too late because being a good Catholic girl she had defied all the church's teachings and given him her much-prized virginity. By the time he said that he was engaged elsewhere, she was on the point of telling him that she was pregnant. In the circumstances she didn't say anything and your Guy came back here not knowing anything about it. Father Gonzales guessed though. Isabella's family was persuaded not to throw her out. She kept the baby and a few years later she married a local widower. I think she was moderately happy with him but he died about two years ago.'

He gave her time to absorb the significance of what he was saying. She looked so confused he placed his hand on her arm and repeated, 'Guy Lamb had a baby son.'

When she didn't respond, he continued, 'Anyway, when I discovered what had happened I knew I had to find her and tell her – and her son – about Guy's death. Since he left she had made no effort to contact him. She didn't even know that he had been missing all these years.'

He bent forward again, forcing her to look at him. 'I felt really bad about doing this to you. I know you thought he was some sort of saint. He wasn't. He was just an ordinary bloke, miles from home, with a pretty woman working next to him day in and day out. What happened was no reflection on his feelings for you.'

Shirley shook her head. 'I can't believe it,' she started. All the time another message was racing though her mind. She, Isabella, isn't Frank's wife or girlfriend. She was Guy's . . . She stopped the thought short.

She asked, 'So you decided to bring her – Isabella – to stay with you?'

'I felt I had to. She hasn't got much money. They couldn't afford a hotel and the paper won't spend out too much. Her son, Guido, is a student so he couldn't just leave but we picked him up from the airport yesterday. I – I think perhaps you should meet him.'

Guy's son? All these years and she hadn't known. It was as if she was on quicksand, all her remaining certainties tumbling beneath her.

'What relationship is she to you?' she asked.

'Who?'

'Isabella.'

He shook his head. 'You haven't been listening. She's nothing to do with me. I just thought that, well, if her child is Guy's son he should know about his inheritance.'

She flailed around to find anything to hang on to. After a moment something else occurred to her. 'What about you then? If what you said was true, aren't you still the one with the best claim to Cartegena?'

His lips turned down in a derisive smile. 'I suppose my claim does precede his but . . . what would I really be wanting with this old house? It's a millstone.'

She stifled the disappointment at his lack of feeling for the house. She tried to think of the implications of what he was saying. She asked, 'If that's the case, what will they do with it? They won't be able to afford to live here.' Perhaps he was being selfish, presenting them with what would ultimately be a burden. She tried not to imagine what she would feel if Guy's son moved in.

He said, 'We hope, if the house can be sold, they should get some residual money. They really are quite poor. Besides, the boy deserves to know who his father was.'

His father. Shirley felt a momentary stab of betrayal but it was quickly overlaid with something else. Frank hadn't brought his mistress back to taunt her. He was here to see fair play done. He was worried that the truth would hurt her.

After a moment he said, 'I'm sorry. It's not that I don't want the house but I could never afford the upkeep. I know how much it means to you.'

She nodded and a single tear of remorse lingered at the corner of her eye.

'Are you all right?' He gave her a gentle smile.

She nodded. Yes, she was all right. She was more all right than she had been for a very long time.

Looking to her for reassurance, Frank said, 'I dropped Isabella and Guido in the grounds before I came to pick you up. They're both pretty stunned as you can imagine. Edward Benningfield has been very helpful. He's going to arrange a DNA test to confirm Isabella's story.'

Shirley nodded. Of all the things she might have heard today, this was the most unlikely. As Frank started the car again and turned into the driveway she felt some of the old apprehension come back. She didn't know how she would react when she actually met Guy's son. The existence of such a child was a fantasy she had often dreamed of, only with herself as the mother. She suddenly felt angry on Florence's behalf, for all this time the old lady could have had a longed-for grandchild. But there was no changing anything.

As Cartegena came into view Shirley felt a sharp pang of loss. Whatever happened it seemed that the house was about to be snatched away for ever. She loved its antiquity, its constancy. Her eyes now brimmed with tears at the certainty of losing it. Mistaking her grief for other losses, Frank squeezed her hand.

'Come on, let's go and find Guido Garcia.'

They found mother and son on the parterre. They were seated on the stone steps leading down to the formal garden with its ornamental pond and fountains. Statues of Greek gods formed an avenue leading on towards the lake and bridge. The view was achingly familiar.

At the sound of their footsteps both mother and son stood up. Shirley caught her breath as the young man turned towards them.

'My God,' she whispered. 'It's Guy again.'

Frank slipped his arm through hers and squeezed her to him. 'Are you OK with this?'

'Yes.'

The young man came forward hesitantly, brushing back a lock of fair hair that hung over his forehead. The mannerism was so familiar she found it difficult to breathe.

'Isabella, Guido, this is Shirley.'

They all nodded, speech deserting them.

'Tell him he is exactly like his father,' said Shirley, suddenly strong.

Frank translated and the boy looked gratefully at her. On impulse she went forward and hugged him, full of compassion for this young reincarnation.

For a moment they were all silent then taking charge, Shirley said, 'I expect they would like to see inside the house.'

'You think . . . ?'

'He's Guy's son. That much is obvious.' She felt in her bag for the keys, beckoning them to come with her.

Frank spoke to them briefly and they followed.

Guido said, 'Is very strange for us. Often I wonder about my father but my mother, she do not know where he is. One day I think I will find him but . . .'

Ruefully Shirley thought that he had been dead even before his son was born.

They did a complete tour of the house. In the library Shirley showed them photographs of the family. 'Grandmother,' she said, pointing out Florence. Looking at the picture of young Florence she was reminded of the inexorable passage of time. The Florence in the picture was someone she hardly knew – a wife and mother, the most influential woman in this small corner of the country. Her Florence was old and alone and frag-ile, victim of a cruel accident that neither her position nor money could protect her from.

Shirley made up her mind. Finding the key, she led the way to Guy's bedroom. She unlocked the door and stood back.

'Your father's room,' she said. 'It has not been changed since he left for Colombia.'

She indicated that Guido should go in. From the doorway she saw the long-remembered bed and shelves and carpet. It was another world, somewhere she had returned to a thousand times in her thoughts. Now it was just an unoccupied room, stuffy from lack of use.

She turned to Isabella. 'This must be very hard for you.'

Frank translated and the woman turned to her. Her face wore the scars of her difficult existence.

Isabella spoke and Frank turned back to Shirley. 'She says that she is sorry if she caused you pain but she did not know. She didn't know about you. When she found out she realized that it was you that Guy loved.'

Love was a slippery creature indeed.

'You stay,' she said to Guido and took the others to the kitchen where she made coffee. As she boiled the kettle she wondered if this would be the last time she would come to this room. There was so much grieving that had gone on here. She looked at Frank, who was beginning to grow restless.

'We have an appointment with Edward Benningfield at two,' he said. 'I really think we should go.'

Shirley nodded and he went to call Guido. When they came back, the younger man was clutching a book. 'Would I be permitted to borrow this?' he asked. It was a copy of *Don Quixote*. 'This book it has the name of my father inside. I would like to read what he reads.'

'I'm sure that will be all right.' Shirley gave him a smile, shaken by the so familiar features.

Once outside, Shirley said, 'I think I would like to walk back. I've got quite a lot to think about.'

Frank nodded. 'I'll call you.' He edged her a few steps further away. 'I'm glad that you aren't too upset. How you would cope has been tormenting me ever since I realized what had happened.'

When she thought about it, there was of course regret at the loss of all the years. There was some anger too that another woman had enjoyed the fulfilment of childbirth that she had always believed Guy would bequeath to her, but for the moment the anger was not directed at anyone. Anyway, she had grieved enough. She felt sad that Frank might have had the house in his possession but as he had already implied, he would only have had to sell it. The idea of living here with him was a fairy tale. Meanwhile the hopelessness of the past weeks was suddenly turned upside down. All was not lost. He was still here, still thinking about her. She smiled at him.

'Let me know how you get on,' she said. 'Soon.'

'I will.'

As they drove down the driveway Shirley was left alone with her thoughts.

'You bastard,' she said to the absent Guy. 'You rotten bastard.'

'Where did you dash off to?'

Shirley walked into the cottage to find Maud at the sink peeling potatoes. She glanced at her mother's gnarled hands, surprised to see her managing so well. This and cooking breakfast were unusual activities. Her overwhelming thought, though, was how to explain what had happened.

'I've just learned something amazing,' she said.

'What's that?'

'It seems that there is a surprise heir to Cartegena.' Shirley took off her coat and flung it on a chair. She kept her face away from Maud, not wishing to let her mother see her tension.

Maud let her hands rest in the water where the potatoes waited to be peeled as Shirley said, 'It – it seems that Guy had a son, out in Colombia.'

'I don't believe it. Why haven't we heard anything about this before?'

'Because his mother never told Guy that she was pregnant. She knew nothing about his disappearance or anything.'

'Well how come she has turned up now?'

Here Shirley hesitated. 'Frank Agnew found them.'

'Why? Where? What has it got to do with him? Trust him to stir up trouble.'

215

Thinking of Frank's claim, she thought, It's got more to do with him than you'll ever know. Aloud, she said, 'It isn't trouble. He wanted to find out more about Guy's time in Colombia. He met the priest where Guy worked and he told him.'

Maud sucked her false teeth speculatively. 'That man's bad news.'

Shirley spoke out strongly. 'No. He's not. He thought the boy had a right to his father's estate.'

Maud turned to her daughter, as if remembering. 'And what about you? What do you feel about this? To think that all the time he was away that Guy was two-timing you. I always warned you. You can never trust the aristocracy.' Shirley remained silent. 'And what about this Frank? He doesn't seem to have had much consideration for your feelings or he would have kept quiet.'

'Perhaps the truth is more important than my feelings.' Shirley stopped and then added, 'But the thing that matters most is that Frank has come back. I've missed him. I hope I'll see a lot more of him.'

Maud made no comment, picking up the half-peeled potato and attacking it again. 'What sort of a woman was this mother then? Was she a native?'

Shirley hadn't given the matter any thought.

'I should think her ancestors were all Spanish,' she said.

'Well, is she some sort of a gold digger?'

'No. She seems very nice, very respectable. It was a tragedy for her.'

'Hmm.' Maud sniffed. Taking another potato, she said, 'I don't know what Lady Florence would have said.'

'I think she would have been delighted. The only tragedy is that she never knew.'

'A strange life,' said Maud and placed the potatoes on the stove to boil.

Shirley echoed her thoughts. A strange life indeed.

Frank rang shortly afterwards.

'Everything's underway. Guido will give a DNA sample tomorrow and it can be matched against tissue taken from

Guy's body.' He hesitated. 'We are going out for a meal later. Will you come?'

She wanted to see him so much but then she thought of Maud. 'I can't. My mother is cooking a meal.'

'I see.' Again he hesitated. 'I'd like to invite you round here but, well, it's rather crowded and I can't really go out and leave them. I want some time alone with you.'

The thought surged through her like quicksilver. She asked, 'Have you any idea how long they are staying?'

'Just long enough to establish Guido's identity.'

'And you?'

'I'll stay on, at least until this is sorted. Besides, it's you I have come to see. I need some time with you. I think there is a lot to talk about – that is, if you want to?'

Before she could frame an answer, he said, 'You seem to have become very friendly with Ed Benningfield.'

It took her a moment to think of the solicitor as Ed. It conjured up someone quite different from the person she thought him to be.

She said, 'He's been very helpful to me since I inherited Lady Lamb's estate – you did know about that?'

'Not until this morning. Congratulations. You'll be a lady of property then.'

'Probably not. It's nice, though, having some money.'

'So he's just been helpful, has he? I thought he looked very much at home hanging on to your arm.'

'That's just his way.' She took a risk and added, 'I don't have any feelings for him, other than as a friend.'

'Do you have any *feelings* for anyone else then?'

Carefully she said, 'It might be too early to say.'

He gave a small grunt to show that he understood. 'Funnily enough I've been thinking along the same lines. Look, come and have lunch with us tomorrow. Bring your mother. She'll enjoy the excitement.'

'All right, I will.'

She was about to ring off when he asked, 'Shirley? When are you coming to France?'

'I . . . don't have a passport.'

'Let's get a form then, and I can do you a couple of photos. We can get Ed to sign them.'

'All right.' A panorama of possibilities opened up before her.

'Good night, then.'

'Good night.'

Neither of them actually put down the receiver. At last, as Shirley did so she could feel Frank still at the other end. She hoped that the day would never come when he was further away than this.

Twenty

The news that a mystery heir to the Cartegena estate had turned up soon spread throughout the village. Speculation filled every street corner and meeting place. Disbelief gradually gave way to naked curiosity as it was confirmed without doubt that this stranger, Guido someone, a foreigner, was the son of Guy Lamb. Shirley became an object of curiosity. Had she known? What did she feel? Were the other relatives going to challenge the claim? The gossip went on.

Seeking refuge, Shirley phoned Jean.

'I can't believe it,' her aunt said, as she stumbled to the end of a near incoherent explanation. 'What do you think?'

'To tell the truth I feel a bit of a fool. I can't believe I wasted all those years like some Greek heroine awaiting the return of her Odysseus.'

They were both silent and Shirley knew that Jean was pondering a similar mystery.

'What about Frank, then?'

'Frank's back.' Shirley felt the pleasure bubbling up inside her. 'He's still busy right now because he has Isabella and Guido staying with him but—'

'Are you going to see him then, in France?'

'He's taken some passport photographs. I am going to get them signed tomorrow then I'll send off the form.'

After a moment, Shirley asked, 'How are things with you?' She could feel Jean sorting out an explanation.

She said, 'Rod's wife is still in hospital. It's more of a nursing home really. She needs specialist care. He goes there every day to be with her. His youngest daughter is away travelling at the moment so he is on his own.'

She left Shirley to make her own conclusions. 'You see a lot of him then?'

'Enough.'

The man's wife was dying. Jean would not want to appear selfish and uncaring but the time was near when she and her Rod would be free. She thought it must be like the approaching end of a prison sentence.

'How's Maud?' Jean asked.

'Quite well.'

'I meant what I said about her coming to stay.'

'Thanks.'

As Shirley rang off, the phone rang again. It was Edward Benningfield. He said, 'Glad to have caught you. I have found out something about the sonnet and I wondered if you might like to come over.'

'Tomorrow morning?'

'I was thinking more about this evening – for a drink?'

Shirley couldn't think fast enough. Since Frank's arrival she had assumed that Edward recognized some existing rapport between them and had wisely withdrawn his interest. Perhaps she was wrong.

'It's rather late,' she started.

'It's seven o'clock. I'll drive over and pick you up if you like.'

'No, it's OK, I'll walk.'

Why she had agreed she wasn't sure. Curious as she was about what Edward had found out, she had no desire to intensify their association, such as it was.

Still pondering, she went into the lounge where Maud was watching a programme about lions. 'Lovely animals,' she said by way of greeting, 'but I do wish they wouldn't show them killing things.'

'I'm just going to pop out for a while,' said Shirley.

'Going to see Frank?'

There had been a dramatic change in Maud's attitude to Frank since the day they had been to lunch with Isabella and Guido. Maud had been charmed by the visitors, naturally respectful to older people, and overwhelmed by Guido's resemblance to his dead father.

'Such a handsome boy,' she kept saying. 'You can see that he is a Lamb.'

Frank had been charming too. Attentive and considerate, it did not take him long to win Maud over.

'My daughter has been badly treated,' she warned, heady on sparkling wine. 'I don't want to see her let down by another man.'

'Mother!' Shirley groaned inwardly but when she looked up it was to see Frank grinning.

'Don't worry, Mrs W, my intentions towards your daughter are purely honourable. That is to say—'

'I know what you're thinking, you naughty boy. Just don't go breaking her heart, that's all.'

Afterwards Shirley and Frank had laughed about it but suddenly serious, he said, 'I meant what I said. The ball's in your court, Shirley. As soon as the visitors go home, I want to spend every minute I can with you.'

'Haven't you got any work to do?'

'Nothing I can't do around here.'

Ever since, she had felt strangely content.

To her mother, she said, 'I'm going to see the solicitor about some papers.'

'At this time of night?'

'It's only seven o'clock.'

'Well, don't you go giving him the wrong idea. Don't go hurting Frank, either.'

'Mother! I thought you didn't approve of Frank.'

'All the same, it doesn't pay to two-time a man.'

Smiling to herself, Shirley set off. Edward's house was a modern bungalow built at the top of an incline. A paved path threaded through the rockery and up to the front door. As she picked her way, a security light came on and she could see the muted colours of a leaded glass panel in the door. The door opened as she reached the top step and Biggles gave a baritone bark.

Frank wore a white shirt and grey trousers. The shirt was open at the neck but she noticed that he still had cufflinks. This was as far as his concession to casual dress went. 'Come along in.'

As she did so she looked around at the pale wooden flooring, the large picture windows and the sparse furniture. This was a house arranged with precise and careful thought.

Edward poured a glass of very cold, dry white wine and invited her to sit on the oatmeal-coloured sofa. Shirley wondered how on earth it kept its colour with such a big dog in residence.

'Well . . .' Edward sat in one of the matching armchairs and sipped on his drink. 'There's bad news, I'm afraid, about the sonnet. I took it initially to the local record office and they assure me that it is not by Shakespeare. In fact, they say that it is not Elizabethan but probably written around 1750. A shame, really, but there you are.'

Shirley gave a philosophical shrug. 'It would have been exciting but it's not important.'

Edward offered her some canapés and olives on a small silver tray, complete with linen napkin. As she scooped up a couple she wondered again if she was doing the right thing. Should she have taken only one? Should she put her glass down between sips? The fact that he always aroused these uncertainties underlined how unsuitable any serious relationship between them would have been.

She said, 'I hope you don't mind but I have some passport photos here. I wonder if you'd mind signing them for me?'

He held out his hand. Shirley fumbled for them in her bag then passed them over. As he studied them she felt as if she was having a test paper marked.

'Not a very good likeness,' he observed.

She bit back the desire to defend Frank's work.

He stood up and went over to a writing desk in the corner. She watched as he rolled back the top, seated himself and unscrewed the lid of a fountain pen. The preciseness of his actions irritated her.

'You are planning on going abroad?' He signed with a flourish.

'I'm hoping to go to France.'

'I see.' He handed them and the forms back without comment.

'You aren't planning on visiting Frank Agnew?'

She wanted to say that it was none of his business but she confirmed that she was.

She was aware of a stiffening in his posture. 'I hope you will be careful,' he observed. 'He seems to be the sort of man who moves around a lot.'

'You sound like my mother.' At the last moment she held back her annoyance.

Quickly she swallowed back the wine. 'I – I think perhaps I should be getting back. My mother—'

He did not move. 'There is something else I think you would want to know. It has important implications for everyone.'

Mystified, she sat back down.

'Do you recall a young man by the name of John Chambers?' he started.

Shirley frowned. 'I don't think so.'

'He works for the National Trust.'

She then remembered the representative who had come to inspect Cartegena. She smiled at the memory of his enthusiasm. 'I do now,' she said.

'Well, it seems that the Trust is very interested in the house. They would like to acquire it, but only on condition that the artefacts remain as they are. It seems that its undisturbed history makes it a unique property.'

'You think they will buy it?'

'We are a long way from that point. First we have to sort out the ownership – although there is little doubt that the Garcia boy is the natural heir. Then all the details of inheritance tax and stamp duty and such matters have to be agreed.' He glanced at her. 'Finally, there would be the question of the furniture and décor and the price.' He hesitated and underlined the importance of his next statement. 'The Trust is adamant that everything would need to remain in situ.'

Slowly it dawned on Shirley what he was asking. 'You mean that they want Lady Florence's things?'

'There are certain items that they would wish to retain.'

She shrugged as if it was of little importance. 'As far as I am concerned they can keep everything – except perhaps a little Staffordshire dog.'

Edward visibly relaxed, dismissing the dog as of no importance. 'Your agreement would make the sale that much easier. I
know that the Garcias are primarily interested in having some
money. Like you they might settle on some small souvenir from
the house but – well, the continuity of Cartegena would go
along as it always has.'

She smiled. 'That's good news. I have been really worried
about what would happen to it.'

There was an awkward silence then he said, 'Perhaps I
should have your keys back now?' He looked uncomfortable at
asking but Shirley felt calm.

'Of course. I have them here.' She found them and held them
out. The feel of them was like a cherished, farewell handshake.

'Right, thank you.'

Edward then stood up and it was clear that the meeting was at
an end. As they reached the front door, Shirley said, 'Thank you
for all you have done for me. I really appreciate all your help.'

He inclined his head with a tight smile. 'I'll be in touch as
soon as your estate is finalized then I'll get you to come and sign
some papers. You might like to find a financial adviser to help
you with any future investments.'

'Thank you, I will.'

He was dismissing her, making it clear that their relationship
had changed. She was sorry if she had hurt him but what he
was losing was nothing in comparison with what she would be
gaining.

As she set off she wondered whether to walk round to
Frank's but then she decided against it. She looked up at the
navy sky, for once an endless panorama of stars. As they
blinked their way along some unknown journey, Shirley made
her own optimistic route towards Hawthorn Cottage.

So far she and Frank had had no time to themselves. She was
hungry for him but it was the sort of hunger that could be
assuaged by thoughts of the meal to come. In a couple of days
Isabella and Guido would be making their return journey, then
they would be alone. And after that? She found herself smiling
into the darkness.